RUINED BY THE TON

Misfits of the Ton
Book Two

by
Emily Royal

ARE YOU SIGNED UP FOR DRAGONBLADE'S BLOG?

You'll get the latest news and information on exclusive giveaways, exclusive excerpts, coming releases, sales, free books, cover reveals and more.

Check out our complete list of authors, too!

No spam, no junk. That's a promise!

Sign Up Here

www.dragonbladepublishing.com

Dearest Reader;

Thank you for your support of a small press. At Dragonblade Publishing, we strive to bring you the highest quality Historical Romance from some of the best authors in the business. Without your support, there is no 'us', so we sincerely hope you adore these stories and find some new favorite authors along the way.

Happy Reading!

CEO, Dragonblade Publishing

Additional Dragonblade books by Author Emily Royal

Misfits of the Ton
Tomboy of the Ton, Book 1
Ruined by the Ton, Book 2

Headstrong Harts
What the Hart Wants, Book 1
Queen of my Hart, Book 2
Hidden Hart, Book 3
The Prizefighter's Hart, Book 4
All I Want for Christmas is My Hart, Novella
Haunted Hart, Novella

London Libertines
Henry's Bride, Book 1
Hawthorne's Wife, Book 2
Roderick's Widow, Book 3
A Libertine's Christmas Miracle, Novella

The Lyon's Den Series
A Lyon's Pride
Lyon of the Highlands

Dedication

for Jasmine

PROLOGUE

Hampshire, July 1817

B EATRICE SAT UPRIGHT, her heart thumping against her chest. A thin sliver of light marked the bottom of the door to her bedchamber, and the dull glow of embers pulsed in the fireplace.

What had woken her?

One of the guests, perhaps? Or maybe the footman she'd set to guard her chamber from marauding guests, such as James de Bruin, who'd been over-attentive of late. Handsome he might be, but she had resolved that no man would come near her again, unless he wanted to lose his manhood at the blade of her knife.

She waited, her eyes growing accustomed to the darkness. But the only sound was her breathing.

She relaxed back into the bed. Why did she have to be so skittish?

Crash!

She froze, her gut twisting in fear.

The noise hadn't come from outside. It had come from the chamber next to hers.

The chamber that had been locked for the past two years.

She reached under the pillow, fumbling in the dark until her fingers met the familiar, solid shape.

Then she heard the sound of wood scraping against wood, as if someone was rifling through a chest of drawers, followed by footsteps.

Someone was inside the adjoining chamber.

She drew the pistol from under her pillow and aimed it toward the adjoining door.

"Who's there!" she cried. "Come out, you coward, and show yourself!"

Her eyes now adjusted to the darkness, she was able to pick out the shape of the door handle; the light from the embers of the fire highlighted the pattern etched into the brass.

Then the handle moved.

She tightened her grip on the pistol, her heart hammering, willing her body to stop shaking.

The handle dipped, and, with a creak, the door swung inward to reveal a tall, dark shape in the doorway.

Beatrice swallowed her fear.

"Wh-who's there?"

The intruder approached the bed. He seemed to increase in size as he moved, his powerful frame dominating the bedchamber, and her stomach cramped in terror.

"Stop!" she cried. "Or I'll shoot!"

He took another step forward. Beatrice cocked the pistol with her thumb, and the intruder stopped at the loud click.

"That's right," she said, curling her finger around the trigger. "I'm armed, and won't hesitate to shoot you. Stay where you are!"

He remained still, but did not speak.

"I demand you tell me who you are!" she cried. "You've no right to enter a lady's chamber uninvited."

He moved closer, and she caught a flash of cold silver eyes.

"That's where you're wrong, my dear," a voice said—a deep male voice…

…a very *familiar* voice.

"I have every right to enter your chamber, invited or not."

"No…" she whispered.

"Oh yes, my dear."

Standing in her bedchamber was her husband.

The man who, two years ago, had broken her heart and walked out of her life.

CHAPTER ONE

London, May 1815

"WHAT YOU NEED, dear boy, is a wife."

Augustus lifted the brandy glass to his lips to disguise his frown.

A low chuckle came from his left. "I don't think he appreciates your meddling, Monty."

Augustus glanced at his friends. Peregrine, Viscount Marlow, continued to laugh while he sipped his drink. Next to him sat Alexander Ffortescue, heir to the duchy of Sawbridge. On the end sat Montague FitzRoy, Duke of Whitcombe.

"You seem overly keen to thrust me into the parson's trap, Monty," Augustus said, "given that you've always declared your aversion to the marriage state."

"That's because, at your age, you should be thinking about securing an heir," Whitcombe said. "You're not getting any younger."

Augustus sighed. He should have known, the moment he returned from the Continent, that his friends would be circling him like vultures. He'd barely entered White's, and they had crowded around him, wanting to set him up with a woman.

Not that he *minded* women, of course. Women gave him great pleasure in bed, with their soft, pliant bodies and silky flesh. But the women he preferred were the faceless doxies who demanded nothing more than a coin or two in return for pleasuring him, after which they went on their way to service another.

Women were all the same—grasping doxies out for what they could get from a man. Kathleen was the epitome of that. But, unlike the doxies who serviced him in the brothels, his late wife had draped herself in the veneer of respectability that all debutantes wore, reeling him in like a prize trout, only to toss him aside as soon as he'd fallen into her net.

"I'm not in the mood for a wife," he said.

"Not all women are like—" Marlow began, but Augustus interrupted him.

"Mention that woman's name, and you'll be wearing this brandy."

"You must want an heir, though," Ffortescue said. "*Natural* children don't inherit the title."

"You'd know all about that, wouldn't you, Alex?" Augustus snarled. "Given that the country's littered with your bastards."

"I say, old boy, there's no need for *that*," Whitcombe said. "We're here to help you."

"I don't need help finding a wife," Augustus said.

"That's where you're wrong," Marlow said. "We've been inspecting the wares on display this Season to find the perfect partner for you."

"The *perfect partner*?" Augustus snorted. "She doesn't exist."

Marlow placed a hand on his arm. "She does," he said, "though you might need to mold her to suit."

"Mold her?"

Ffortescue leaned forward. "Some women are blank canvases on which you can paint the image of your ideal wife."

Whitcombe nodded. "Exactly. What we have in mind for you is an impressionable young girl—the timid sort, who hangs on to her chaperone's skirts. That sort of woman's apt to do anything to please, and she can be trained into the perfect, obedient wife."

"You mean an innocent?" Augustus asked.

"Exactly," Marlow said. "One who can be fashioned into the biddable little wife you want—who will take care of your estate and bear your children with the minimum of fuss."

An obedient little mannequin, with no mind of her own, trained to do exactly what he wanted.

The exact opposite of *her*.

Augustus shook his head. "It all sounds a little *false*."

Whitcombe laughed. "Would you rather marry for love?"

"Good Lord, no," Augustus said. "I have no intention of taking *that* path again."

"Then why not tread the road in the opposite direction?" Ffortescue suggested. "There's bound to be a mindless little ingénue willing to marry the first man who flatters her. That's what you need, isn't it, Gus? A wife who won't object to being left to take care of the family estate while you continue your travels across Europe and indulge in excesses with Italian goddesses."

"A broodmare for your family line," Whitcombe added, "a submissive wife who'll part her thighs as soon as you unbutton your breeches."

Augustus wrinkled his nose at his friend's crude expression.

Whitcombe laughed. "We all want one of those!" He drained his glass. "And, Gus, you want a wife who'll bear *your* children, rather than those of her lovers."

The other two drew in a sharp breath simultaneously.

"Monty…" Marlow said.

The brandy glass slipped out of Augustus's hand and landed on the floor, shattering on impact.

"*Shit!*"

A chorus of tuts, and the rustling of newspapers, rippled through the clubroom. A footman appeared and deftly picked up the shards of glass, collecting them on a tray, his face impassive, as if it were a daily occurrence.

Which it probably was, knowing the members' reputation for rowdiness when they gathered to toast each other's conquests.

In fact, most members of White's had likely toasted Kathleen at least one time, given how many men she'd spread her legs for.

"That was a low blow, Monty," Ffortescue said. "The late Lady Hardwick was—"

"A whore," Augustus said, wincing at the bitterness in his own voice. "Isn't that what you all think? And I was a poor, cuckolded fool, naïve enough to fall in love with her."

"Apologies, old boy, I meant no harm," Whitcombe said. "But you've always wanted an heir. And if you bag yourself an impressionable little thing who will obey you at every turn, then you'll be assured of an heir and won't spend the rest of your life wondering whether or not it's *yours*."

"If that's your way of making me feel better," Augustus said, "I—"

"Save your breath, Gus," Marlow interrupted. "We all know that a serial shagger such as Monty here has no intention of slipping his neck inside the parson's noose. But *you*, my friend, are a different animal. You want an heir more than anything, and therefore, we will help you in your quest."

"Like I need help!" Augustus scoffed.

"You're not getting any younger," Whitcombe said. "Didn't you complain of rheumatism last week?"

Augustus sighed. "A slight ache, nothing more, and it's only because I'm unused to the London weather. Italy's much warmer this time of year. Besides, thirty isn't old."

"It is if you want to keep a young wife entertained."

"I'll have no trouble with *that*, I assure you," Augustus said. "I picked up one or two tricks in Rome."

"Oh, spare me the tales of your Italian doxies," Whitcombe said. "Though perhaps I should take a trip to Rome myself. I could teach them a thing or two."

"I don't doubt it," Marlow said, laughing. "So, Hardwick, do you have any particular requirements for a wife?"

Augustus shook his head. "Not really. She must be genteel, of course. And demure—not one of those bright young things who attracts a good deal too much attention from the young bucks."

"Naturally. You wouldn't want to have to fight off the competition at your age."

"She needn't be beautiful," Augustus continued. "As for a dowry—a woman with a large dowry will have an overinflated opinion of herself, and will harbor expectations over how it is spent."

"Good Lord, man! At least take a wife with enough cash to make it worth your while."

"Rich wives place too many demands on their husbands," Augustus said.

Kathleen's dowry had been twenty thousand. But with it came the expectation that he'd give her free rein to do what she liked.

And fuck whom she liked.

"So, you're after someone plain, dull, and poor." Whitcombe laughed. "There's plenty of wallflowers to choose from. We can make a start tomorrow night."

"What's happening tomorrow night?" Augustus asked.

"Lady Bunting's ball."

"I've not been invited."

"Pah!" Ffortescue exclaimed. "Who needs an invitation nowadays? Besides, you can regale the hostess with tales of your trips around Europe. She's half Italian, you know, and I'm sure a few choice words about *La Bella Roma* will stand you in good stead."

"*Do* say you'll come," Whitcombe said. "Lady Bunting will be most impressed if we bring a friend who speaks Italian."

"Let me guess—you want to court Miss Bunting," Augustus said.

Whitcombe let out a snort. "I've no intention of *courting* any woman."

"Shag her, then?" Marlow asked.

"Good lord no! Her face is so horselike, I hear Lord Bunting has to keep her away from the stables when the mares are in season." Whitcombe nudged Augustus. "Do say you'll come."

Augustus let out a sigh. "I might as well. I've nothing better to do. As well as being colder than Rome, London's bloody dull. I'd forgotten how dull."

"All the more reason to find a wife to warm your bed," Marlow said. "So that's settled. Tomorrow, we'll start window-shopping for your bride."

Augustus drained his glass, then rose to his feet and bade his friends goodbye. Then he exited the clubroom, dropping a tip to the footman on the way out.

His friends—Marlow, Whitcombe and Ffortescue—might be overly fond of debauchery, but they were right.

He needed a wife.

In any case, that was why he'd returned to England—to put the tragedy of his first wife firmly behind him, and set about the task of producing an heir.

And, to do that, he needed a woman he *wasn't* in danger of falling in love with. Marriages based on love led to heartbreak and tragedy.

And Augustus had no intention of experiencing love again.

CHAPTER TWO

"A REN'T YOU DANCING tonight, cousin?"

Beatrice's guardian towered over her, determination in his eyes.

"I've yet to see anyone I wish to dance with, Giles," she said.

"Nonsense! There's plenty of respectable young men here tonight."

She glanced across the ballroom, where the dance was in full swing. Couples moved smoothly across the floor to the music—ladies decorated in bright silks and tall feathers, the brighter the better in order to attract partners, and gentlemen prowling the room, sizing up their prey.

None of them looked respectable. Since the events of last Season that had threatened to ruin her family name, Beatrice had lost faith in her judgment of character. The women she viewed as rivals eager to discredit her respectability in order to make themselves appear in a more favorable light.

As for the men…

The men she saw as predators, eager to snare a dowry and a female body, whether or not the female was willing.

"Giles, darling, must you plague Beatrice quite so much?"

A light hand caught hers, and Beatrice turned and looked into the eyes of her chaperone.

Henrietta was the only woman capable of making Giles listen to reason. Theirs was a love match between two strong-willed characters, and Beatrice couldn't help admiring Henrietta's ability to convince Giles of her point of view each time they disagreed—particularly when it came to Beatrice herself. Giles had a reputation for strictness, but he was, Beatrice knew, ruled by his wife. Had it not been for Henrietta, Giles would have married Beatrice off to the first man who asked. He believed he had her best interests at heart, but Beatrice had no wish to marry a man she couldn't trust.

And it was doubtful whether she'd be able to even *consider* trusting a man again.

"Henrietta, my love," Giles continued, "Beatrice will never find a husband if she—"

"I *am* in the room, cousin," Beatrice said. "Can I not answer for myself?"

"You don't always know what's best for you, Beatrice," he replied. "Since your antics of last Season, your reputation is at risk."

Beatrice's cheeks warmed with shame. Why did Giles always have to remind her of her failed elopement when he wanted to make a point?

"That's enough, Giles," Henrietta said. "Why don't you fetch Beatrice and me a drink?"

"You shouldn't be drinking in your condition," he replied.

Henrietta placed a hand over her belly, and Beatrice looked away, unable to contain her envy.

"Water for me, please, Giles, darling," Henrietta said, "but I believe Beatrice deserves something stronger, given that she's had to weather your instructions tonight."

Giles bowed, then headed toward a footman brandishing a tray and several champagne glasses.

"Your cousin has your best interests at heart, Beatrice," Henrietta said, "even if he's incapable of articulating anything with any degree of sensitivity."

"I wish he'd leave me alone," Beatrice said. "It's bad enough coming here tonight. I've not been to a party since…"

Henrietta nodded. The sentence didn't need finishing. Tonight was the first time Beatrice had ventured out since her elopement with Phillip Meredith, a dashing son of an earl who'd swept her off her feet with pretty speeches, gallant compliments, and the promise of adventure. Henrietta had managed to put paid to the rumors, and the gossipmongers had turned their attention to other poor souls' indiscretions. But the echo of the rumor remained, like a stain on a white muslin gown that could never be completely removed.

"You're not obliged to dance tonight," Henrietta said. "But not all young men are like—"

"Please don't mention his name!" Beatrice cried.

"There will come a time when you'll *have* to mention his name without flinching," Henrietta said. "Only then can you say you're fully recovered." She placed a hand over Beatrice's. "Perhaps I'm being too hasty. I only want you to be happy, my dear. And Giles does too, of course, though he has his own unique way of showing it."

The dance concluded, and a young man approached.

"Lady Thorpe, a pleasure to see you," he said. "I trust you're well?"

"Perfectly, as you see, Mr. Yates," Henrietta replied.

"May I have the honor of an introduction to your lovely companion?"

Henrietta wrinkled her nose, but her smile remained. "Of course," she said. "Mr. Yates, this is my husband's cousin and ward, Lady Beatrice Thorpe, daughter of the late Lord Anthony Thorpe." She turned to Beatrice. "Beatrice, this is Mr. Yates, lately come to London from Cambridge, and, if I recall right, he has recently purchased a commission in the militia."

Beatrice rose and held out her hand. The young man took it and brushed his lips against her skin. Then he glanced up at her, his eyes glittering in the candlelight. Beatrice shivered inwardly at the predatory gleam in his eyes. She snatched her hand free, then resumed her seat.

"Would you partner me for the next dance, Lady Beatrice?"

"No, thank you," she replied crisply.

His eyes narrowed, and his mouth slipped into a grimace before the smile returned. Then he bowed and slipped away, moving toward a young lady in a bright green silk gown sitting beside a dowager resplendent in purple and an abundance of diamonds and feathers.

"Poor Mr. Yates," Henrietta said. "Giles has a good opinion of him. Did you have to disappoint him?"

Beatrice gestured across the room. The young man was bowing over the hand of Miss Green Dress, and, shortly after, she rose and he escorted her to the dance floor.

"*His* disappointment was short-lived," Beatrice said. "Unlike Giles's disappointment."

"What do you mean?" Henrietta asked.

Giles approached them, brandishing two glasses, a frown darkening his features. He glanced toward Beatrice, then to the dance floor—where Mr. Yates was holding his partner's hand—and back again.

Beatrice stared back at him with defiance.

Your little scheme has failed, cousin.

He handed them a glass each, then sat beside his wife and fixed his gaze on the dancers. Beatrice waited for the admonishment.

At length, it came.

"Mr. Yates is an excellent dancer, is he not?" he said. "The poor fellow has a challenge on his hands with Miss Beauchamp. Ignoring the fact that the particular shade of green does nothing for her complexion, I swear she's in possession of two left feet."

"Then I pity her for being at the mercy of your opinion," Beatrice said. "Having benefited from your opinions myself, I could advise her on how to weather your scorn."

"Beatrice…" he began, but Henrietta silenced him.

"Giles, that's enough."

"But Mr. Yates is—"

"Perfectly respectable, I know, Giles," Henrietta said, "but, as I said last night, *you're* not the one who has to dance with him."

Beatrice rolled her eyes.

Better and better…

Not content with trying to arrange a partner for her on his own, Giles had drawn Henrietta—Beatrice's only ally—into his scheme.

"You've entrusted *me* with Beatrice's care this Season," Henrietta continued. "Therefore, you must trust my judgment."

"You mustn't overtax yourself, my love," Giles said.

"Good heavens, Giles!" Henrietta cried. "I'm with child, not on the brink of death." She winked at Beatrice. "Your cousin seems to think that my condition renders me incapable of functioning unaided. It may surprise him to learn that I was able to brush my own hair last night without fainting. But I will admit that I cannot fight off every undesirable man who plagues you with offers to dance."

"Oh, yes you can, my love," Giles said, "but, at present, your weapon is a hard stare capable of slicing through the toughest cut of beef, rather than your sword."

Beatrice flushed at the reference—yet another damnable reference—to last Season, when Henrietta had brought her home after her elopement attempt having challenged Phillip Meredith to a duel for her honor. But had it not been for Henrietta, Beatrice would have found herself ruined—or worse, married to a man who didn't love her.

As if she sensed Beatrice's discomfort, Henrietta gave her hand a gentle squeeze. Then she glanced at Giles, a determined set to her jaw.

Giles nodded and rose to his feet. "I think I'll have a word with Lord Bunting, if you ladies will excuse me?"

"With pleasure," Henrietta said, a little too quickly.

"I can tell when I'm not wanted, my love." He bent down and placed a kiss on Henrietta's forehead. The two of them exchanged a smile, and Beatrice looked away. Though she loved them both dearly—and it filled her with joy to see her cousin so happy with the woman he loved—it only served to emphasize her own situation. Would that she could find someone to love her— someone that she could love, and trust, in return!

"Forgive us, my dear," Henrietta said. "Giles was so set on having you dance with Mr. Yates that he quite forgot to consider your views. If you have no wish to dance, then we'll say no more on the matter."

Beatrice glanced toward the center of the ballroom, where Mr. Yates was steering Miss Green Dress about, his teeth gritted, as if in pain.

"It's not that I don't want to dance," she said. "But I wish to be discerning in my choice of partner. I only want to dance with someone I can *trust*. You can understand that, can't you?"

"Of course, my dear," Henrietta said. "You're wise to exercise caution. But you're unlikely to know whether or not you can trust a man when you first meet him. Sometimes one must experience a man's company for a little while before forming a valid opinion on his character."

"Is that what you did with Giles?"

"We loathed each other on sight!" Henrietta laughed. "But I always knew I'd never love another. And you'll feel the same."

Beatrice shook her head. "I'm not sure."

"It may take you longer than the usual pampered miss to find your partner," Henrietta said. "Most young ladies will settle for any man as long as he has a title and carriages of his own, of which they can boast to their rivals. When you find the right partner, he'll be worth the wait."

"I don't think I'll ever find someone I can trust," Beatrice said. "Not tonight, at least."

"How can you be so sure when you've hardly spoken to anyone?"

Beatrice glanced about the room. "I can tell by looking," she said. "It's the eyes."

"The eyes?"

Beatrice nodded. "There's something—I can't quite describe it—in a man's expression. I should have noticed it in"—she swallowed her discomfort, trying to dispel the unwelcome memory—"in *his* eyes. It reminds me of a pack of dogs circling a rabbit just before the kill."

"You liken all men to wolves?"

"Perhaps I'm being overcautious," Beatrice said, "but I only wish to dance with a man who has kind eyes." She shook her head, her cheeks warming. "I'm being foolish, aren't I?"

"Of course not, my darling," Henrietta said. "There's wisdom in your words. Our eyes convey our innermost thoughts and desires, and while most of us are capable of pulling a face that's contrary to our true feelings, it takes a certain skill to prevent our eyes from betraying those feelings. Which is, of course, why most children, for example, will stare at their shoes when attempting to deny their transgressions to their parents."

"Is that so?"

"Of course!" Henrietta laughed. "My dear papa always says that I spent most of my childhood either looking at the floor when uttering a falsehood, or staring at him in defiance when confessing the truth."

Still holding Beatrice's hand, Henrietta glanced about the room. Then her eyes lit up with joy.

"Eleanor!" she cried. "I didn't think to see you here."

A young woman approached them, dressed in a plain gown of white muslin. Most would describe her as unremarkable, save for the intelligent expression in her green eyes. Eleanor disliked being looked at, and hardly made eye contact with anyone. Not due to any falsehood on her part, but because she loathed the attention of anyone save her closest friends. And, by virtue of last summer's scandal, Beatrice understood Eleanor's discomfort.

"How are you, Henrietta?" Eleanor asked. "Should you be attending a party, given your state of health?"

Henrietta laughed. "Giles has just been admonishing me. Are you in league with him?"

The two women chatted, engaging in the easy banter of good friends who had no need to stand on ceremony. Though Beatrice was fond of Eleanor, the bond of friendship that existed between Henrietta and Eleanor was something Beatrice had yet to experience with another. She adored Henrietta, but since Henrietta had married Beatrice's cousin and taken on the role of chaperone, a barrier had formed, confirming the distinction between them…

The distinction between a married chaperone and an unmarried young woman…

Or that between a respectable countess and a lady of *doubtful reputation.*

With Henrietta's attention focused on Eleanor, Beatrice set aside her drink and glanced about the room, her gaze following the smooth lines of the dance. She smiled to herself as she caught sight of Mr. Yates tripping over Miss Green Dress's hem.

Three men stood beside the doorway, staring at the dancers. Beatrice recognized the tall blond figure of Lord Marlow and the darkly piratical features of the Duke of Whitcombe—two of the most predatory males who'd ever existed. Their companion she did not recognize.

He was dressed in a dark gray jacket and cream breeches. His hair was jet black, save for a few speckles of gray that, if anything, gave him a distinguished air. Though his build was athletic—his jacket serving to accentuate, rather than conceal, his toned body—his stance did not exude the easy grace of a powerful man. A tension seemed to vibrate through his body, as if he were ill at ease.

Then her gaze shifted to his face. Her heart gave a flutter, and the breath caught in her throat.

Those eyes…

She had never seen anything like it—such an extraordinary shade! Pale gray, with a faint hue of blue. The color of slate, or a stormy sky.

Then he blinked, and his gaze settled on her.

Her heart shuddered in her chest, and she caught her breath. His eyes held an intensity that conveyed intelligence and a deep soul. They were the eyes of a man capable of eliciting the truth from the most determined liar with a single stare.

But something else resided in his eyes—a deep sorrow. They spoke of a man who'd had his heart broken—a man capable of the most intense, fierce loyalty, which rendered him vulnerable to the unscrupulous.

They were a deep gray ocean into which she would willingly throw herself, to be engulfed in their depths.

Never before had she seen eyes capable of rendering her so helpless, and so desperate to ease the pain that lurked behind their expression.

And though they elicited a deep fear from within—the fear of having her soul laid bare before him—they differed from any pair of eyes she had seen in her life.

Because they were the eyes of someone whom she knew, deep inside, that she could trust.

For a moment, she simply stared at him, immobilized by the intensity of his gaze. The rest of the world dissolved into obscurity. The music dissipated into the air and the bright silks and jewels faded into insignificance, overshadowed by the purity of those gray eyes.

Beatrice…

A soft voice whispered in her head as she continued to gaze at him. Was he calling to her mind, or did his soul whisper to hers across the chasm while he held her in his thrall?

A hand touched her wrist and broke the spell, and she looked away.

"Beatrice, what's wrong?"

Henrietta stared at her, concern in her expression. Eleanor was nowhere to be seen.

Dear Lord, how long had she been staring at the stranger like a lovesick fool?

"You look troubled," Henrietta said. "For a moment, I

thought you'd stopped breathing. Has something upset you?

"N-no," Beatrice stammered. Then she glanced down. Her hands were curled into fists, grasping her skirts.

"Are you sure you're all right?"

Beatrice didn't reply, but she was unable to temper the tremors in her body.

She glanced up again, but the man had gone.

Perhaps he'd been a figment of her imagination. She had dreamed, for so long, of the perfect man—someone she could trust completely—that her fevered mind had conjured one up, like a phantom, to taunt her with.

She picked up her drink and took a sip, focusing on the sharpness of the champagne against her tongue.

"Yes, I'm fine," she said. "Just a little overwhelmed, being at a ball again. I'd forgotten what noisy affairs they were."

"Poor Beatrice," Henrietta said. "Things will improve in time. Perhaps if Giles and I host a small event, you might not find it quite so daunting?"

Beatrice nodded. "I'd like that," she said. "I could help with the organizing, so you don't overtire yourself."

"Your aunt Euphramia would be happy to oblige in that quarter," Henrietta said. "She's always telling me about the magnificence of the parties she held when Giles's father was alive. I hear they were a little outrageous, but tempered with your good sense, I'm sure that she could organize something that even Giles cannot object to."

"You don't think Giles would mind?"

"He'll love it," Henrietta said. "Oh, here he comes now. Giles, darling, what do you think of our holding a ball? Just a small one? I thought Euphramia could have a hand in the organization."

Beatrice sipped her drink and kept her gaze focused on her glass as footsteps approached.

"Anything you wish, my love," Giles said, "provided you don't overtax yourself. Mother would be delighted, I'm sure.

What say you, Hardwick, to the prospect of hosting a ball?"

"If balls must take place, I'd rather be a guest than a host," a deep voice said.

"Then you shall be the first to have an invitation, Hardwick," Giles said. "May I introduce you to my wife and cousin?"

Beatrice looked up, then froze.

Standing next to Giles, his gaze fixed on her, was the man with the gray eyes.

CHAPTER THREE

S HE WAS, WITHOUT doubt, the loveliest thing he'd ever seen.

Augustus couldn't take his gaze away from her. Almost as soon as he stepped into the ballroom, his eyes had been drawn to the figure sitting on the edge of the ballroom along with the chaperones and wallflowers.

But she looked utterly unlike any wallflower he'd seen before.

It was obvious that she was a young woman of breeding. Even sitting down, the way she moved told him that—the delicate turn of her head as she swept her gaze across the room, and the smooth gesture she made with her hand when sipping her drink. Only years of tuition at the hand of a stern governess hellbent on teaching her charge the attitude of a young aristocratic lady could instill such a demeanor.

And her gown was simple and elegant, a pale lilac, unlike the gaudy frocks of the young ladies desperate to secure the attention of a man. By its very simplicity, her gown stood out among the rest—the cut of the silk, the embroidery around the bodice, and the pearls dotted in her hair, which was fashioned into a plain, smooth style, with a single curl adorning her shoulder.

Warm eyes the color of chocolate scanned the room, their expression guarded, wary even, as if she were a fox hiding among the bracken.

Or a broken angel.

Her expression bore neither the haughty expectation nor the

frantic desperation of other young ladies. Unlike them, she had not come tonight in search of a suitor.

Then what *had* she come for?

"Seen anything you fancy, Hardwick?"

Augustus turned to his companions. Marlow stood, champagne glass in hand, staring around the room, evidently hunting for a particular lady. "There's several young ladies here tonight who'd make fine partners. What say you, Monty?"

Whitcombe leaned against the wall, a bored expression on his face. "Good Lord, Marlow, your standards couldn't get any lower," he said. "I see nothing here to lead me into temptation."

"I wonder why you bothered to come at all if you aren't going to dance," Marlow said.

"I intend to indulge myself at the gaming tables," Whitcombe said.

"I pity the man who plays against *you*," Augustus said. "Whom will you drive into ruination tonight?"

"A man has no business playing the game if he cannot afford the price of failure."

"Are you speaking of cards, Monty, or matters of the heart?" Augustus asked.

"Both," came the reply. "You of all men should know that."

"Leave him alone, Monty," Marlow said.

Augustus returned his gaze to the broken angel. A young man approached her, bowed, and offered his hand. An unremarkable young buck.

He found himself smiling as she declined with a shake of her head. The woman next to her, presumably her chaperone, leaned over and whispered in her ear. The young woman flushed a delicate shade of rose, then looked down, as if ashamed.

He found himself intrigued.

"Ah, I see my quarry," Marlow said.

Augustus followed his friend's eye line until his gaze fell upon a blonde woman with strong features and an air of mischief about her. "Who the devil's that?" he asked.

"The honorable Lavinia de Grande."

"Lord de Grande's daughter?" Augustus asked. "Don't tell me that old fossil's still alive."

"Barely," Whitcombe said. "He's hardly been seen in public since losing his fortune. Don't tell me you're after his daughter, Marlow? I'll wager there's no dowry there."

"Perhaps not, but there's something about her," Marlow said.

"*I* don't see it," Whitcombe said, the bored tone returning to his voice.

"*You* wouldn't," Augustus said. "But mark my words, Monty. One day, a woman will catch your eye and you'll have to play at being the suitor in order to captivate her."

Whitcombe shook his head. "I have no intention of falling into the parson's trap," he said. "I only have to look at *you* to see the fruits of falling in love."

Augustus sighed. Why did his friend persist in needling him? He glanced back toward the young woman he'd noticed before, and caught his breath.

She was watching him.

Her eyes widened, and, for a moment, she held his gaze. Then her chaperone leaned toward her again and she startled and looked away, her blush deepening. Distress lined her features, and she picked up her glass and drained it.

"Oh, I say!"

He looked around at the shrill voice. Two young ladies emerged from the crowd and were bearing down on Augustus and his friends in the manner of she-wolves who'd scented a particularly tasty piece of meat. One was pretty enough. But the other was exquisitely beautiful—though it was plain from the expression on her face that she was fully aware of her beauty.

"Oh *bugger*," Marlow cursed.

"What's wrong?" Whitcombe asked.

"I forgot I'd offered to partner Lady Irma Fairchild in the quadrille," Marlow said.

"Why the devil would you do that?"

"Gallantry, Monty. You should try it some time."

Whitcombe snorted. "I see no merit in anything so ludicrous as *gallantry*. If a woman's interested, then she'll part her thighs whether I dance with her or not. And I prefer the thighs of a doxy to those of a debutante."

"Why, because they part more easily?"

"Because they come at a lower price," came the reply. "A few coins, as opposed to a lifetime of servitude."

"Ha! I can't imagine *you* being in servitude to a woman," Marlow said.

The two ladies joined them and dropped into curtseys.

"Lady Irma, a pleasure," Marlow said.

"The pleasure's all mine, I'm sure." Lady Irma's companion nudged her, a frown turning her beautiful features quite ugly for a moment. "You know Miss Juliette Howard, of course," Lady Irma said. "Aren't you going to introduce us to your friends, Lord Marlow?"

Marlow gestured toward Whitcombe. "My friend here you know, of course," he said, "Montague FitzRoy, Duke of Whitcombe."

"Your Grace." Miss Howard, the prettier of the two, stared at Whitcombe, hungry desperation in her eyes.

Augustus sipped his drink to hide his smile.

"And this is Earl Hardwick," Marlow continued, "lately returned from Italy."

Two pairs of female eyes looked at Augustus with interest.

"Hardwick," Miss Howard said. "Of Hardwick Hall?"

"The very same."

"I hear it's one of the finest estates," Miss Howard said. "A beautiful building, or so the Duke of Dunton has told me."

"You're too kind," Augustus replied, "though I wouldn't say it's particularly remarkable."

"I *always* appreciate a fine building, don't I, Lady Irma?" Miss Howard said. "And gardens. I quite adore a beautifully landscaped garden. I couldn't live in a house without a landscaped garden."

"Are you fond of gardens?" Augustus asked.

"Oh, yes." Miss Howard fixed her predatory gaze on him. "I'm fond of dancing, also."

Whitcombe let out a snort, then disguised it as a cough.

"I'm fond of a landscaped garden myself," Marlow said. "In fact, there's a young man I've heard of who's particularly talented in designing them."

Miss Howard wrinkled her nose. "Oh really?"

"Yes, Baxter's the name. Lawrence Baxter. He's the son of a prizefighter, if I recall."

"Good Lord!" Miss Howard cried. "You couldn't have someone like *that* managing your garden."

"Why ever not?" Augustus asked.

Miss Howard cast him a sharp glance, her pretty little nose wrinkled in disgust. Then she smiled and gave a laugh. "Oh, Lord Hardwick, you do amuse!"

"If you'll excuse me," Whitcombe said, "I'm required elsewhere." He bowed, then slipped into the crowd and disappeared, presumably on his way to earn a fortune at the card tables.

Augustus gritted his teeth.

Whitcombe was a swine. Once Marlow had taken Lady Irma onto the dance floor, Augustus would be left on his own, at the mercy of Miss Howard, who was looking at him expectantly.

Honor demanded that a gentleman capable of dancing did not leave a lady without a partner if she had indicated her desire to dance.

Honor be damned.

Miss Howard reminded him of Kathleen, with her hard-eyed beauty and avaricious gaze. Beautiful enough to adorn a gentleman's arm, but a harridan nonetheless—the type of woman not content with securing a man's hand, but someone who'd take delight in securing his heart, then crushing it.

But his heart was not for the taking. Not again.

He glanced about the room in search of aid, and his gaze fell upon a familiar shape.

With a tall, athletic figure, Earl Thorpe was just as striking as he had been when Augustus last saw him, when they'd shared a brandy at White's, shortly before Augustus departed for the Continent.

The years had been kind to Thorpe. The once-stiff demeanor had gone, and he looked less careworn.

In fact, he positively glowed.

Augustus caught Thorpe's eye, then lifted his hand in salute. In truth, his gesture was akin to that of a man in a shark-infested ocean raising his hand to a passing ship in a plea for sanctuary.

Thorpe glanced at Miss Howard, and his lip curled into a smile of understanding. The cry for help had been acknowledged, and Augustus's savior sauntered over.

"Hardwick!" he cried. "You old devil! How long has it been since I saw you last?" He bowed to Marlow, then gave a cursory nod to the ladies. "Miss Howard, Lady Irma, a pleasure as always," he said, in a tone that implied the opposite.

"It's been five years, at least," Augustus said. "I arrived in London last week."

"Do you find it much changed?" Thorpe asked.

"In many ways it's just the same," Augustus said. "My valet informs me that I need to refresh my wardrobe lest I wish to be mistaken for a troubadour, but the predatory nature of balls such as this is no different to when I last set foot in a ballroom."

"I'm sure the unattached ladies in Italy are just as eager to hook their talons into an eligible man," Thorpe said, casting a sidelong glance at Miss Howard.

"Which, perhaps, explains why Hardwick has returned to London," Marlow said. "He's looking for the *right sort of girl*. Whitcombe and I have pledged to find such a girl for him."

"For marriage or pleasure?" Thorpe asked.

Both ladies colored, and Miss Howard drew in a sharp breath and glared at him.

"If you'll excuse me, *gentlemen*," she said, her tone leaving nothing to the imagination in regards to the degree of offence she'd taken, "I have a megrim. Lord Marlow. Would you be so kind as to escort me to a seat before the dance begins?"

Augustus bowed, as did Thorpe, while Miss Howard inclined her head, then, with a flourish of her skirt, she swept past them and crossed the dance floor. The unfortunate Marlow followed in her wake, Lady Irma clinging to his arm.

"Megrim, indeed!" Thorpe scoffed. "That's a lady's excuse to remove herself from a conversation when she knows she cannot get the better of the other party. But perhaps I spoke out of turn."

"Good Lord no," Augustus said. "I can only thank you for rescuing me. I feared I'd be obligated to ask Miss Howard to dance."

"I had the misfortune of experiencing rather too much of her company last Season," Thorpe said. "Not something I'd wish on any man who values his peace of mind."

"You must admit she's rather easy on the eye," Augustus said.

"I'll call her back if you wish to engage her for a dance."

"Heavens, no!" Augustus laughed. "My taste in jackets may have remained unchanged over the past five years, but I'd like to think I'm more discerning than I once was in my requirements for a partner. There's more to the perfect wife than a pretty face and a dowry."

"I couldn't agree more," Thorpe said, his eyes sparkling.

Augustus shook his head in disbelief. Before him stood a very different creature to the staid man he'd known before—a man who'd inherited a title before his time and always looked as if he carried the cares of the world on his shoulders.

"What is it with you, Thorpe?" Augustus asked. "Don't tell me you've found the perfect wife."

"That I have," Thorpe said, gesturing across the room. "There she is!"

Augustus's heart sank.

Thorpe was pointing toward the broken angel.

"My Henrietta," Thorpe said, "who made me the happiest man in the world last year."

"Why aren't you dancing with her?" Augustus asked.

"Her condition prevents it. She's a lively little thing, and keeps me on my toes. But even she sees the sense of waiting until after the birth of our child."

Damn.

Augustus swore under his breath. Lady Fortune had seen fit to stab him in the heart again. Giles Thorpe, on the other hand, was one lucky bastard.

"Oh, forgive me, Hardwick!" Thorpe cried. "How insensitive you must think me, given what happened with your..." He hesitated and colored.

"My late wife?" Augustus asked. "I've had five years to reflect on what happened. And it would be a very bitter man who expected everyone around him to share his misery. Good news should be shared, and celebrated."

"I'm glad you think so," Thorpe said. "What do you think of her? Is she not the most delightful creature in the room?"

"The young woman in the lilac? Aye, she's exquisite."

"Good Lord!" Thorpe let out a laugh. "Don't let my wife hear you say that! The young lady in the lilac is my cousin and ward. My *wife* is sitting next to her—in the blue."

Augustus suppressed a sigh of relief.

"Come, let me introduce you," Thorpe said. "But you mustn't repeat what you said just now. No chaperone wishes to be told that she's been outshone by her charge—not even a charge who's disinclined to dance."

"Disinclined to dance?" Augustus asked. "I thought every young woman was eager to dance. Is that not the purpose of attending a ball?"

Thorpe opened his mouth to reply, then hesitated and closed it again.

Augustus followed Thorpe across the ballroom, ignoring the hopeful glances of the unattached young women they passed. His broken angel was staring at her lap, but Lady Thorpe looked up and smiled, her expression filled with love, as her husband approached.

"Giles, darling," she said, "what do you think of our holding a ball? Just a small one? I thought perhaps Euphramia could have a hand in the organizing."

The young woman beside her focused her attention on the drink in her hand.

"Anything you wish, my love," Thorpe said, "provided you don't overtax yourself. Mother would be delighted, I'm sure." He turned to Augustus. "What say you, Hardwick, to the prospect of hosting a ball?"

Augustus suppressed a shudder. He couldn't think of anything worse.

"If balls must take place, I'd rather be a guest than a host," he replied.

"Then we shall issue you the first invitation, Hardwick," Thorpe said. "May I introduce you to my wife and cousin?"

The broken angel looked up. Lovely she may have been from a distance, but at close quarters she was breathtaking. Augustus could hardly tear his gaze from her. She was younger than he'd first thought, but what captivated him was the beautiful expression in her eyes. They were the color of liquid chocolate, a rich, dark brown that spoke of a warmth of heart and soul...

...and a deeply hidden sorrow that belied her youth.

She understood pain and heartbreak. Perhaps she'd experienced it herself.

Her chest rose and fell as she drew in a sharp breath, then her lips parted, and he discerned a slight tremor in their plump softness.

Thorpe gestured toward his wife.

"Hardwick, this is my wife, Lady Thorpe. Henrietta, my love, this is Earl Hardwick, lately returned from the Continent, and I have it on good authority that he's on the lookout for the right sort of girl."

Augustus tore his gaze from the angel and toward the woman sitting next to her. "Lady Thorpe, delighted to make your acquaintance," he said, bowing.

She fixed her gaze on him, her hazel eyes radiating sharp intelligence. Then she offered her hand, and he lifted it to his lips.

"And," Thorpe continued, "my cousin and ward, Lady Beatrice Thorpe."

Augustus turned his attention to the young woman. Her face flushed a delicate shade of rose as she offered her hand.

Beatrice. *Bringer of joy.*

The name suited her. He couldn't imagine anything more joyous than having her in his arms.

He took her hand and drew in a sharp breath at her touch. Warm and soft, her fingers slid over his, and he curled his fingers around hers, relishing the silky-smooth skin.

She let out a sigh, and his skin tightened as her warm breath caressed the back of his hand.

Sweet Lord, what was happening to him? He wasn't some callow youth experiencing his first infatuation. He was a man who'd experienced enough of the world to understand that *love at first sight* was a foolish concept used by authors to sell novels, and chaperones to persuade their charges to accept an offer of marriage.

"Lady Beatrice," he whispered.

Her eyes widened, and their color deepened until they were almost black.

He brushed his lips against her skin and closed his eyes. Then he inhaled, and a delicate fragrance caressed his senses—rose and honey, the sweet scent of innocence.

He lifted his head and opened his eyes once more, to find her looking directly at him. A spark of light shone in her eyes—a flash of gold, like the sun's rays penetrating the depths of a dark pool.

"Lord Hardwick."

Her voice was soft and rich—the warm tones of a woman who had no expectations of others around her. It was the sort of voice that mothers soothed their children with when they wanted them to know that, despite all the hurt in the world, they were loved and protected.

It was voice to soften the hardest of hearts.

Then she curled her lips into a shy smile, and he was ensnared.

He blurted out the question before he could stop himself.

"Lady Beatrice, would you partner me for the next dance?"

Thorpe's eyes widened, and he shook his head. Lady Thorpe frowned at Augustus, then exchanged a glance with her charge. She took Lady Beatrice's free hand and gave it a gentle squeeze.

There was no mistaking the silent message between the two women.

You don't have to dance with him if you'd rather not.

A ripple of fear crossed Beatrice's expression, as if she were afraid to refuse. Augustus couldn't deny his disappointment, but he had no wish to distress her.

"No matter, Lady Beatrice," he said with a smile. "Your guardian will no doubt regale you with tales of my inability to move across the dance floor without treading on my partner's feet at least ten times. You've had a lucky escape. And besides, I'm being most selfish in asking you to stray from your chaperone's side." He glanced toward Thorpe's wife. "I understand congratulations are in order, Lady Thorpe."

"N-no," a soft voice said.

He resumed his attention on Lady Beatrice.

"I quite understand your refusal," he said. "It only remains for me to apologize for such a presumption. Having spent the past five years on the Continent, I'm afraid I've forgotten the rules of decorum. You must think me something of a savage."

He withdrew his hand, but she curled her fingers around his and tightened her grip.

"No," she said. "You misunderstand me. My cousin has no need of me..." She glanced toward Lady Thorpe. "Do you, Henrietta? I should like to dance."

"If you're sure," Lady Thorpe said.

Lady Beatrice nodded and rose from her seat.

"I promise to take the greatest care of your charge, Lady Thorpe," Augustus said.

"Even her feet?" Thorpe asked with a wry smile.

"You're at liberty to call me out, Thorpe, if your cousin has the slightest complaint with regards to my behavior."

"I believe I'm unlikely to have any complaints," Lady Beatrice said, in her soft voice.

Augustus led her onto the dance floor, his blood warming at the feel of her hand in his. Then he glanced back at the Thorpes, both of whom continued to watch him.

They were protecting Lady Beatrice.

But from what?

The dancing began. To his shame, Augustus realized that he'd forgotten the steps. But his partner was accomplished enough to steer him across the floor and prevent him from stepping on her, or anyone else's, toes.

Though he longed to know more about her, she reminded him of a skittish filly, needing to be coaxed into trusting him.

About halfway through the dance, she spoke. Her voice, though soft, penetrated his thoughts, despite the music and the ever-present chatter in the room.

"So, you're a traveler, Lord Hardwick?"

"I am," he said. "I spent the past five years on the Continent, mostly in Italy."

"Oh, Italy!" she cried. "I've always wanted to see Rome. Is it as magnificent as they say?"

He smiled at her wide-eyed enthusiasm. "The architecture is to be admired," he said, "but I prefer the countryside. Cities are crowded, filled with people come to stare open-mouthed and declare how pretty the buildings are."

"And you don't think the buildings are pretty?"

"I appreciate the workmanship that's gone into a beautiful building," he said, "but I prefer objects that were fashioned to suit nature rather than seek to conquer it. Mankind is all too apt to force natural curves into straight lines."

She gave a shy smile. "Would you say that, where beauty already exists, it should not be compromised by a quest for aesthetics?"

"You seem remarkably well informed for a young woman embarking on her first Season," he said.

Her smile disappeared. "This isn't my first Season."

"Forgive me," he said. "I meant no offence. I'm afraid I've lost the talent for flattery. My friends see me as something of a savage, having been out of London for so long."

"Perhaps that renders you *less* of a savage," she said. "London Society might be perceived as the pinnacle to which men and women aspire, but I find it a somewhat small and exclusive environment."

"You disapprove of exclusivity?"

"I loathe it," she said. "It enables those who view themselves as paragons to perpetuate that view by surrounding themselves with either like-minded snobs or sycophants."

What a jaded view of the world she had! What had she experienced to gain a degree of cynicism to match even his own?

"I agree with you, Lady Beatrice" he said.

"Are *you* a sycophant, Lord Hardwick?"

Then she blushed, her eyes widening with distress.

At that moment they were separated in the dance, and Augustus found himself hand in hand with Lady Irma for the next few steps, while Marlow took Lady Beatrice's hand. Marlow looked pointedly at Lady Beatrice, and back to Augustus. Then he winked.

When Augustus found himself once more attached to his partner, she seemed to have diminished, despite her tall frame, and she appeared disinclined to talk. By the time the dance had finished, her eyes glistened with moisture.

Rather than return her to her chaperone, he guided her toward a footman holding a tray of glasses, plucked two from the tray, and handed her one.

She nodded in thanks and took a sip.

"Did you enjoy the dance?" he asked.

"Of course." The tone of her voice belied her words.

"I would prefer sincerity to civility, Lady Beatrice," he said. "I myself found the dance rather tedious."

"Forgive me."

"There's nothing to forgive," he said. "You had no wish to give offence. Perhaps you dislike the dance because of my inability to waltz without bruising your feet?"

The flicker of a smile returned. "My feet are still intact, I assure you," she said. "No, I wanted to apologize for calling you a sycophant earlier. I meant no offence."

He squeezed her hand. "I took none," he said. "I find myself honored to have secured a dance, if you're not fond of the activity."

"It's not the dancing I dislike," she said. "It's the whole idea of a ball. People crammed in a room merely to find a partner for life."

"Perhaps you'll learn to enjoy parties."

She shook her head. "I prefer to be outdoors," she said. "When the world is so beautiful outside, I cannot understand the need to remain indoors, parading about a ballroom following the exact same steps that men and women have taken for years."

"I couldn't agree with you more," he said. "There is more to be gained by exploration. A man should follow his own path in life, for only then will he learn and grow. What is the purpose in following a path that's been trodden by others for generations? There's safety in tradition, but little fulfilment."

"Oh, you understand!" she cried, her distress seemingly forgotten.

He smiled at her outburst of enthusiasm. "Do I?"

"I'd much rather run barefoot in the garden than be led by a man around a dance floor."

"Oh dear," he said.

A glint of mischief shone in her eyes. "Present company excepted, of course, Lord Hardwick, even if I was placing my toes at risk."

He let out a laugh.

Her blush deepened. "I-I'm sorry, I meant no offence."

He took her hand. "My dear Lady Beatrice, will you grant me a request?"

The hunted look returned, and she glanced across the room toward her chaperone. "Forgive me, I-I don't…" She hesitated.

"I only request that you refrain from asking my forgiveness at every turn."

Her eyes widened.

He raised his glass. "In fact," he said, "I insist. There's nothing to forgive, Lady Beatrice. I find your frankness charming, and quite rare among our class. May I propose a toast to honesty— that is, at least, honesty between you and I?"

She eyed his glass. "You value *complete* honesty?" she asked. "Even when the truth can be painful?"

He nodded. "I think, perhaps, Lady Beatrice, we are alike, in that we both carry the weight of past histories on our shoulders."

He caught a flash of fear in her expression.

"You must remember, Lady Beatrice," he said, lowering his voice to a whisper, "that past history is just that. It's in the *past*. What's happened before matters not when we're of a mind to follow our own path into the future. Do you not agree?"

He tipped his glass toward her and smiled, and the fear in her eyes faded. She lifted her glass, touching the rim against his with a delicate clink.

"To honesty—between us," she said, lifting the glass to her lips. Then she lowered it again, and he caught sight of a droplet of moisture on her lower lip. Unable to conquer his instincts, he lifted his hand and placed it on her cheek. She drew in a soft breath, and her gaze flicked up to meet his—the color of her eyes warm and inviting.

He caressed her cheek with his thumb, moving against the corner of her mouth, and she parted her lips—sweet, plump lips, asking to be kissed…

Then he withdrew his hand.

What the devil was he doing, in the middle of a ballroom?

"Forgive me, Lady Beatrice," he said.

He caught a flash of disappointment in her expression. Surely she hadn't wanted him to continue?

"Might I make the same request," she said, "that you don't ask for forgiveness when there's nothing to forgive?"

Sweet Lord…

The seed of warmth—that had ignited in his body from the moment he took her hand—coursed through his blood, inflaming a need he hadn't experienced for some years. It surpassed the need that had drawn him to Kathleen seven years ago, for it was a need of his soul, not merely his body.

How was it that such perfection existed?

And he'd been on the brink of compromising her.

If Thorpe had seen him, he'd be placed in the objectionable predicament of having to make her an offer.

Not that objectionable…

In fact, he couldn't think of anything more delectable.

A seed of longing rippled through his body as the image flashed before his mind—that of having this sweet creature in his life, and his arms.

And in his bed…

A hand touched his arm, and he jumped, spilling his drink.

"Did I startle you, Hardwick?"

Thorpe stood before him. He glanced toward Lady Beatrice, then back at Augustus, and raised his eyebrows in the manner of a lawyer cross-examining a witness.

"I trust you're taking care of my ward."

Though Thorpe's voice was quiet, there was no mistaking the underlying threat.

What the devil could Augustus say? That he was dreaming about compromising her?

"Of course he's taking care of me, Giles," Lady Beatrice said. "We were having a perfectly good conversation about gardens before you interrupted us. I was going to ask if Lord Hardwick might like to join us for a walk tomorrow."

"Beatrice!" Thorpe scolded. "It's most improper for a young woman to make such a suggestion. Have I not said—"

"Forgive me, Lord Thorpe," Augustus interrupted. "It was entirely *my* fault. I asked Lady Beatrice if I might call on her tomorrow morning, and she was just telling me that I should ask your permission."

"Oh." Thorpe glanced at his ward, the stern expression fading. "And you consent to this, Beatrice?"

She glanced at Augustus, then smiled. "I do."

"Far be it for me to refuse," Thorpe said. "But you must take Kitty as chaperone. Henrietta's tired, and I wish to take her home. I believe her excursions must be curtailed until our happy arrival."

"Oh, poor Henrietta!" Lady Beatrice glanced across the room toward Lady Thorpe. "We must take her home, of course, if you'll excuse us, Lord Hardwick?"

Augustus took her hand and lifted it, pressing his lips against her skin. "Until tomorrow."

Shortly after the Thorpes departed, Marlow appeared at Augustus's side.

"Found yourself a biddable little woman yet, Hardwick?"

"Don't be crass, Perry," Augustus said.

"Ha! That means you have. I take it the delectable Lady Beatrice is your choice?" Marlow's smile broadened. "There's no need to answer, Gus; I see it in your eyes. Excellent choice. Charming little thing, and her guardian's strict enough to support you in your efforts to mold her into exactly the kind of wife you want."

"I think she's perfect as she is." Augustus sighed.

"Oh, bloody hell." Marlow shook his head. "Promise you'll not give your heart too easily. I wouldn't have you repeat the mistake you made with your first wife."

"Lady Beatrice is nothing like Kathleen," Augustus said.

"She's an innocent. I cannot compare her to that deceitful harridan who'd already taken several lovers before she manipulated me to the altar."

"Of course not," Marlow said. "I meant no offence."

"I've learned from my mistake," Augustus said.

Nonetheless, Lady Beatrice had caught him unawares, and was already on the way to capturing her heart.

But his friend gave good counsel. With his first wife, Augustus had fallen headlong into an infatuation, and agreed to her suggestion of an elopement. Only after their hasty marriage had he realized the reason for her urgency—that she carried another man's child.

This time, he would court Lady Beatrice properly.

CHAPTER FOUR

THE WATERS OF the Serpentine sparkled in the afternoon light—tiny jewels dancing across the surface, broken by the occasional ripple as a fish swam toward the surface, then dived down again.

The swans, which Beatrice loved to watch, were nowhere to be seen. Aunt Euphramia had told her that swans mated for life, that once they'd found their true love, they remained together until the day they died.

Aunt said they were like people in that respect—they only loved once. Those unable to find their soul mate must either settle for second-best, or remain faithful to their ideal and live out their lives in loneliness.

Aunt Euphramia had been widowed several years, and she'd been true to her word, living faithfully to her husband's memory.

As for Beatrice's own mama and papa…

They had adored each other. Never in her life had she heard a cross word from either of them.

She blinked back a tear. Though she adored Aunt Euphramia—and Giles and dearest Henrietta, of course—the pain of losing her parents would never fade. The agony that shattered her heart on learning of their deaths had diminished over time, but the wound would never completely heal.

More than anything else, she wanted a love like theirs. She longed for it, and feared it at the same time. What if she found someone to love, and who loved her in return, but then she lost them?

"Lady Beatrice?"

She looked up to find Lord Hardwick staring directly at her.

She clung to his arm. Since last Season's scandal, she found the proximity of men discomfiting. But Lord Hardwick had a different air about him. She found comfort in his presence, though she'd known him barely a fortnight. Each time he paid a call and took tea with her under Henrietta's watchful eye, her discomfort had lessened.

Now, she found herself drawn to him. That morning, she hadn't been able to stop herself from looking out of the window in anticipation of his arrival. This softly spoken man with clear gray eyes might be that rarest of creatures…

A man to be trusted.

She smiled to reassure him, but he was not easily fooled.

"You smile, but I see melancholy in your eyes," he said. "What distresses you on such a beautiful day?"

His insight unsettled her, and she resumed her attention on the water. At that moment, a pair of swans appeared and glided across the surface in unison—twin souls as one.

She let out a sigh, and he placed his hand over hers.

"I was thinking about happiness," she said.

"Aren't you happy?"

"I'm happy enough," she replied, "but everything—life, fortune—ebbs and flows like a tide."

"And you therefore fear that once you've found happiness, then misery will follow?"

She drew in a sharp breath. How could he read her mind so easily?

He smiled, the sunlight dancing in his eyes, and her stomach somersaulted at the expression—one of regard, affection…

…and desire.

"Such is life," he said. "Without the pain, we can never truly appreciate the pleasure. Sometimes great risks must be taken in order to win great rewards."

"Oh!" she cried. "That's what Henrietta says. She's an advocate for adventure, though tempered by good sense, now that she's nearing her confinement."

"Ah, yes," he said. "Lady Thorpe told me of the adventure you shared last Season."

She stiffened as a cold hand clutched at her stomach. *Dear Lord*, did he know of her elopement? Giles had been so strict about her behavior. He'd said that if the rumors that had almost ruined her last year were to circulate again, there was nothing he could do to restore her reputation, and she'd be ruined.

Then he laughed. "I've no wish to distress you, Lady Beatrice. I find it amusing that two young ladies whisked themselves off to the seaside in search of a little freedom. There's nothing untoward in *that*."

Beatrice averted her gaze to conceal her relief.

"Lady Thorpe said you indulged in a little sea bathing during your excursion."

That, at least, was true.

"We did," she said.

"How did you find it?"

"Cold," she replied. "I discovered that I'm not much of a swimmer. Henrietta, on the other hand, is a marvel. She swims better than anyone I know, better even than Giles. I quite adore her."

"That's most unusual," he said.

"A woman showing greater prowess than a man?"

He laughed again. "No—Lady Thorpe's a remarkable woman. I meant that it's unusual to see a young lady on such friendly terms with her chaperone."

"Henrietta's the best friend I've ever had," Beatrice said. "I'll miss her so much when I…"

She broke off and looked away.

When I marry.

What had caused her train of thought to wander toward

matrimony?

"Henrietta taught me to climb trees!" she continued, a little too loudly. But if Lord Hardwick noticed her discomfort, he showed no sign. She pointed ahead. "That one there, for example. I could climb it almost to the top."

His eyes widened. "Really?"

"Oh dear," she said. "I'm not much of a lady, as you see."

"If I'm permitted to contradict you," he said, "I think you're charming. Artless honesty must always be valued over sophisticated deception. Your chaperone should be proud of her protégée."

A delicious warmth coursed through her body at his words and the expression in his eyes as he looked at her.

"I love Henrietta," she said, "and I fear for her confinement. You hear such horror stories about childbearing, but I have promised to help her in any way that I can."

Lord Hardwick drew in a sharp breath, and his body stiffened. Beatrice caught a flash of fear in his eyes.

"Confinements can, indeed, be dangerous," he said quietly.

"But they come with great rewards," she said. "Henrietta will make a wonderful mother, and I adore children."

He took her hand and held it to his breast. Out of the corner of her eye, she saw Kitty staring at them both, concern in her expression.

"Do you want children, a family of your own…Beatrice?"

Her heart skittered at the familiarity of his address, and she looked up and met his gaze. What she saw unsettled her—hunger, desire, and a deeply rooted need.

It was a need that called to her on a visceral level. His gaze fixed on her, he lifted her hand to his lips and kissed it. A flash of silver shone deep within his eyes, a spark of need, while their color darkened.

"Sh-should you be asking me such"—she hesitated—"such an *intimate* question, Lord Hardwick?"

"I find myself unable to refrain from such intimacy with you."

He lifted his hand to her face, the same gesture he'd made at the ball before Giles interrupted.

But this time there was nobody to interrupt them. He placed his hand on her face; his skin was warm against her cheek.

"Beatrice," he said, "I…" He shook his head. "I don't know if I should say it."

"Please," she whispered. "There's nothing you could say that would cause offence."

He smiled, uncertainty in his gaze, then nodded. "I said myself, only a moment ago, that one must take risks in order to win rewards. Therefore, I shall take a risk now."

He caressed her skin with his thumb, and a secret thrill coursed through her body.

"You may think me overly hasty," he said, "but I shall ask nonetheless. When a man stumbles across the path to true happiness, even if it's sooner than he expects, he should set foot upon it at once, should he not?"

She shook her head. "I-I don't understand…"

"Let me enlighten you," he said. "Beatrice, I have been in London only a short while, but I am happiest when I'm with you. I shall not press you for an answer, but I find myself unable to contain the question any longer. Beatrice, would you do me the honor of becoming my wife?"

Beatrice's heart fluttered, and she stepped back. She had felt a connection between them, as if an invisible thread bound them together. But she'd thought it was a figment of her imagination, or the product of a girlish hope that the first man she believed she could trust would fall in love with her.

Then her heart sank. He *couldn't* have fallen in love with her after such a short acquaintance. He must be proposing a marriage of convenience, sanctioned by the traditions of Society.

She withdrew her hand. "Why do you ask such a thing of me, Lord Hardwick?"

His eyes narrowed with hurt. "Forgive me for such forwardness," he said. "To find myself in love after so short a time—

believe me, I've questioned it myself. But in love I am, and I see no need to refrain from declaring it. After all, we pledged to be honest with each other, did we not?

"Y-you *love* me?"

His eyes crinkled with a smile. "I believe I do, Beatrice," he said. "Of course, I couldn't hope to expect an answer from you now, but may I be permitted to live in hope that, one day, you might consider accepting my hand in marriage?"

Her heart swelled at the sincerity in his eyes. He was so unlike the last man to court her, who'd been all pretty smiles and flattery—the man before her now spoke from the heart. Only after experiencing deception did she recognize sincerity.

"Lord Hardwick," she began, but he interrupted her, the hope in his eyes fading.

"Forgive me. I should not have asked."

"Hush." She placed a finger on his lips.

"You're right, my lord," she said. "Just because love has blossomed over a number of days, doesn't make it any less genuine than a love that takes years to form. Why should we wait to declare love when our hearts are already filled with it?"

Hope shimmered in his eyes, and her heart was ensnared.

"Yes," she whispered. Shyness overcame her, and, unable to meet his gaze—to look into those eyes that seemed to know so much—she looked away. "Yes, I will marry you, Lord Hardwick. I-I find that I return your love."

He cupped her chin and tilted her head up. "My name is Augustus," he said. "Will you not look at me, Beatrice, when you give me your answer?"

Conquering her shyness, she blinked then met his gaze.

"I love you—Augustus," she whispered. "I'll gladly be your wife."

His eyes glowed almost silver in the afternoon light and captured her heart.

The sounds of the park—the wind through the trees, the swans in the distance, and the far-off sound of children laughing—

faded into obscurity until there was nothing left in her world.

Except him.

At that moment, her world was him. And he was everything.

Then he lowered his mouth to hers.

His lips were warm, and they slid over hers with the smooth, practiced grace of an experienced lover—of a man who knew what he wanted and took it. But despite his powerful frame, and the barely suppressed desire trembling in his body, he held back, waiting to be invited.

She parted her lips in invitation. With a low growl of approval, he slipped his tongue between her lips and stroked the inside of her mouth—teasing, coaxing, until she responded, and their tongues circled each other in a smooth dance of seduction.

Her body hummed with life. Wicked sensations resonated through her bones, pooling in her center, which gave a little pulse in recognition.

The breath caught in her throat. What was happening? One moment she was having a rational conversation, then her body sparkled with a primal need. A need for what, she couldn't fathom, but a voice inside her mind told her that only *he* could satisfy that need.

A fizz of desire tingled across her skin, and she became acutely aware of the fabric of her gown against her nipples, which had stiffened into hard little buds.

She arched her back to chase the sensation. Then he slipped his hand inside her gown, and she cried out as a fizz of desire ignited in her center as his fingertips brushed against her sensitive little bud.

"Oh, heavens!" she cried. "I-I…"

"Beatrice?"

"Wh-what's happening?" she said. "I don't understand…"

Almost at once, he withdrew his hand.

"*Dear Lord*, Beatrice, forgive me! I had no intention of behaving in such a manner."

"There's nothing to forgive," she said. "I felt…" She shook

her head. "I can't describe it, but it was wonderful."

"When we're married, you'll discover how wonderful love-making can be," he said. "But I shan't compromise you before then. We have the rest of our lives to explore the pleasures that a man and woman can share."

The rest of our lives…

He offered his arm, and she took it, this time relishing the feel of his body against hers, and they retraced their steps along the path and headed for home, Kitty following a few paces behind.

Lord Hardwick. A name she'd not even heard until a fortnight ago. This man, this beautiful man who had entered her life as swiftly as a storm, was set to give her everything she had wished for. A family, children of her own…

And someone to love.

After the tragedy of her parents' deaths two years ago, and the scandal of last year when she'd had her heart broken, she never believed she could experience such happiness.

Yet here, and now, she was the happiest woman in the world, with a bright future ahead of her with a man who did not judge her for her past mistakes, but who loved her for who she was.

CHAPTER FIVE

A UGUSTUS HAD NO idea which was the more astonishing—the fact that he'd succumbed to love after such a short acquaintance and offered for Lady Beatrice…

…or the fact that she'd accepted him.

Did she have a reason for accepting such a hasty marriage proposal?

He glanced at the woman on his arm. Her lips were curled in a serene smile, her eyes warm with joy, and she seemed to skip along the path. The hunted expression he'd first seen in her at Lady Bunting's ball had disappeared.

Then he admonished himself. Just because he'd been taken in so readily before, that did not mean that all women were the same.

Lady Beatrice was the opposite of Kathleen. She represented the purity his first wife had lacked. Not even he was unlucky enough to be taken in a second time.

As they approached Lord Thorpe's townhouse, the maid maintaining a respectable distance behind, Lady Beatrice tightened her grip on Augustus's arm.

"Are you going to ask my cousin's permission for my hand today?"

"Do you think Lord Thorpe will refuse?"

"N-no…" She hesitated. "But he might remark on how short a time we've been acquainted."

His heart gave a flutter. Was she already regretting her decision? Or perhaps she feared her guardian would refuse. Giles Thorpe was an imposing man with a reputation for sternness. And he might object to their difference in age, even though such age gaps were commonplace in Society marriages. Augustus was thirty-four. Lady Beatrice couldn't be much more than nineteen.

"Perhaps we should wait," he suggested. "I'm prepared to wait if you think propriety, and Lord Thorpe, demand it."

"No, I wish to be married as soon as possible."

As soon as possible…

Augustus winced inwardly.

Beatrice had unwittingly used the exact same phrase Kathleen uttered when he'd offered for her, though Kathleen followed it with a suggestion that they elope.

He glanced at her, a voice of suspicion whispering in his head. Then she colored and the hunted expression returned in her eyes.

"Forgive me," she said. "It was unseemly of me to suggest such a thing. But I see no occasion for subterfuge. I would rather Giles be told of your—*our*—intentions than conceal the truth. I've been less than honest with my cousin in the past, and it's only caused him pain. I have no wish to disappoint him."

She looked away, her lip trembling, and he placed his hand over hers.

"I understand, Beatrice," he said, "and I commend your regard for your cousin. It only serves to convince me that I've made a wise choice. If you're able to show such regard for me, then you'll make me the happiest of men."

She turned her gaze to him, and his heart melted at the affection in her eyes. In time, he hoped, that affection would turn into the deepest love.

As they ascended the steps to the Thorpe townhouse, the doors swung open to reveal a liveried footman.

"Ah, Lady Beatrice," he said. "Lady Thorpe was just wondering where you had got to." He gave a pointed glance at Augustus.

"Thank you," Lady Beatrice said. "Is Lord Thorpe at home?"

"He's in his study," the footman said. He eyed up Augustus once more. "Will your guest be staying for tea?"

"Of course," Lady Beatrice said. "Would you have some brought into the parlor?"

The footman bowed, then retreated toward the back of the house. Beatrice removed her pelisse and handed it to the maid. Then she led the way to the parlor.

Lady Thorpe was sitting beside the fireplace, her pregnancy visible beneath the blanket over her knees.

Augustus felt a pang of jealousy. Lord Thorpe was a lucky bastard—with a beautiful wife who clearly doted on him, and a child on the way.

Then he glanced toward Lady Beatrice—soon, he hoped, to be *his* Beatrice. Her gaze was fixed on him, her eyes dark with desire, and he uttered a silent prayer of thanks for his good fortune.

Provided, of course, Lord Thorpe accepted his petition for her hand.

Lady Thorpe glanced up as they entered the morning room. "Beatrice, dear!" she cried. "I trust you had a pleasant walk?"

"I did, Henrietta, thank you."

"And Lord Hardwick," Lady Thorpe said. "Are you staying for tea? You must forgive me for not accompanying you on your walk today. Giles is such a stickler for propriety. I swear he's of the opinion that ladies of delicate sensibilities will faint at the sight of me. A pregnant woman must not be seen in public, for her body is evidence of unsavory deeds."

"Henrietta!" Beatrice laughed. "I'm sure Lord Hardwick has no wish to hear such things."

Lady Thorpe colored. "You must forgive me," she said. "Giles continually reprimands me over my improper remarks. I trust you'll attribute it to my mind having been addled by what he calls my *delicate condition.*"

"I find your frankness refreshing," Augustus said. "Having spent many years on the Continent, I am used to a much freer form of speech than, say, at Almack's, I assure you."

"I wouldn't know," Lady Thorpe said, a twinkle of mischief in her eye. "I have not traveled outside England, and I am never likely to be granted a ticket to Almack's."

Shortly after, a maid entered the room holding a tray. She placed it on the table in the center of the room, then dipped into a curtsey.

"Thank you, Molly, dear, that will be all," Lady Thorpe said. "Beatrice, would you mind awfully seeing to the tea?"

"Of course." Beatrice approached the table and picked up a cup and saucer.

"Do sit down, Lord Hardwick," Lady Thorpe said.

"I wonder," Augustus said, "might I have an audience with Lord Thorpe before I take my tea?"

Beatrice blushed, and the crockery rattled in her hand. Trembling, she set her cup aside. Lady Thorpe glanced toward her, then fixed her gaze on Augustus.

"Do you have a particular reason for wanting to see my husband?"

The tone of her voice was that of a nursemaid having caught her charge appropriating something that didn't belong to him. But he met her gaze head-on. He'd done nothing wrong, and, in truth, he found much to admire in Lady Thorpe's protectiveness of her young cousin.

"I do," he said.

"Might I ask what it is?"

So frank a question, and on a matter usually settled between men, was the last thing he'd expected from her.

But if what Marlow had said was right, Lady Thorpe had been something of a tomboy, who rode and wielded a sword like a man. It was only logical, then, to assume that she'd wish to negotiate a marriage contract like a man.

"You're too insightful not to understand why I seek an audience with your husband, when I have been courting Lady Beatrice," he said. "But I trust you'll permit me the indulgence of observing tradition. I respect Lord Thorpe too much to ignore what is considered his due as Lady Beatrice's guardian."

"A pretty speech, indeed," Lady Thorpe said, "which conveys your intent without expressing it overtly. I commend your intelligence, at least, which surpasses that of most men." She turned to her cousin. "Beatrice, dear, is this what *you* wish?"

Beatrice was blushing so violently that the tips of her ears had turned pink. The hem of her skirt rippled with the tremors of her body. Pained to see her distress, Augustus moved to stand beside her. He took her hand and lifted it to his lips. Her body stilled, and she drew in a deep breath. Then she let out a sigh, relaxing against him, and his heart swelled at the gesture of trust.

"Yes, Henrietta," she said. "It is my wish."

"You don't think it rather hasty?"

"I respect your wish to protect your cousin, Lady Thorpe," Augustus said, "and if I must wait to claim Beatrice's hand, I'm prepared to do so. But, rest assured, I love Beatrice, and will do everything in my power to make her happy."

"Then I see no reason why you shouldn't discuss the matter with my husband," Lady Thorpe said. "Do you intend to settle in London?"

"No, at my estate in Hampshire," he said. "With my travels overseas, I see little point in keeping a house in London. The rooms I rent are adequate for my needs."

"But you'll have a wife to think about."

"Which is why we'll settle in the country," he said.

"I don't mind," Beatrice said. "I prefer the country to London. As do you, Henrietta."

"Quite so," Lady Thorpe said. Then she resumed her questioning. "Do you intend to continue your travels, Lord Hardwick?"

He nodded. "I have some business interests overseas."

Lady Thorpe turned to Beatrice. "And are you content to be abandoned in the country while your husband travels?"

"Henrietta, please!" Beatrice cried. "Lord Hardwick is entitled to travel if he wishes. I'm not so selfish as to expect him to curtail his lifestyle. Giles went to Paris last year and you didn't object. In fact, you said you took great pleasure in a month of peace and quiet without his getting under your feet, and you can't wait for him to venture abroad again."

Now it was Lady Thorpe's turn to blush. "Forgive me, Lord Hardwick," she said. "I'm excessively fond of Beatrice, and only wish to satisfy myself that you'll make her happy."

"Am I not the best person to decide what, and *whom*, will make me happy?" Beatrice asked.

"Beatrice, if you recall—"

"Henrietta, please!"

The two women exchanged a glance, then Lady Thorpe nodded.

"Forgive me, Beatrice—I speak only out of my love for you. Here, help me up, would you?"

Beatrice rushed to her side and helped her to stand. Lady Thorpe approached Augustus and offered her hand.

He took it, and she curled her fingers around his wrist in a surprisingly strong grip.

"If you're true to your word, and intend to ensure Beatrice suffers no hurt, then I wish you every success in your audience with my husband."

A rather strange little speech, but he took it in the spirit in which it was meant and bowed over her hand, brushing his lips against her skin.

"Thank you, Lady Thorpe," he said. "You have my word that I'll do nothing to hurt Beatrice."

Lady Thorpe nodded, then withdrew her hand. She crossed the floor to the bellpull and gave it a sharp tug.

Moments later, the footman appeared.

"Would you be so good as to show Lord Hardwick to my husband's study?" she asked.

"Very good, ma'am," he replied. "Come with me, sir."

Augustus followed the footman out of the morning room.

Lady Thorpe had shown some mettle in questioning him over his intentions, but, given Lord Thorpe's reputation for sternness, the real ordeal lay before him.

※※※

As the footman ushered Augustus into the study, its occupant rose from his seat behind a large mahogany desk and offered his hand.

"Hardwick! Did you have a pleasant walk with my cousin?"

"Very."

"And now you're come to see me. To what do I owe the pleasure?"

"I wondered if I might have a moment of your time."

"That sounds serious."

"I believe it is."

"You'd better take a seat." Thorpe gestured to the chair in front of the desk, and Augustus took it.

"Brandy?"

Augustus nodded.

Thorpe poured two glasses and handed one over. Augustus took it, swirling the amber liquid, watching it bead on the inside of the glass.

Despite being the elder of the two, Augustus couldn't help the feeling of apprehension, as if, for the first time in his life, he was exposing himself to the judgment of a superior man—someone who possessed the power to prevent him from achieving his heart's desire.

Good heavens, I've really fallen for her!

"What can I help you with?" Thorpe lifted his glass to his lips with one hand while drumming on the desk with the fingers of the other, like a master waiting for a servant to petition him for a favor.

"I'm not one for clever speeches," Augustus said, "so I'll come straight to the point. I'm come to ask for Lady Beatrice's hand in marriage."

Thorpe spluttered on his brandy. Coughing, he set his glass aside, wiping his mouth. "You *what?*"

"I'm asking for—"

"Yes, yes, I heard," Thorpe said, refilling his glass. "I'm just astonished, that's all."

"Is it so unusual that someone should want to marry a lovely young woman such as your cousin?" Augustus asked.

"Perhaps not," Thorpe said, "but why *you?*"

"It's quite simple, really. I've fallen in love."

"You're in *love* with her?" Thorpe shook his head. "After how long—two days?"

Was the man deliberately trying to insult him?

"It's two weeks, and well you know it," Augustus said. "Why wouldn't I be in love? It might seem hasty, but in matters of the heart, there are no rules to dictate how long it takes for love to blossom. Love happens at its own pace."

"Have you asked her?"

"Of course," Augustus said. "It's only right that I seek her opinion first. After all, it's her fate that's at stake, not yours."

Thorpe leaned back, and his mouth twitched into a smile. "I quite agree."

"Lady Thorpe has also voiced her opinion."

For the second time, Lord Thorpe engaged in a coughing fit, and droplets of brandy sprayed onto the desk. "Ha! I bet she bloody did. Did she threaten to cut off your vitals with her sword?"

"No."

"Then I consider that her seal of approval," Thorpe said. "Threatening unwelcome suitors with a sword has become something of a habit where my Henrietta is concerned, and I doubt something as trivial as a pregnancy would stop her."

"Is it an everyday occurrence, then?" Augustus asked.

"What? Being threatened with a sword? Or Beatrice being accosted by unwelcome suitors?"

"Has Lady Beatrice had suitors before?"

Thorpe averted his gaze and hesitated. Then he sighed and set his glass aside.

"If you're going to marry my cousin, it's only right that you know the truth," he said. "I would not have you say that we attempted to deceive you. And if you love Beatrice, then it won't matter, will it?"

Augustus drew in a sharp breath as his stomach twisted in apprehension. What the devil did he mean?

"Does she love another man?"

"Good Lord, no," Thorpe said, "but…" He let out a sigh. "At one time, she thought she did."

"And…he died?"

"No, he's very much still alive," Thorpe said, "though Henrietta has threatened to rectify that should he approach Beatrice again." He leaned forward and refilled Augustus's glass. "Beatrice is an impressionable young woman," he said. "I presume you know the circumstances under which she came into my care?"

Augustus nodded. "Lady Thorpe told me that Beatrice lost both her parents."

"She did," Thorpe said, "and I was, perhaps, a little overindulgent with her, on account of the tragedy she'd already experienced. Last year, that overindulgence culminated in an episode I'd rather forget—that we'd *all* rather forget."

"Was that when she disappeared to the seaside with Lady Thorpe?" Augustus asked. "I see no harm in a little adventure. In fact, I told Beatrice I admired her spirit."

"A seaside holiday is the story we circulated," Thorpe said. "Few people know the truth."

"The truth?"

"Last season, Beatrice ran off with a young man. It was my wife who discovered them"—Thorpe lifted his gaze to Augustus—"after two days."

Two days…

Good Lord!

Augustus took a mouthful of brandy to remove the bitter taste in his mouth. At last, the reason why she'd accepted his proposal had become clear.

Beatrice had given herself to another. As a ruined woman, she'd have to accept the first marriage proposal that came her way.

So *that* was why she was so ready to accept his hand.

Thorpe's expression hardened. "I know what you're thinking, Hardwick."

Augustus set his glass aside. "I doubt that."

Thorpe let out a sharp sigh of irritation. "Like every other man who insists upon perfection in a woman, despite your own shortcomings, you've assumed that Beatrice somehow tricked you into making her an offer." He leaned back, his mouth set in a hard line. "Nothing could be further from the truth. Beatrice was led to fancy herself in love by a libertine who only wanted her for her title and fortune. She regretted her elopement almost as soon as they left London."

"And what part did your wife play?"

"Henrietta brought Beatrice home to me." Thorpe's expression softened, and love shone from his eyes. "It was she who insisted on our spreading the rumor that she'd taken Beatrice on vacation. I was determined that Beatrice marry the young man, but Henrietta persuaded me otherwise."

"Why?" Augustus asked. "Surely marriage would have preserved her reputation."

Thorpe banged his fist on the desk, making Augustus jump. "Because he would have made Beatrice miserable!" he cried. "Having already suffered tragedy, my cousin didn't deserve to spend the rest of her life married to a man who cared nothing for her, merely for the sake of propriety. Henrietta taught me that it's far better to be happy than proper."

The anger in his eyes fading, Thorpe massaged his hand and leaned back, giving a sigh of resignation. "Beatrice has never fully recovered from her ordeal," he said. "She withdrew into herself and lost her enthusiasm for life. When she first agreed to dance with you at Lady Bunting's ball, I saw it as a sign that she might begin to trust again."

Augustus picked up his glass again and stared at its contents. Beatrice hadn't played the temptress. Far from it—she'd been demure and shy. The look in her eyes had spoken of pain and fear, rather than cunning. He was either the greatest simpleton in the world and had been taken in by a very clever woman, or…

Or Beatrice had genuinely fallen in love with him.

"If Beatrice has, indeed, accepted your offer of marriage," Thorpe continued, "then it's for no other reason than she believes that you will make her happy."

Silence fell while Thorpe waited for a response.

At length, he sighed. "Of course, Hardwick, if you wish to withdraw your offer, you're at liberty to do so. Beatrice's welfare is my greatest concern, and I would not have her marry a man who cannot love her as she deserves to be loved. If the…*incident* of last year makes you think less of her, then tell me now, and leave Beatrice to my care."

Augustus opened his mouth to reply, but Thorpe held up his hand.

"If I may finish, I will only say that I am fully aware of the circumstances of your first marriage. The first Lady Hardwick had something of a reputation. I think even you must acknowledge that *you* made a mistake, and fell in love with the wrong person— someone who married you for material reasons, and had no love for you. If Beatrice is guilty of anything, then it's of having made the same mistake as you. But, as a woman, she will be subject to judgment rather than understanding."

Thorpe was right. If Augustus could make such a catastrophic mistake, then a young, impressionable girl shouldn't be vilified for having done the same.

At last, he understood the hunted look in her eyes, and he appreciated the true meaning of the trust she'd placed in him. His Beatrice—his broken angel—had trusted him enough to give him her heart. It was up to him to show that her trust had not been misplaced.

It was not Beatrice who was unworthy of him—but *he* who was unworthy of her.

Augustus lifted his glass. "Then," he said, "it only remains for me to, once more, promise that I will love, honor, and keep Beatrice, and to ask for your blessing."

Thorpe's mouth curled into a smile, and he lifted his glass. "Welcome to the family."

⟫⟫⟫⟫⟩⟨⟨⟨⟨⟨

WHEN AUGUSTUS RETURNED to the morning room, together with Lord Thorpe, Beatrice was drinking tea with Lady Thorpe. Two pairs of eyes watched him as he entered, one quizzical, the other wary.

Thorpe strode toward Beatrice, hands outstretched. "Well, my dear cousin," he said. "I believe congratulations are in order.

She leaped to her feet and threw her arms round his neck. "Oh, Giles, thank you!" she cried. "You've no idea how happy I am!"

"Beatrice! Decorum, please," Thorpe said, but Augustus could hear the laughter in his voice.

Then she broke free and glanced toward Augustus. His heart fluttered at the expression in her eyes—the warmth and love radiating from them. Gone was the hunted look, the undertone of fear. It had been replaced by the charm of youth.

He'd been struck by her beauty the moment he first set eyes on her. But now that she had thrown off the cloak of melancholy…

Now, she was a goddess.

And she was his—all his.

"I think this calls for something a little more celebratory than tea," Lady Thorpe said. "Perhaps, Lord Hardwick, you might care to dine with us tomorrow night?"

"Alas, I have a prior engagement," Augustus said, "but may I call on Lady Beatrice tomorrow morning, for a drive in the park?"

"Of course," Lady Thorpe said, "if Beatrice would like to."

"I'd love to!" Beatrice cried.

Augustus lifted her hand to his lips and kissed it. Lord and Lady Thorpe exchanged a smile and held hands. Her expression was filled with joy, then Augustus caught another look in her eyes as she glanced at Beatrice.

A look of relief.

CHAPTER SIX

BEATRICE DROVE THE needle into her embroidery and winced at the sharp stab. A red droplet swelled on the tip of her thumb, and she lifted it to her mouth.

"I think you should leave your needlework until you're more composed, Beatrice, dear," Henrietta said. "There's still five minutes before Lord Hardwick's due to arrive."

Were her feelings that obvious?

Setting her needlework aside, Beatrice rose to her feet and approached the window overlooking the street.

An enormous open-topped carriage had just drawn up by the front door, bearing a crest she didn't recognize. A black leather hood concealed its occupant.

"Look!" Beatrice cried.

Henrietta appeared at her side. "What a beautiful barouche! Your betrothed is to be commended."

My betrothed…

Beatrice had woken in the middle of the night, almost paralyzed with fear. In her dreams, Phillip Meredith had told Augustus that she was a ruined woman. Then Augustus had abandoned her and forced her into Phillip's arms.

Poor Kitty had entered her chamber just after dawn, to find her mistress racked with tears.

Though it was only a dream, the memories of last summer's scandal had resurfaced since Giles told her that he'd related the story to Augustus. She had struggled to eat more than a few mouthfuls at breakfast. But Henrietta's assurances had calmed her nerves. Augustus had done nothing to make her believe that he'd forsake her. Still, she could hardly contain her relief on seeing the carriage.

Henrietta took her hand. "There!" she said. "Did I not say he'd come? Though I was skeptical at first, he seemed quite genuine when he petitioned for your hand."

A hand appeared and opened the carriage door. Then the subject of their discussion descended from the carriage, carrying an enormous bouquet. He issued an order to the driver, smoothed down the lapels of his jacket, then approached the steps.

Beatrice caught her breath as her heart gave a little flutter. His athletic frame filled out his suit to perfection. His eyes seemed to glitter in the sunlight, which shone on his dark mane, picking out the touches of silver that gave him a distinguished air. His jacket, a dark blue, seemed to emphasize the color of his eyes, which were akin to a stormy sky. The roses he carried were white, their absence of color giving them an elegance that brighter blooms lacked.

He glanced toward the window, and Beatrice shrank back, ashamed to be caught watching him like a love-struck teenager.

But that's exactly what she was. Only this time her love was genuine, and the object of her affection loved her back.

The morning room door opened, and a footman appeared.

"Lord Hardwick for Lady Beatrice."

He stepped aside to reveal her fiancé, and her heart somersaulted in her chest again.

Augustus entered the room, and Beatrice caught the aroma of exotic, woody spices. Then he smiled, and a liquid heat coursed through her veins at the desire in his eyes.

"Beatrice…" He offered the bouquet, and she took it, running her fingertips over the pure white petals. She inhaled the sweet scent of rose. "Lady Thorpe," he said, bowing to Henrietta. "A pleasure to see you again."

"Lord Hardwick, you've quite outdone yourself," Henrietta said. "I had no idea you were in possession of such a beautiful barouche."

"It's on loan from a friend," he said. "The Duke of Whitcombe. Perhaps you know him?"

"I know *of* him," Henrietta said, her smile slipping. "He has something of a reputation."

"I fear it's deserved," he said, "but we were at Eton together, and sometimes loyalty to a friend means that one must ignore a man's faults and concentrate on his more redeeming features."

"Such as being in possession of a barouche?" Beatrice asked.

He let out a laugh. "Exactly, my love." He offered his arm. "And now, if you've no objection to the reputation of its owner, shall we partake of its delights?"

She handed the bouquet to Henrietta and took his arm, and he led her outside to the barouche, where the driver was wrestling with the hood to lower it.

"It's such a fine day, I thought you might enjoy the open air," Augustus said. "And, I must admit, I'm eager to show off my bride-to-be."

Beatrice cringed at the notion of everyone's eyes on her, but she couldn't deny him the pleasure. Her heart swelled at the pride in his voice. She'd never have believed that a man would be *proud* to love her. After last year's scandal, perhaps that was what she needed to silence the doubts in her mind.

She climbed into the barouche, then Augustus followed, settling on the seat beside her.

"Drive on."

They set off, the horses' hooves clip-clopping on the street.

"I trust you're not cold," Augustus said. "I've a blanket should you need it."

She leaned against him and smiled. "I have everything I need right here." She tipped her face up, anticipating the kiss, but he turned his head away, raising his hand in salute to a couple across the street.

"Westbury and his wife," he said. "I've not seen them since I left England. Charming fellow, if a little brusque. His wife's an extraordinary creature. Somewhat forthright, if I recall. She gifts him with a cravat each Christmas, decorated with embroidered holly, and makes him wear it. Can you credit that?"

"Perhaps it's because she loves him," Beatrice replied. "I shall resolve to buy you a whole drawerful of cravats for our first Christmas together."

"Do you impugn my taste in cravats?" His eyes twinkled with mirth, then he patted her hand. "The sentiment is appreciated."

He rattled on, commenting on their surroundings and the people they passed, as if he were a Society gossip. As the driver steered the barouche through the gates leading to the park, Beatrice noticed that the smile in her fiancé's eyes had gone.

A flicker of fear rippled inside her. Did he have doubts, now that he knew the truth about her past?

"Lord Hardwick?"

He focused his gaze on her and frowned. "Now we're engaged, I hoped you would address me with more familiarity."

"Augustus."

"That's better." The smile returned.

"May I apologize for yesterday?" she asked.

"Yesterday?" He raised his eyebrows. "Yesterday you agreed to become my wife. I see nothing to apologize for in that regard."

"I mean about my"—she hesitated, feeling the heat rising in her cheeks, then lowered her voice—"my *elopement*. Giles said that he'd told you the truth."

"He did. May I ask why you didn't tell me yourself?"

"I-I was afraid," she said. "Giles insisted on my not telling anyone. He said that reputations are ruined on far less, and that I must behave as if it had never happened. But I had no wish for there to be secrets between us. I'm sorry." Her voice caught as she fought back tears. "I'm so ashamed of my folly. I-I didn't love him. I have only recently realized that I *couldn't* have loved him."

"How come?" he asked. She tried to withdraw her hand, but he held it firm. "Won't you look at me, Beatrice?"

She lifted her gaze, her vision blurred with tears. Though his expression was intense, she saw no anger, only curiosity.

"Y-you made me realize," she said. "I began to understand what love felt like—when I fell in love with you."

He lifted his hand and placed it on her cheek. She closed her eyes and leaned toward him, relishing the feel of his skin against hers—the callouses on his palms that contrasted with her smooth skin.

A tear spilled onto her cheek, and he brushed it away with his thumb. "You forget your promise, Beatrice."

"P-promise?"

"Aye, your promise to stop asking my forgiveness," he said. "Did I not say that we both carry the weight of past histories on our shoulders? I must also shed the weight of my past, and learn to trust again, if I'm to be happy."

Had his heart been broken? She knew little about the circumstances surrounding his first marriage, but so eligible a man must have had a reason for remaining unmarried for five years since his first wife's death. He must have loved her a great deal.

The pain in her heart caught her unawares. She had no wish to hear about his love for another.

She glanced about the park, then spotted the familiar figure of Eleanor Howard, a dear friend who rarely ventured abroad due to her dislike of crowds. She was viewed as something of an oddity among Society, but she had the kindest heart, and the sharpest wit, though she concealed it well.

To Beatrice's disappointment, Eleanor was not alone. Arm in arm with a young man, a few paces ahead of Eleanor, was her younger sister Juliette.

Beatrice didn't recognize the man, though he was extremely handsome. Together with Juliette—who, for all her unpleasantness, was one of the most beautiful ladies in London—they made an attractive couple. He was dressed ostentatiously, and most certainly *expensively*, in a bright blue jacket with wide lapels, cream breeches, and highly polished boots. His white-blond hair and pale blue eyes were so striking that Beatrice could hardly take her eyes off him.

Juliette glanced at the barouche, then at Beatrice. Her eyes narrowed for a moment, before glimmering with their usual predatory expression.

"Lady Beatrice!" she cried. "How pleasant to see you." She curled her lip into a sneer.

Beatrice stiffened, and a warm hand took hers. Augustus gave the order to stop the carriage. Then he drew Beatrice closer, as if to protect her from Juliette's spite.

"Is that the Whitcombe crest on the carriage?" Juliette asked. "I see no sign of His Grace."

Eleanor drew to a halt and glanced about her, discomfort, or even terror, in her expression, as if she expected the duke to spring out from the nearest bush.

"His Grace is, I believe, at home," Beatrice said.

Eleanor visibly relaxed. What had distressed her?

"It must be so unfortunate not to have a barouche of one's own," Juliette continued, "as charitable as His Grace's gesture might be."

"Monty's an old friend," Augustus said. "Shall I give him your regards when I next see him?"

Juliette had the grace to blush, and she glanced at her companion, but he was staring at the path ahead, a bored expression on his face.

"Will His Grace be joining you later, Lord Hardwick?" Juliette asked.

"He has the good sense not to," Augustus said. "Even Monty knows when he's not wanted."

Juliette frowned. "How so?"

"We have some news that I'm sure you'll be delighted to hear," Augustus said. "Beatrice, my love, would you like to be the one to tell your friend?"

"Of course," Beatrice said. Ignoring Juliette, she gestured to Eleanor. "Eleanor, I am…that is…Lord Hardwick and I are to be married."

"Oh!" Eleanor let out a cry of joy, her usually reserved manner dissolving as she approached Beatrice and held out her hands.

Beatrice leaned over the edge of the carriage, and Eleanor kissed her on both cheeks.

"What joy!" Eleanor cried. "First Henrietta, and now you. I'm so happy for you!" She turned to Augustus. "Lord Hardwick, you're a lucky man to have secured my friend's affection."

"Eleanor!" Juliette snapped. "Must you be so indecorous in your expression?"

Eleanor flushed bright pink and stepped back, mumbling an apology.

"I find your sister's enthusiasm refreshing, Miss Juliette," Augustus said, before pointedly addressing Eleanor. "Miss Howard, I'm sure Lady Beatrice would appreciate your calling on her, perhaps to discuss the wedding. I understand when ladies are good friends, they like nothing better than to gossip and discuss trousseaux."

Eleanor gave a shy smile. "I should like that," she said.

"Perhaps tomorrow?" Beatrice suggested. "I know Henrietta would love to see you."

"Are you sure she's up to visitors?" Juliette asked.

"She's not at home to visitors generally," Beatrice said, glancing toward Juliette, "but she'd make an exception for *Eleanor*."

Ignoring the slight, Juliette turned to her companion, who had shifted his attention, and was now staring at Beatrice, an intense expression in his pale blue eyes.

"Permit me to introduce you to Mr. Moss," Juliette said. "He's the heir to Sir William Moss and has a remarkable estate in Hertfordshire. "Mr. Moss, this is Lord Hardwick and Lady Beatrice Thorpe."

Mr. Moss freed himself from Juliette's grip and took Beatrice's hand.

"Lady Beatrice." He lifted her hand to his lips. Then his tongue flicked out against her skin, and she felt his teeth graze against her flesh. She tried to withdraw, but, for a moment, he tightened his grip before releasing her. An uncomfortable heat bloomed in her cheeks, and she felt the urge to rub the back of her hand, to remove all trace of him.

"Mr. Moss." Juliette's nasal tones cut through the air as she held out her hand. "Would you be so kind?"

Her voice had taken on a harsh note of jealousy. Beatrice shrank back against Augustus's warm body as Mr. Moss resumed his place beside Juliette and took her arm. But his gaze was still focused on Beatrice, and she suppressed a shudder.

Mr. Moss, whoever he might be, was a rake.

Augustus gave the order to drive on, and the barouche resumed its path.

"Your friend seems happy for you," he said.

"Oh, Eleanor," Beatrice said. "I quite adore her."

"But her companions not so much?"

Beatrice blushed. "It's uncharitable of me, I'm sure, but I cannot like Juliette. As for Mr. Moss, I can't abide him." She shuddered.

"You know him?"

She hesitated, then Augustus drew in a sharp breath.

"Is…is *he* the one whom you ran off—"

"No!" she cried. "I've never met him before."

"Yet you've already formed an opinion of him?"

The suspicion in his tone cut through her heart.

"Have you not sensed that someone cannot be trusted the moment you meet them?" she asked. "I didn't like the way he looked at me."

"Aren't you being a little harsh at a first meeting? You might be mistaken."

"I sensed that I could trust *you* from the moment I met you," she said. "Or am I mistaken there as well?"

He closed his eyes and shook his head. When he opened

them again, his expression was filled with guilt.

"Oh, Beatrice, forgive me," he said. "What a fool I am. I only seek to protect you from…" He hesitated and gestured in the air. "From…"

"Phillip Meredith," Beatrice said. "His name was Phillip Meredith. He was sent to the militia, and I have no wish to see him again. But if I do, I trust I'll be able to face him without relying on another to defend me."

He bowed his head like a penitent sinner. "I'm unworthy of you, dearest Beatrice," he said. "My late wife was not faithful to her vows. It's no excuse for my behavior, but it's the reason for it." He broke off, his voice cracking, and she caressed his hand.

"You don't have to tell me if it pains you," she said.

"I do," he replied. "I owe you the truth, dearest Beatrice."

He bent his head and kissed her knuckles, and her skin tightened with need at the feel of his lips—soft, inviting, and loving.

"I was captivated by Kathleen's beauty, and believed myself in love." He shook his head. "No, I owe you the truth—I *was* in love. So blinded was I that I was prepared to do anything to make her mine. I acceded to all her demands, and after she threatened to break off our engagement, I consented to an elopement." He kissed Beatrice's knuckles again. "So you see, my love, I have no right to judge you for being persuaded into an elopement, for I'm guilty of the same action. Only I went ahead with it and married her."

He drew in a deep breath, then let out a sigh.

"What happened?" she asked.

"It became clear that she loved another—or, I should say, *others*. How many lovers she had, I knew not. I heard that she'd broken off five engagements before I offered for her. Monty even told me that she'd offered herself to him. Imagine that—one of my oldest friends!"

"Perhaps he lied to make you jealous," Beatrice suggested.

He shook his head. "A man of Monty's prowess has no need for falsehoods. Besides, whatever his reputation as a rake, to his friends he's as loyal as they come. No—Kathleen had shared her favors with many before I married her. As for the child she carried…"

Beatrice let out a gasp. "She was with *child*?"

"Aye." He nodded. "Part of me hoped the child was mine. But I soon realized my folly. She continued to take lovers after our marriage. I was content, and resigned to raising another man's child as my own. A child shouldn't suffer for the sins of its parents. As she neared her confinement, her resentment of the child grew, but I was determined to love it for the both of us. I told her that once the child was born, I'd claim it as mine, then she could live as she wished, provided she kept her affairs quiet. But, alas, it was not to be. Though she provided me with a son, she didn't survive the birth."

"Oh Augustus, I'm sorry," Beatrice said.

"I hardly mourned her," he said, "so happy I was to have the child. Benedict, I called him, after my father. I saw him as my miracle—my reward for enduring months of an unhappy marriage."

"So…you have a son?"

He blinked, and a sheen of moisture glistened in his eyes. Then he looked away.

"The child lived for three days," he said. "He died before he was due to be baptized."

The stoicism with which he uttered the words sliced through Beatrice's heart more than any outburst of emotion could have done. She took his hand. "Augustus, I'm so sorry," she said. A tear splashed onto the back of her hand, and she wiped her eyes.

"Do not cry for me," he said softly. "I deserve no such consideration."

She shook her head. "I shed tears to acknowledge the tears you cannot shed yourself," she said. "Is that not what a woman does for the man she loves?"

He nodded and held her hand to his breast. "Forgive me for doubting you earlier," he said. "Your love is the greatest gift that

Fate can bestow on me, and I promise that I will treasure it."

"Do you think a man can love twice in a lifetime?"

He drew her to him.

"Yes," he said, "and the second time will be greater than the first, I promise."

CHAPTER SEVEN

"HERE'S TO AUGUSTUS, the seventh Earl Hardwick, on the occasion of his loss of liberty!"

Whitcombe raised his claret glass. "Come on, gentlemen! It's not often we get to toast a man's *second* foray into incarceration."

Marlow and Ffortescue lifted their glasses.

"To you, Hardwick," Marlow said. "Don't listen to Monty. He's a jaded fool with no notion of love."

"Love? Ha!" Whitcombe barked. "I've lent Gus my barouche to parade his doxy round the park. What more do you want? A sonnet? Very well..." He cleared his throat. "There once was a virile young buck, who had multiple ladies to f—"

"That's enough!" Ffortescue cried, with a laugh. "You'll get us thrown out."

Augustus glanced around the dining room, but the other diners were too occupied with their meals to hear them.

"Doxy, eh?" Marlow laughed. "Lady Beatrice seems a very respectable young woman."

"I'm surprised you've noticed," Whitcombe said, "given that you've been mooning over that de Grande girl."

"Don't be a fool," Marlow growled.

"Boys, please!" Augustus cried.

"*Boys*, is it?" Marlow said.

Whitcombe let out a snort. "You forget, Perry, Gus here is nearing his infirmity. To an aged fellow such as him, we're nothing but boys."

"Don't be a fool," Augustus said. "You're, what—three years younger than me?"

"But I'm not weighed down by the ravages of matrimony," Whitcombe said.

"Leave him alone, Monty," Marlow said. "He's in love, can't you tell?"

"Ugh, *love*," Whitcombe said. "Women are for bedding, not wedding."

"So speaks the rake without a heart," Augustus said.

"At least I'm not in danger of having my heart broken," Whitcombe replied. "Are you sure you know what you're doing? Your engagement seems awfully hasty. I don't mean to impugn your choice, but wasn't Lady Beatrice embroiled in some scandal or other last Season?"

"That's right," Ffortescue said. "Disappeared for a week, so I heard."

"She took a vacation with Lady Thorpe, that's all," Augustus said, cringing inwardly at the falsehood.

"Are you sure? Usually when a young woman runs off in secret, it's with a young man."

"Monty, that's *enough*," Marlow said. "Can't you see Hardwick's in love?"

"Then he ought to know, at least, whether the waters he intends to sail up are uncharted. I trust nobody got there before you?"

Augustus rose to his feet. "Didn't you hear Marlow?" he cried. "He said that's *enough*!"

A volley of coughs rippled around the dining room, and a footman appeared at Augustus's elbow.

"Is there anything you require, sir?"

"Another bottle of claret, if you would," Marlow said, "and make sure it's on Whitcombe's ledger."

Whitcombe sighed, then gestured to Augustus. "Sit down, old boy, you're making the place look untidy." He nodded to the footman. "Make it two bottles, and put the entire meal on my ledger."

After the footman exited the dining room, Whitcombe leaned toward Augustus. "Sorry, old boy," he said. "If you are really in love, then I wish you all the best. For what it's worth, your wife-to-be seems a charming little thing." He raised his glass again. "Here," he said. "Let me drink to honor Lady Beatrice Thorpe. Soon to be Lady Hardwick."

Marlow and Ffortescue followed suit.

"To Lady Beatrice!"

Augustus raised his glass and took a sip. The rich ruby wine warmed his throat.

His friends meant well—even Whitcombe, who believed that women had only one purpose.

But he couldn't help the voice whispering in his head. He'd pledged honesty to Beatrice, yet here he was, having to uphold a falsehood in front of his best friends. How many times would he have to lie for her?

CHAPTER EIGHT

"O H, *MADEMOISELLE BEATRICE, vous êtes très belle!* The green sets off your complexion beautifully, *n'est-ce pas?*"

Beatrice stood before the mirror and gazed at her reflection while the modiste held a bolt of silk against her.

"*Regardez* the color of the silk! It brings out the color of your eyes. And I have the most beautiful lace for the trim—would you like to see?"

"Yes please, Madame Dupont," Beatrice said. She held up the modiste's sketch. "Henrietta, what do you think?"

Henrietta smiled from her vantage point in a chair beside the mirror. "I think madame has excellent taste. I love what she's proposing with the cut of the sleeves. Madame, you're an artist."

"*Merci*, Lady Thorpe!" the modiste said. "You're too kind. Of course, I save my best silks for my very *favorite* customers."

Henrietta let out a laugh. "I'm sure you say that to every lady who walks through your door," she said. "But I appreciate the sentiment."

"Thank you, madame." The modiste scribbled in her notebook then snapped it shut. "And, of course, I shall attend you for the fittings, Lady Beatrice. Dear Lady Thorpe mustn't venture out, given that she is *enceinte*."

"I'm quite well enough to walk, I assure you, madame," Henrietta said.

"No, I insist. A wedding is an exciting affair, *n'est-ce pas?* You must conserve your strength. Now…” The modiste turned to Beatrice. “Shall I show you the lace I have in mind?”

Beatrice nodded. “Thank you, Madame Dupont.”

“I’ll be just a moment,” the modiste said in her singsong voice, then she disappeared into the back of the premises.

About a minute later, the doorbell tinkled, and a small group of ladies entered the shop.

“Oh, I say!” a familiar nasal voice cried. “It’s Lady Beatrice, and dear Lady Thorpe, also.”

Standing in the doorway, flanked by two young ladies, was Juliette Howard. To her left stood Lady Irma Fairchild, and to her right, Lady Arabella Ponsford. The latter should elicit sympathy, given that she’d been recently orphaned, as Beatrice had been a year ago. But her personality was even more unpleasant than Juliette’s, something Beatrice wouldn’t have thought possible. Rumor had it that Lady Arabella was seeking to attach herself to the Duke of Dunton, which made her Juliette’s chief rival.

By rights, therefore, Juliette should loathe the young woman, but for Arabella’s one redeeming feature.

Her wealth.

Rumor had it that Lady Arabella had a fortune of fifty thousand pounds, which she came into on her twenty-first birthday, at which point she’d attract the attention of every avaricious man in the land.

Perhaps Juliette was following the old adage to keep one’s enemies close.

As for Lady Irma…

At one point, Giles had thought to make her an offer, until he was reunited with Henrietta. Beatrice herself had ensured that the engagement did not take place.

But she had done it at great cost.

For she had confessed to her elopement in front of Lady Irma. It had the desired effect—Lady Irma turned her attentions away from Giles. But since that day, Beatrice had lived in fear of Lady Irma spreading gossip, despite Giles’s warning Irma that he’d seek retribution if she did.

But as Beatrice knew, there was no need for Irma to be explicit. A sly whisper here, a wink there, and her secret would be out.

And there were none so proficient at sly whispers than the three women who stood before her now.

"I had no idea you frequented Madame Dupont's," Juliette said. "I'd have thought her style a little flamboyant for a creature of your tastes."

"On the contrary," Henrietta replied. "Madame has a reputation for making the finest wedding gowns in London. Naturally, we wish Beatrice to have the best. Madame designed the most exquisite gown for the Duchess of Westbury, who's a very dear friend of mine. Perhaps you know her?"

Juliette colored and looked away, but Lady Irma let out a laugh. "That common little fortune hunter!" she cried. "I wouldn't be proud to call *her* a friend. She's rumored to have taken part in a duel and shot a man."

"I admire her spirit," Henrietta said. "I've only ever fought with a sword, not a pistol."

Her words had the desired effect, silencing Lady Irma, who fanned herself as if suffering a fainting fit. But Beatrice looked away, ashamed. The only duel Henrietta had fought was against Phillip Meredith, the man Beatrice eloped with.

Henrietta met her gaze and mouthed an apology.

"So," Lady Irma said, regaining her composure, "you're to be *married*, Beatrice?" A cold smile curled her lips, and a small shiver of fear rippled along Beatrice's spine.

Surely Lady Irma wouldn't reveal her secret?

Out of the corner of her eye, Beatrice saw Henrietta straighten her back, as if readying herself for a fight. Irma glanced in her direction, and her eyes widened. Beatrice could almost hear the message Henrietta conveyed.

Go on, Irma. If you dare…

"Oh, yes!" Juliette cried. "I saw the couple myself in the park the other day. A rather fine catch, dear Beatrice—and, of course, you have no concerns about your husband-to-be being inexperienced in the ways of the world."

"How come?" Irma asked.

"Why, he must be forty if he's a day!" Juliette said. "He's going quite gray, you know. Of course, it gives him a more mature air, and I understand some young women are quite drawn to that sort of thing, particularly if they yearn for fatherly affection."

Henrietta leaned forward, her eyes glittering with anger, and Beatrice placed a hand on her arm. As loathsome as Juliette might be to make reference to her deceased parents, Beatrice had no wish to see Henrietta distressed in her condition.

"Are you going to enlighten us as to the identity of the man fortunate enough to have secured Beatrice's affection?" Lady Irma asked.

"Earl Hardwick," Juliette said.

A glimmer of envy shone in Irma's eyes as she focused her gaze on Beatrice. "Fortunate indeed," she said.

"Of course," Juliette continued, "a man of his age will have to maintain his vigor if he's to be your perfect match, and not just because of the difference in age."

"Whatever do you mean?" Arabella asked, speaking up for the first time.

"Well, our dear Beatrice here is something of an adventuress," Juliette said. "Both she and Lady Thorpe disappeared during last season on an impromptu vacation, and caused something of a stir."

"Well, *really!*" Arabella wrinkled her nose in disgust, but Irma's mouth curled into a smile, her eyes glittering with malice.

"Oh, is *that* what happened?" she asked. "I heard something quite different." Then she gave a light laugh and waved her hand dismissively. "I confess, I hear so many different accounts of events during the season that I never know what to believe. What say you, Beatrice, dear?"

"I have never been interested in gossip," Beatrice said.

"We cannot all share the same interests," Irma said. "Gossip is only truly enjoyed by those who do not invite scandal. Those embroiled in scandal are less likely to indulge in gossip themselves."

At that moment, Madame Dupont returned holding some samples of lace.

"Ah! Lady Irma!" she said. "And you've brought Mademoiselle Juliette with you, and another young lady. How delightful! Have you come to see the new silks I've had delivered, or do you have something particular in mind?"

"I'm in need of a new gown, Madame Dupont, for Lady Moss's ball," Irma said, "and I'm anxious for Arabella to pay you a visit, since she's new in Town. Do you know Lady Arabella Ponsford, daughter of the late Duke of Southerton?"

The modiste dipped into a curtsey. "Lady Arabella, a pleasure! I heard of your father's passing. How tragic, *ma pauvre fille!* You have something in common with Lady Beatrice, *n'est-ce pas?*"

Arabella inclined her head politely, but the sour expression on her face spoke of her disdain at the notion of having *anything* in common with Beatrice. Unlike Beatrice, whose heart always stung whenever she thought of her parents, Lady Arabella didn't seem to care at all.

"Now, ladies," the modiste continued, "might I invite you to admire the silks which have just arrived? If you wish to choose a fabric, I'll be with you directly once I have finished with Mademoiselle Beatrice."

The three ladies nodded, and Madame Dupont guided them to the back of the shop, where the bolts of silk were aligned in neat rows according to color.

When she returned, she placed the different samples of lace against the green silk, until Beatrice agreed on one to adorn her gown. Then, after writing more notes in her ledger, the modiste bade them farewell, and they exited the shop.

Beatrice slipped her arm into Henrietta's, and they set off for home.

"It's a fine day today," Henrietta said. "What say you to a stroll in the park, then perhaps tea? There's a shop beside the entrance that sells the most delightful cakes."

"No, thank you," Beatrice said. "We should get back."

"I'm feeling quite sprightly, if that's your concern," Henrietta said. "Dr. McIver said I should continue to take light exercise before my lying-in."

"Nevertheless, I'd rather go home."

Henrietta drew to a halt. "What's upset you, Beatrice, dear?" she asked. "Surely you're not taking any notice of what that dreadful Juliette girl and her friends say?"

"Of course not," Beatrice said, "but I can't help but wonder whether Irma won't reveal the truth about my elopement."

"What harm can it do?" Henrietta asked. "Lord Hardwick knows the truth, and he's not concerned by it."

Beatrice shook her head. "I know, but something tells me not to trust those women. I can't place what it is—but I have a feeling of dread, as if something terrible is going to happen."

"Such as what?"

Beatrice opened her mouth to answer, but her throat constricted with an overwhelming sense of fear, and tears pricked her eyes.

A warm hand took hers, and she glanced up to see Henrietta looking directly at her.

"Oh, Beatrice!" she cried. "You really love him, don't you?"

Beatrice bit her lip and nodded, the motion releasing a tear, which spilled onto her cheek. "It's foolish, I know," she said, "but I've grown so fond of him! He's so kind, and for the first time, I feel I can trust someone—*really* trust them. Am I naïve to think so?"

"No, my dear," Henrietta said. "You're not naïve. You're just in love. And while I'm a little surprised that love has blossomed so quickly, I can understand it. After all, I was in love with Giles for years, even though it took me a long time to recognize it. If you're able to recognize your love now for what it is, then you can enjoy the wonder of being in love rather than spend years denying it."

She placed a kiss on Beatrice's forehead. "You've nothing to fear, my dear, from those unpleasant young women. You are in love, and that love is returned. And, because of that, nobody can touch you."

"I know," Beatrice said, "and I know Augustus doesn't care about what happened last Season, but I can't help but be concerned. What if Irma decides to gossip? I care not for myself, but I do care for him. Augustus has suffered such heartbreak with his first wife—how he recovered from her betrayal, I know not. It would break my heart to see him distressed further." She sighed. "More than anything, I want to ensure he's never hurt again."

"Then you are truly in love," Henrietta said, "for only the deepest form of love makes us place the welfare of others before ourselves." She took Beatrice's hand. "Come, my dear—we'll return home and take tea. Cook made some excellent shortbread today, and I'm concerned that Giles will eat it all if we're not quick."

The two of them resumed walking.

Henrietta was right: Augustus had made it clear that he cared not about Beatrice's past, and he'd given her every sign that he loved her.

But a voice kept whispering in her mind that now she had reached the pinnacle of happiness, there was only one direction her fortunes could turn.

CHAPTER NINE

THERE WAS NO doubt about it: his fiancée was the most beautiful woman in the room. It wasn't her striking looks—the fact that her tall, slender frame stood out among all the other ladies at the ball. Neither was it the exquisite color of her gown—the ocean blue that shimmered in the light, shifting to a deep green. Nor was it the way her eyes seemed to deepen with desire each time she looked at him…

It was, as he had begun to admit to himself over the past fortnight, the fact that he had fallen utterly in love with her.

How could a woman be so perfect? And why had he been so unfortunate as to not have known her earlier? Perhaps he might have been saved from Kathleen's predatory charm.

Perhaps it was a lesson in life that he'd needed to learn—to suffer heartbreak at the hands of a woman who despised him. Because, now, he could appreciate the pleasure of finding a woman with a purity of soul that made him want to weep—a woman who loved him in return.

He was, indeed, the most fortunate of men.

And tonight, she was in his arms. Her delicate hand with its long, slender finger curled round his, as if to mark her possession of him, as surely as he possessed her in turn.

This was their third dance in a row. Twice was acceptable, but a third time conveyed to the whole room that he had claimed her as more than a mere dance partner.

It had not gone unnoticed, and he couldn't help the beast that resided inside his mind roar with possessiveness every time he saw the hungry glances of the unattached men as he guided his fiancée across the dance floor.

The dance concluded, and he steered her toward the edge of the room where Lady Thorpe sat, her pregnancy visible even through her shawl.

Almost as soon as they sat, a young man appeared, dressed in a flamboyant jacket of dark purple, with a brightly colored, striped waistcoat and cravat trimmed with lace. He eyed up Augustus with a slight sneer on his lips, his pale blue eyes glittering in challenge, and his expression turned to one of hunger as he shifted his gaze to Beatrice.

Heath Moss. The young man they'd encountered in the park a fortnight ago, eldest son and heir to their host, Sir William Moss.

He returned his gaze to Augustus, like a young buck challenging the stag for possession of the females.

Or, in this case, one female in particular.

But Heath Moss was no stag. He was, at best, a strutting peacock who thought himself desirable by virtue of frills and frippery.

"Lady Beatrice," he said, his thin, nasal tone filled with affectation. "I believe you now belong to *me*." He glanced at Augustus, a smirk on his lips before offering Beatrice his hand. "For the next two dances, at least."

Two dances? Really?

Heath glanced back at Augustus. "Yes, that's right," he said.

Damn, he'd said that aloud.

"Lady Beatrice was most accommodating in letting me fill her"—Heath licked his lips, his eyes taking on a predatory look—"her dance card."

Augustus curled his hands into fists, fighting the urge to smash the smugness out of Heath's expression. The cocky young buck fancied himself a little too much.

"Lady Beatrice," Heath continued, giving her a dazzling smile, "you've been quite neglected. Shall I fetch you a drink?"

"I'm quite capable of fetching my own, Mr. Moss," she said.

Augustus felt a surge of pride in his Beatrice, in how she refused the false gallantry of the young puppy.

Undeterred, Mr. Moss bowed and offered his hand.

"I like a woman who's unafraid to take what she wants. Permit me to escort you to the punch bowl."

She rose and let him guide her across the dance floor, and Augustus swallowed the surge of rage. They made a handsome couple, and Heath Moss was Beatrice's age—a virile young man, the kind that young ladies flocked to. Youthful, charming, dashing, dazzling…

Everything that Augustus was not.

He continued to watch while Mr. Moss talked animatedly to Beatrice, and she smiled and laughed, nodding in agreement at whatever inanities he threw her way. Miss Juliette Howard and Lady Irma Fairchild joined them, and, though Augustus knew Beatrice loathed both ladies, her smile hardly wavered.

The music struck up again, and Mr. Moss led Beatrice onto the dance floor, where the couples were, once more, lining up.

"They dance well together," a voice whispered.

He turned to see Marlow at his elbow. Augustus gave a snort. "Don't be a fool, Perry. I'll wager that young coxcomb does little else than prance about the room and discuss the latest style of lace-trimmed waistcoats with his valet."

"Ah, I thought I'd detected an air of Othello about you."

"What do you mean?" Augustus asked.

Marlow waved toward the dancers. "A much younger, beautiful wife, giving another man her attention."

"And I suppose you fancy yourself something of an Iago?"

"Good Lord no!" Marlow laughed. "My dear Gus, I've no intention of inciting jealousy when there's no justification for it. All the world can see how Lady Beatrice adores you. But you must understand that now the lady has secured an offer of marriage, she has also secured the attention of the rest of the world. In the eyes of most other young men, she is desirable. For what can be more tempting for a hungry suitor than the forbidden fruit?"

"She hasn't just secured an offer, Peregrine," Augustus said. "In two days she'll be my wife."

"Which makes her even *more* of a temptation," Marlow replied, "for there's so little time left for young men to be gallant to an unattached woman. Lady Beatrice is hardly likely to dance with another man again once she becomes your countess."

"You think so?"

Marlow raised his eyebrows. "Heavens, Gus!" he cried. "Surely you don't suspect Beatrice of returning Mr. Moss's regard? This Season she has been the model of decorum. She's young, and a little malleable, and will honor her vows of obedience. You'll be able to fashion her into the perfect wife, which is what you said you wanted."

Young and malleable—qualities that, at first, he'd deemed perfect. But when such malleability stretched to other young men...

Damn Marlow! While he'd meant to reassure him, the seed of doubt threatened to sprout in Augustus's mind.

"Do you expect Miss de Grande to be as malleable, Perry?" he asked.

Marlow's smile slipped. "You and I are different, Gus," he said. "I could never be satisfied with a biddable wife. I relish the challenge too much. And Miss de Grande could never be described as malleable. In fact, she's disappeared again tonight."

"Is she not dancing?"

"She was dancing with Thorpe during the quadrille, but I've not seen her since."

"Does she have a habit of disappearing during parties?" Augustus asked.

"On occasion," Marlow said, "but she always reappears."

"Looking guilty, I imagine," Augustus said. "When a single

lady is nowhere to be seen, one must make assumptions that, more often than not, are true."

"Unless she's accompanied by her chaperone."

"I can see Miss de Grande's aunt sitting close to the punch bowl, as usual," Augustus said. "The lady in question is not with her." Marlow's smile slipped, and Augustus let out a laugh. "Perhaps you're the one to wear Othello's mantle tonight," he said. "At least my quarry is still within my sights."

He glanced across the room to where Beatrice was still dancing with Mr. Moss. The dance was coming to a close. Soon she'd be back by his side, and he longed to claim her again to quash the doubt that Marlow had inadvertently placed in his mind.

Perhaps he'd defy decorum and kiss her in front of the guests. After all, they would be man and wife in two days, and it would be natural for a couple so much in love to be overcome by the struggle to contain their passion for each other.

"Ah, *there* you are," another voice said, and Augustus turned to see Whitcombe standing before him, champagne glass in hand, a smirk on his savagely handsome face. "Not dancing, Augustus, old chap? The company seems exceptionally cordial tonight."

Augustus let out a snort. "I see *you're* not dancing, Monty," he said. "But then, you loathe the prospect of standing up with a woman, don't you?"

"Oh, I don't know." Whitcombe's mouth curled into a cocky smile. "Standing gives one just as much pleasure as any other position." He sipped his champagne, then wrinkled his nose. "Ugh. The rumors must be true. Sir William Moss is suffering from a lack of funds." He lifted his glass and inspected the contents. "No man of means would serve such ditchwater at a ball."

"Perhaps his palate lacks sophistication," Augustus suggested. "A family trait—after all, his son has an appalling taste in waistcoats."

Whitcombe set his glass aside. "Young Master Heath considers himself something of a womanizer. Of course, a man has to appeal to the female sex in order to claim that title, otherwise he's nothing but a lecher. Not even a pink waistcoat can compensate for a lack of sexual appeal."

"The one he's wearing tonight is sporting green stripes," Augustus said. "I can't imagine any self-respecting tailor making a *pink* waistcoat."

"You'd be surprised," Whitcombe said. "But I can't see him at the moment."

Augustus cast his gaze across the ballroom. Mr. Moss seemed to have disappeared.

A ripple of apprehension threaded through him.

Beatrice had disappeared also.

At that moment, footsteps approached.

"Lord Hardwick!" a thin, nasal voice cried. "You must come quickly!"

Juliette Howard stood before him.

Augustus raised his eyebrows. What the devil did *she* want?

She frowned when he didn't respond. "It's Lady Beatrice," she said. "She's been taken ill. You're to go to her immediately."

"Where is she?" he asked.

"In the library," came the reply. "Let me show you."

Whitcombe let out a snort. "That's one way to entice a man into a liaison," he said. "I wish you luck."

Before Augustus could respond, Whitcombe sauntered off. Augustus met Miss Howard's gaze as she arched her eyebrow expectantly.

"Very well," he said. "Lead the way."

He followed her out of the ballroom and into a corridor. The strains of the music grew fainter, until he could hear another sound.

An unmistakably *primal* sound.

Deep, throaty male rasps, and the shrill sounds of female pleasure.

"What the devil's going on?"

"Oh, mercy me!" Miss Howard cried.

The surprise in her voice was a little too forced.

Augustus grasped her wrist and pulled her close. "Is this some trick?"

A flash of fear shone in her eyes, and she shook her head. "Beatrice is in the library, I swear," she said, gesturing to a door about halfway along the corridor. "Let me show you."

"No," he said, pulling her back. "*I'll* go first. If you're toying with me, there will be consequences. I care not whether you're a woman."

"Very well," she said. "Go ahead."

As he neared the door, the sounds increased, and he caught sight of shapes moving in the shadows at the far end of the corridor.

"Who's there?" he cried.

The shapes moved, and a face came into the light—a face Augustus recognized. Lord Ian Short, a man with a reputation for debauchery.

"Ah, Hardwick, isn't it?" Short said. "Come to join our little ménage?"

"You boor!" Augustus cried. "Have you no respect for your hosts?"

Short let out a laugh. "I forgot, you're past rutting age, aren't you, old man?"

Before Augustus could reply, he heard voices coming from the library—a deep male voice, filled with lust, and a shrill female voice.

He pushed open the library door and recoiled at the sight before him.

In the center of the room, a woman lay sprawled on a table. A man leaned over her, cradling her in his arms.

"What the bloody hell's going on?" Augustus roared.

The man turned around and smiled.

It was Heath Moss, his pale blue eyes glittering with relish. "Well, well, it's the cuckold," he said. "Making quite a career out of it, aren't you, old man?" Then he adjusted his cravat and winked.

The woman sat up and let out a cry, and a shaft of pain tore through Augustus's heart.

It was Beatrice.

His Beatrice had lain back on the table, spread her legs, and offered herself to another man, lying in exactly the same position he'd once caught Kathleen in six years ago.

Once again, the woman he loved had betrayed him.

CHAPTER TEN

THE FOG OF terror lifted as Beatrice pushed her assailant back. How could she have been so foolish as to have trusted him? The nausea that had overcome her during the dance still ebbed and flowed, like a tide. Mr. Moss had been so gallant, offering to take her outside for air, steering her along the corridor while she struggled to retain her balance. Then she'd found herself pushed back, while he coaxed and flattered her. What had, at first, seemed laughable soon brought about a terror inside while she tried to fight him, but found her limbs unable to move.

But oh, what blessed relief when she heard the voice of her savior!

"Augustus!" she cried. "Thank goodness!"

She blinked, struggling to focus on the man standing in the doorway, like a knight come to her rescue.

Augustus stared at her, his expression hardening. Jaw set firm, teeth gritted, he gestured toward Heath. "Get your hands off my fiancée."

Though his voice was quiet, it held a note of barely contained fury.

Shaking her head to dispel the dizziness, Beatrice pushed Heath back. He resisted, the loathsome smirk returning to his expression. She lifted her leg and rammed her knee into his groin.

"You heard him!" she cried.

Heath staggered back, raising his hands in supplication. "Oh, very well," he said, "but you can't blame a fellow for trying when you received my attentions so prettily."

"I did no such thing!" She smoothed her skirts, trembling, then tried to stand, but the world slipped sideways, and she staggered back against the table.

Heath reached for her, then a pair of hands grasped him by the shoulders and pulled him back.

"I *said*, get your filthy hands off her, or I'll break your damned neck!" Augustus roared.

Beatrice shrank back. She'd never seen Augustus so angry. His usually gentle, staid demeanor gone, he exuded raw fury. He grasped Heath by the lapels and threw him against the wall, knocking over a vase, which landed on the floor and exploded into shards.

"All right!" Heath cried. "I'll go!" He shook his head. "That was a Ming vase. How the devil will I explain it to Pater?"

"Tell him you got hit by an old man," Augustus sneered.

Heath adjusted his cravat, then exited the room. Only then did Beatrice notice the other occupant in the library.

Juliette Howard stood in the doorway, triumph glittering in her eyes.

"Augustus," Beatrice said, "thank heavens you came when you did. I—"

He raised his hand to silence her. "I'm in no mood for tales, Beatrice," he said in a quiet, even voice.

She rose to her feet and stumbled as the world slipped sideways again. He reached out and caught her, but when she looked up to thank him, he stared at her unsmilingly.

"How much have you had to drink?"

Why did he have to sound so accusing?

"Two glasses, maybe three. I can't recall exactly," she replied. "I-I saw no harm in a few glasses. Then, when I felt unwell, Heath offered to take me outside…"

"I *beg* your pardon?"

"I said—"

"I know what you said," he interrupted, "but since when have you taken the liberty of addressing Mr. Moss in such a familiar manner?"

Behind him, Juliette let out a little huff, her lip curled into a sneer.

He whirled around. "Leave us, Miss Howard," he said. "We don't exist for your amusement. Rest assured, if I hear any gossip relating to tonight, I'll know who's responsible. I have no qualms about punishing a woman for her misdeeds."

Juliette paled, then nodded and fled.

"Beatrice, tidy yourself up," Augustus said. "You don't want anyone else seeing you in that state."

Beatrice fought back the tears. "How can you be so unfeeling?" she cried. "Mr. Moss tried to compromise me tonight."

"Did he succeed?"

Her gut twisted. "What exactly are you accusing me of, Augustus?"

"You know full well," he said. "What will your cousin do now, Lady Beatrice? Will he demand that Mr. Moss be packed off to the militia in order to quell any scandal—like he did with Phillip Meredith?"

She blinked, and a tear splashed onto her cheek. "How can you say such things, Augustus? I've told you what happened. Surely you can't think the worst of me?"

He shook his head and sighed. "I don't know what to think."

"You've made it perfectly clear what you think," she said bitterly. "Would you believe him over the woman you profess to love?"

"I cannot help what I saw."

"How dare you!" She raised her hand to strike him, but he caught her wrist.

"Beatrice!" a voice cried.

Henrietta stood in the doorway, cradling her swollen belly, her face creased with distress.

"Henrietta, what are you doing?" Beatrice said. "You mustn't wander about in your condition."

"Lavinia saw you leave the room," Henrietta said. "She told me you looked unwell." She glanced at Augustus, her eyes widening. "Oh, forgive me, have I interrupted you?"

"No, Lady Thorpe," Augustus said. "We're finished here."

"Is everything all right, Lord Hardwick?"

"Of course," he replied. He steered Beatrice toward Henrietta, his touch so gentle that she could almost have believed his previous outburst had been a figment of her imagination.

"I'll leave you two ladies now," he said. "Lady Thorpe, I must go home, and I suggest you take Lady Beatrice home also."

He gave a stiff bow, then walked away, leaving Beatrice alone with Henrietta.

The tears flowed freely now, and, trembling, Beatrice clung to Henrietta.

"Whatever's the matter, my dear?" Henrietta asked.

"It's Mr. Moss!" Beatrice cried. "I came across all dizzy during the dance, so he offered to take me for a walk to clear my head, then…then h-he tried to compromise me, and"—she caught her breath, fighting back the sobs—"and Augustus came in, and thought we…" She drew in a sharp breath, unable to contain the sob that escaped. "Oh, Henrietta! Juliette Howard was there. She saw everything!"

"Juliette Howard?" Henrietta's eyes narrowed. "I'll wager that loathsome creature had something to do with it."

"What about Augustus?" Beatrice asked. "Is he…" She hesitated, unwilling to voice her fear. "Is our engagement broken?"

"Of course not!" Henrietta said. "You're getting married the day after tomorrow. Did he say anything to indicate that was the case?"

"Not explicitly."

"There you have it," Henrietta said. "I daresay he'll have a good sulk tonight, then tomorrow he'll visit, bearing gifts and pleading your forgiveness. Each time Giles makes a fool of himself he showers me with gifts. It's come to such a state that whenever he brings me a gift, I ask him what transgression he's committed that he feels the need to compensate for. Usually, the finer the gift, the greater the transgression."

Henrietta slipped her arm through Beatrice's. "Come along, my dear; let's get you home. Unless you'd like me to ask Giles to challenge Mr. Moss to a duel?" She smiled at Beatrice, mischief in her eyes.

"There's no need," Beatrice said. "I kneed him in the groin, and Augustus threw him against the wall."

"There!" Henrietta said. "You see? Only a man in love would throw a rival against a wall. You've nothing to fear, my dear. Lord Hardwick will realize the error of his ways, mark my words."

Henrietta spoke sense, but another voice whispered in Beatrice's mind, repeating the words Augustus had said to Juliette.

I have no qualms about punishing a woman for her misdeeds.

Chapter Eleven

AUGUSTUS STRODE OUT of the library. The rutting Lord Short and his doxy seemed to have disappeared, as had Juliette Howard. No doubt *that* particular woman had achieved her objective.

Damn her!

And damn…

He caught his breath, trying to dispel the image of his fiancée spread over the table like an offering.

Adjusting his cravat, he approached the footman in the hallway. "Fetch my coat, would you?"

The footman's eyes widened, then he nodded. "Shall I have your carriage sent round?"

Augustus shook his head. "No, I'll walk."

He needed time, and exertion, to work off the anger simmering inside.

The footman bowed again. "Very good, sir."

After donning his greatcoat, Augustus strode out of the townhouse, barely acknowledging the footman in the doorway. He descended the steps, his breath forming puffs of mist in the air.

It was going to be a cold evening. Perhaps, even, a frost might settle overnight.

How appropriate. It would match the frost that had descended on his heart.

How could he have been such a damned fool—again? Was he so lacking in good sense and judgment? Having sworn never to be duped again, he'd pushed aside his concerns about the rumors that surrounded Beatrice—rumors confirmed by her guardian—and believed in her innocence.

Perhaps he still did. The relief in her eyes when she'd set eyes on him in the library seemed genuine enough. But he'd been duped before by an air of innocence.

Perhaps all women were deceivers.

But—*damn it*—he'd grown fond of her, and had begun to see himself in the family life he'd always dreamed of—seeing his estate prosper at his hands, and the household thrive under his wife.

And seeing his family grow—children he could love and, above all, claim as his.

"Well, well—what's a fine-looking gentleman such as your-self doing out on such a cold night?"

A shape emerged from the shadows—a very delectable shape. Barely clad in a bright red gown, trimmed with black lace, the doxy approached him, swaying her hips with the loose-limbed gait of a practiced seductress.

"Do you perhaps need a little warming up, good sir?"

A lace-gloved hand caught his and strong, bony fingers curled around his wrist as she glanced up at him, her face pale in the moonlight save for an overabundance of rouge on her cheeks and her bright ruby-red lipstick.

"Leave me alone," he said. "I'm busy."

"You look lonely, my lord," she said. "I can ease your pain. My lodgings are not far. I have brandy, a warm fire, and an even warmer bed."

Five years ago, he might have been tempted. The doxy re-minded him of the Italian whores he'd patronized on his travels— glossy black hair, voluptuous curves, and a predatory sensuality.

The exact opposite of…

He recoiled as if her touch burned him.

"Leave me," he said. "Take your trade elsewhere."

"Come now, sir," she purred. "A gentleman such as yourself, all alone, must be in need of a little comfort."

She placed her hand on his waist, then moved it toward his breeches, until she found what she sought and began to caress him, her fingers teasing, coaxing…

But his body did not react.

She stopped, disappointment in her expression.

"Mayhap the gentleman does not prefer a lady's touch?"

"I see no lady."

She frowned, then withdrew, brushing an imaginary speck of dust off her shoulder. "Perhaps I was mistaken when I thought you a gentleman."

"Perhaps you were."

He pushed her to one side, but she merely smiled. Then she curtseyed and sauntered off in the direction of Vauxhall Gardens, where she would, most likely, find better trade.

He thrust his hands in his pockets and continued at a brisk pace until he reached his lodgings.

Once inside, he poured himself a brandy and drained the glass.

Women—damn the lot of them! First he'd been betrayed and forced to watch while the woman he thought he'd fallen in love with gave birth to another man's child—a child he'd sworn to love until it was taken from him. And now, five years later, history seemed doomed to repeat itself.

He poured a second glass, spilling brandy over his hand.

"Damn!"

A sharp pain sliced through the back of his hand where he must have scratched himself in the scuffle with Heath Moss. The brandy made it sting, and his eyes watered.

Damn him! Damn them all.

And damn *her*, for making him fall in love.

His knuckles whitened as he tightened his grip on the glass, his hand shaking. Then he threw the glass against the door, where it shattered on impact, leaving an explosion of brandy staining the wood and a pile of splintered glass on the floor.

CHAPTER TWELVE

"YOU LOOK BEAUTIFUL, Beatrice, dear."

Beatrice took her guardian's hand. She couldn't stop shaking, and she'd struggled to keep her breakfast down. In the carriage on the way to the church, the motion had churned her stomach, causing a wave of nausea to incapacitate her. The stays of her wedding gown seemed to constrict her breathing, enclosing her in a cage.

Unaware of the fear swirling in her mind, Giles squeezed her hand and smiled.

"My lovely cousin," he said. "You cannot imagine how happy you're making me this day."

"Because I'm making a respectable marriage after last year's scandal?" She winced at the bitterness in her tone, and his expression softened.

"No, dear girl," he said. "It's always weighed heavily on me, since your parents died, to see you so lonely. I know Henrietta has been a good friend, and we both love you as if you were our own child, but I've always feared we could never replace the love of your parents."

He patted her hand, then linked arms with her. "I've tried to be a father figure to you, dearest Beatrice," he said, "and nothing makes me prouder than to walk you down the aisle today. Hardwick's a good man. I couldn't wish for a better man for you."

She blinked, and a tear splashed onto her cheek. He lifted his hand and brushed it away.

"Come now, dear cousin," he said. "Henrietta's already been through several handkerchiefs this morning, having adapted well to her role as mother of the bride. But the bride herself isn't supposed to cry at her own wedding, even if they are tears of happiness."

But they were tears born of sorrow, not happiness.

Augustus had not called on her yesterday, and nor had he sent word. In all likelihood he wasn't in the church, and all that awaited her at the altar was humiliation.

The church doors opened, and they stepped inside. The church was almost full. Though the end of the aisle was obscured by the congregation, Beatrice could make out the bright peacock-blue feather Henrietta had insisted on wearing in her hair.

The parson stood waiting, his soft gray hair forming a halo in the light that streamed in through the stained-glass window.

But there was no sign of the groom.

Her fears had been realized. Rather than admonish her, Augustus had chosen a more calculated form of punishment. By not turning up, he ensured she'd be disgraced and ridiculed, for no bride who'd been jilted at the altar would recover a shred of respectability.

She drew in a sharp breath as the world began to spin, and Giles tightened his grip, steadying her.

"Courage, cousin," he said. Then he began to lead her down the aisle.

The walls of the building closed in on her, and she struggled to draw breath.

"G-Giles, I c-can't do it," she whispered. "What will people *think*?"

"Hush, Bea," he replied. "Just walk with me. Hold your head high. You have nothing to be ashamed of, remember that. You were the victim of others' actions. An innocent woman has naught to fear from gossip."

Yes, he was right. If Augustus were to jilt her, let *him* bear the burden of guilt. She could walk through the church with her head held high so as not to elicit anyone's pity.

She nodded, and they walked down the aisle. Though she set her gaze straight ahead, she couldn't help but notice Eleanor Howard sitting among the onlookers, next to her sister Juliette. Both ladies glanced over their shoulders. One gave Beatrice a smile of encouragement; the other scowled.

Juliette's scowl would soon turn into a sneer of triumph, but now was not the time for Beatrice's courage to waver. Henrietta had taught her to stand tall, despite her enemies' attempts to belittle her. And, like a warrior, she would stand tall today, come what may.

As they reached the end of the aisle, where the parson stood alone, a man rose from a pew at the front, stepped forward, then turned to face her.

Clear eyes, the color of steel, fixed their gaze on her, and her heart fluttered at the intensity in their expression. Giles guided her toward Augustus, placed her hand in his, then stepped back.

Unable to contain her relief, she drew in a sharp breath. He smiled and nodded, then resumed his attention on the parson.

Augustus was, indeed, a kind and understanding man. He had seen reason, and loved her enough to still wish to marry her without even demanding an explanation for what had happened.

All was well. She had been afraid for nothing.

A BRIDE'S MISFORTUNE was that she found herself constantly on display, like an exotic bird in a cage for sightseers to gawp at, or a prize hog set on a banqueting table for the diners to pick at and salivate over.

It also meant that, due to having been paraded around the guests during the wedding breakfast, Beatrice had hardly spent a moment in her husband's company.

My husband.

How gentle he'd been as he slipped the ring onto her finger. How softly spoken were his words when he uttered the vows...

...and how warm his lips had been when he brushed them against her forehead after they were announced man and wife!

In short, Augustus had behaved like the perfect gentlemen, the gallant suitor, and the devoted bridegroom.

But since then, he'd spoken hardly a word to her.

She glanced across the dining room, where he was speaking to the parson. The toasts completed, it was almost time to leave, at which point she would be alone with him—as his wife.

He shook hands with the parson and kissed the parson's wife's hand. Then he approached Beatrice, smiling, and offered his arm.

"Shall we?"

Amid cheers, they exited the dining room and stepped outside, where the carriage stood waiting. Giles and Henrietta approached them, and Giles shook Augustus's hand.

"Take care of her, Lord Hardwick," Henrietta said.

"I intend to behave as a husband ought," came the reply.

Henrietta's forehead creased into a frown, then she nodded. She drew Beatrice to her and kissed her on both cheeks. "Be happy, darling."

Augustus steered her toward the carriage and helped her inside. Then he climbed in beside her, rapped the window, and they set off, amid cheers.

He settled back into his seat and closed his eyes.

"Is everything all right"—she hesitated—"Augustus?"

"Yes, of course."

He sounded so polite, so courteous. Like a gentleman on first acquaintance.

Where had the passion gone? Perhaps he kept his passions at bay at such an event, having made a solemn vow before the Almighty. Some men were rumored to find the speaking of such vows overly intimidating, and today was the second time he had spoken them.

Perhaps that was it. Today reminded him of his late wife…

…and the child he'd lost.

After the carriage drew to a halt outside his lodgings, he took her hand and helped her out. Then he led her to the front door and handed his coat to the waiting footman.

"Bring a bottle to the study, would you?" he asked.

The footman bowed. "Yes, your lordship."

He turned to Beatrice. "You must retire, my dear. I'll join you presently. Your maid should be waiting for you in your chamber."

Before she could respond, he bowed over her hand, then turned and walked away, disappearing through a door at the end of the hall.

Beatrice climbed the staircase to where her maid stood waiting.

"Welcome home, miss," the maid said. "Oh, I beg your pardon, I mean your ladyship. You must be tired after such a long day. Shall I show you to your room? It's ever so lovely!"

"Thank you, Kitty."

The maid led her to a sturdy oak-paneled door and opened it.

The room inside was elegantly furnished in pale creams and reds, with a large bed at the far end, opposite the fireplace. But it lacked the soul of a lived-in room such as the one she'd known when she was growing up with Mama and Papa, or her chamber at Giles's townhouse.

This room reminded her of an inn—functional and pleasing to the eye, but with none of the personal touches that identified it as truly belonging to someone. It was a room for passersby.

She stepped inside. Her trunk lay open next to the fireplace. Kitty had set out her nightgown on the bed, and a few personal items on the dressing table, but other than that, her trunk was still full.

"Have you not unpacked my trunk yet, Kitty?"

"No, Lady Beatrice," the maid replied. "Lord Hardwick said I was not to. He was most particular."

"I wonder why."

Beatrice approached the mirrored dressing table and stared at her reflection. No longer a debutante, the woman who looked back at her was a married woman, and a countess. And she seemed to have aged since the morning. Perhaps that was what marriage did to a woman.

She shivered, despite the heat from the fire crackling in the room.

"Perhaps he noticed you were tired, Kitty." She took her maid's hand. Though she had agreed to marry Augustus and remove herself from the family home, her maid had no choice in the matter. Personal servants had to go wherever their masters and mistresses went, no matter how far it took them from friends and family.

"Lord Hardwick's a most kind and considerate man," Kitty said. "Here, let me help you get ready."

Beatrice stood, like an obedient child, while her maid unhooked her dress, slipped it off, then helped her into her nightgown. Then Kitty unpinned her hair, removing the Hardwick family tiara. Beatrice ran her fingertips along the jewels, then closed her eyes, relishing her maid's gentle touch and the bristles of the hairbrush running along her scalp.

When Kitty finished, she placed a hand on Beatrice's shoulder. Beatrice let out a sigh and opened her eyes to see her maid looking at her in the mirror.

"There!" Kitty said, with smile of reassurance. "You look lovely. I'm sure you have nothing to fear tonight. The servants here say that the master is a kind man, and will treat you well."

Beatrice placed her hand over the maid's and nodded. "I hope so, Kitty. You and I are embarking on this adventure together, are we not? We must take care of each other."

"Thank you, Lady Beatrice."

For a moment, they stared at each other, and the air was

filled with the crackling of the fire and the sound of their breathing. Then footsteps approached and muffled voices came from the room next door.

"That'll be his lordship with his valet," the maid said. "He'll be joining you soon, I expect. Is there anything else I can do for you tonight?"

A shiver coursed through Beatrice's veins at the prospect of Augustus joining her. Swallowing her apprehension, she squeezed her maid's hand.

"No thank you, Kitty. I'll see you in the morning."

The maid extinguished the candles, save for a solitary one on the dressing table, then bobbed a curtsey and exited the chamber. Beatrice glanced at the adjoining door, her heart pounding. Picking up the candle, she rose from her seat, approached the bed, and climbed in.

Then she blew out the candle, lay back, and waited.

The flames of the fire glowed a deep orange, shifting, pulsing, as if in time with her heart. The murmur of voices continued next door, and her eyelids grew heavy.

The voices stopped, and she waited, in silence, as shadows moved at the foot of the door.

Then the door opened to reveal the silhouette of a man. He moved closer, making no sound as he crossed the floor and approached the bed. Then he slipped beneath the sheets, making the bed shift under his weight, and lay next to her, facing the ceiling, his eyes glittering in the soft light of the dying fire.

She could bear the waiting no more.

"H-husband," she whispered.

He made no move. Save for the reflection of light in his eyes, which were still open, she'd have believed him to be asleep.

"Augustus?"

He turned his head and looked directly at her, neither smiling nor unsmiling. Her stomach twisted at the expression in his eyes—two cold stars gazing at her from a midnight sky. The raw, primal desire in them sent a shiver through her bones, and a nugget of need swelled and throbbed in her center.

Henrietta had spoken of the marriage bed, and of how, despite what most elegant ladies said, the act could be as pleasurable for the woman as for the man. She had said there was no pleasure in the world like it—that it was like flying through the trees and soaring through the heavens.

But the thought of a man—any man, let alone the one she'd fallen in love with—touching her in the most intimate of places… She blushed at the mere notion of such a thing.

Then he shifted until his body touched hers, and a ripple of apprehension threaded through her body.

He was naked.

Swallowing her fear, she lay still, while he placed his hand on her breast. His body heat seeped through the palm of his hand, and her skin almost burned at his touch—a burning to match the flame in his eyes.

He squeezed her breast, gently at first, and caressed it with his thumb, until her nipple beaded against his touch. Then he rolled the tip between his fingers until it hardened further, sending a fizz of need through her body until a thick ache began to swell deep inside.

Then he withdrew his hand, and she gave a low mewl of frustration and arched her back, in an involuntary gesture of need.

He placed his hand on her thigh and pushed her nightgown up, exposing her legs. Then he ran a light fingertip along her thigh, moving it higher, toward the center of her need, where her body continued to pulse faintly.

He inhaled then exhaled rapidly, and her need swelled at the urgency in his breathing.

He wanted her.

"Augustus, I—"

"Shh…"

He moved his hand higher until his fingertips sank into the nest of curls at her center. Overcome by embarrassment, she bit her lips to suppress a cry, as he ran his finger slickly along her flesh. Then desire swelled within her, and he moved his fingertips back and forth, increasing the pressure, stoking the flame of raw passion.

How could he know exactly where to touch her to elicit such sensations?

The pleasure morphed into an ache, which grew in intensity with each stroke of his expert fingers. A raw need burned within her. But for what, she couldn't fathom. She only knew that he was the one to meet that need, to bring the sweet relief from the madness that hovered just out of reach.

His breathing hoarsened as he inhaled and exhaled in time with the movement of his fingers. And her breathing quickened to match, as if they formed a single creature. Then a shudder reverberated through her body, as the need swelled, forming a mighty wall that climbed higher and higher, until it could go no further, and she parted her thighs, waiting for the release of pleasure…

Then he withdrew his hand, and she gave a low whimper of despair. Her mind was gone, and her body had assumed control, chasing the one thing that remained in the world.

The need for release.

"Hush…"

He shifted on top of her and nudged her thighs apart with his knee. Then she felt him, hard and hot, his tip moving slickly against her center, where his fingers had been, and the sensation swelled until she was a woman no more—she was a mere creature, aware of only pure sensation and raw, base need.

Then he thrust forward, and she drew in a jagged breath at the sharp sting. She shifted position as her body stretched to accommodate him. She reached up and grasped his arms, and he stilled, as if giving her time to grow accustomed to the sensation of his being deep inside her, his breath coming out in sharp puffs, hot and urgent against her cheek.

He moved, withdrawing slowly, then eased himself back into

her. He continued to move, forming a steady rhythm in unison with his breathing. The tempo increased as he plunged in and out. As his movements grew in urgency, the pleasure swelled once more, higher than before, so high she could believe she'd die from it. Then he whispered her name, over and over.

"Beatrice, my Beatrice…"

Pleasure morphed into pain as he continued to move, more urgently now, slamming against her with each movement, as if his life depended on finding the pleasure he sought.

Then he thrust forward once more, and the pleasure exploded inside her.

She let out a scream, then he cried out her name and collapsed on top of her. His body continued to move, the thrusts growing weaker, while she clung to him, her own body vibrating with aftershocks of pleasure, until he lay still, clinging to her as if his life depended on it.

He murmured her name one last time, then he fell silent, his breathing steadying.

She lay back, her own breathing softening. Before she drifted into sleep, she realized that while she had experienced unimaginable pleasure, not once had her husband kissed her.

CHAPTER THIRTEEN

W HEN BEATRICE WOKE, sunlight filled the room. She reached out to find that she was alone in the bed.

"Mistress, you're awake!"

She rolled onto her side. Kitty was already in the room, tidying Beatrice's belongings. She gestured to a gown she'd set out on a chair beside the bed. The wedding gown, which she'd placed on the chair last night, was nowhere to be seen.

"I thought you'd like to wear the blue today," Kitty said. "It brings out the color of your eyes. I'm sure his lordship will love it." She held out her hand. "Here, let me help."

Beatrice blinked, then rubbed her eyes and yawned. "What time is it?"

"It's early." Kitty colored and averted her gaze. "His lordship insisted that you join him in the breakfast room. I'm to take you to him."

She climbed out of the bed, aware of the soreness between her thighs, and blushed at the memory of last night—the wicked sensations she could only have dreamed of.

To think, she would experience such pleasure each night from now on! No wonder Henrietta looked so happy.

Dreaming of a life of ecstasy, Beatrice stood patiently while Kitty dressed her, then she sat at the dressing table. While Kitty arranged her hair, she reached out for the tiara, but it was no longer there.

"His lordship told me to place it in your trunk," Kitty said, twisting a tendril of hair into a curl and fixing it in place with a hairpin.

"Along with my wedding gown?"

Kitty nodded. When she'd finished arranging Beatrice's hair, she stood back with an expression of pride. "You look lovely, Miss Beatrice," Kitty said. "A proper countess." Then she glanced at the clock. "Heavens!" she cried. "You must go now, or you'll be late. His lordship awaits you in the breakfast room."

Beatrice rose and glanced at her reflection.

A countess…

This time yesterday, she was a bride, a young woman in love, and under the care of her cousin. Today, she was a countess, with all the duties and responsibilities associated with the rank, with a household to run…

…and the prospect of children of her own.

She placed a hand over her stomach.

Perhaps, even now, she was carrying Augustus's child.

Augustus…

In the eyes of the world, she now belonged to him. But Augustus was unlike other men. He viewed her not as his property, but as his equal. He would support her in all things so that she might grow accustomed to the enormity of her position. With him at her side, she would never fail.

Kitty approached the door and opened it. Two footmen stood outside, and they bowed as Beatrice exited the chamber and approached the staircase. She glanced back to see them entering the chamber, and shortly after, they emerged carrying her trunk.

"This way, mistress," Kitty said.

Beatrice resumed her attention on the staircase and followed her maid down the steps and along the hallway to a half-open door. Her stomach growled at the aroma of bacon.

Kitty pushed open the door, then bobbed into a curtsey.

"Lady Hardwick, your lordship."

The maid stepped aside, and Beatrice entered the room.

A long table dominated the room. At the far end sat a man, silhouetted against the morning light from the window behind him.

He rose and bowed. "Good morning, my dear."

"Augustus—" she began, but he interrupted her.

"Please, sit." He gestured to the place at the end of the table, and she slipped into her seat in the manner of an obedient child. "Garrett will serve you whatever you wish," he said. "I'd recommend the bacon. I had it sent from my estate."

Shortly after, a plate of bacon was placed before her. She picked up her knife and fork and began eating.

"What do you think?" he asked.

She swallowed a mouthful. "It's very good."

He nodded his approval, then picked up his newspaper and studied it.

An awkward silence descended as she continued to eat, aware of her knife scraping against the plate. The footman approached with a pot of tea and raised his eyebrows in inquiry.

"I can help myself, thank you," she said. He nodded then backed toward the door, where he stood, body stiff, as if he were anticipating a prize for masquerading as a statue.

As she ate her breakfast, she glanced occasionally toward her husband, but he was absorbed in his paper.

He was no longer the gallant suitor, the man who'd declared his love. But theirs had been a short courtship. In truth, she knew very little of him, or what he occupied himself with during the day. And a husband was a very different creature to a suitor.

The wedding was over. It was now time for the marriage to begin.

She finished her bacon and pushed the plate away. Shortly after, the footman removed it.

Her hands shaking, she reached for the sugar bowl and dropped a spoonful into her cup. Though she didn't usually take sugar in her tea, she felt the need for it today. Then, sipping her tea, she waited for her husband to finish his paper. Something held her back from interrupting his reading. Whether it was the knowledge that it was a wife's duty to wait for her husband to decide the turn of the conversation, or the apprehension bubbling inside her, she did not know.

Eventually, he set his paper aside. Though he was silhouetted against the window, his eyes seemed to glow as he fixed his gaze on her.

"Have you finished your breakfast, my dear?"

"Y-yes."

He gave a businesslike nod. "Good."

What had happened to the kind, gentle man who'd professed his love—the man who'd won her heart so easily?

"Is anything amiss?" she asked.

"No," he replied. "Everything's well." He drew out his pocket watch, opened it, then nodded before snapping it shut and returning it to his waistcoat pocket. He rose to his feet. "If you're ready, Beatrice, it's time to go."

"Go? I thought we were to remain in London before traveling to the country."

"My plans have changed. I'll be giving up my lodgings at the end of the month."

"I-I don't understand," she said, pushing back her chair and standing. "That's barely a few days away. Are we leaving for the country today?"

He approached her, his body seeming to block out the light from the window, and a shiver rippled over her skin. He offered his arm, and she took it, then he led her out of the breakfast room into the hallway, where two footmen stood beside the front door. Next to them, holding a valise, was Kitty, her eyes bright with moisture.

Something was wrong.

Beatrice swallowed her fear. "Augustus, what's happening?"

"It's quite simple, my dear," he said. "You are to go to Hard-wick Hall, as is your duty as my countess."

"And…*your* duty?"

"I've done my duty," he said. "It just remains for me to settle my affairs before returning to Europe."

Her gut twisted in fear. *Europe?*

"Are you abandoning me?" she whispered.

A flash of regret shone in his eyes. "I've done more than could be expected under the circumstances," he replied. "I've settled a regular stipend on you, and, provided you employ economy, you'll want for nothing at Hardwick Hall."

"What about *us?*"

"You'll be protected by my name."

Why did he sound so calm, so soulless?

"That's not what I meant!" she cried. One of the footmen cleared his throat and shuffled from one foot to another. Perhaps she was ignoring decorum. But decorum be damned—what the devil was he playing at?

Augustus tightened his grip on her arm. "Please control yourself, my dear,"

"Augustus, please," she said, lowering her voice, "what is all this? I thought we were to be together."

"You know I travel," he replied.

"Yes, but to abandon me the morning after our wedding? Do you think I'd not enjoy the journey to Europe? Why can't I come with you?"

"It's not appropriate under the circumstances," he said. "Now, you really should leave. The carriage is waiting."

He issued a sharp instruction, and the footmen opened the front doors. Beatrice was greeted with a gust of cold, fresh morning air, and the sight of a coach-and-four bearing the Hardwick crest waiting by the steps.

"Come, my dear." With a display of gallantry, he led her toward the door. Out of the corner of her eye, she saw Kitty climb onto the back of the coach, where a footman settled her into a seat with a blanket.

"Augustus, why are you sending me away?"

He let out a sigh, and for a moment, she saw deep sorrow in

his expression. "Surely you must understand why, after what happened. We must all reap the rewards of our sins."

The rewards of our sins…

"Sweet Lord, you don't mean what happened with Mr. Moss?" she asked.

"Lower your voice," he said, glancing at the footmen. "I won't be subjected to servants' gossip."

"There's nothing to gossip about," she said. "Nothing happened—I thought you knew that. Don't you believe me?"

He let out a sigh. "I've seen it before," he said. "I vowed that I'd never place myself in such a position again."

"Then why did you marry me, if you suspect me of having been unfaithful with that vile man?"

He closed his eyes, and when he opened them again, a film of moisture glistened in his eyes, turning the gray to liquid silver.

"Because I had promised myself to you, Beatrice," he said, "and I couldn't bear to see you hurt if I broke off our engagement so close to our wedding day. Given your past history, you'd never recover from the scandal."

"You married me just to maintain *propriety*?"

He shook his head, and the expression in his eyes tore at her heart. "No, Beatrice," he said. "I married you because I love you."

"Then why leave me?" Beatrice winced at the desperation in her voice. But her heart ached at the thought of being all alone, when she wanted nothing more than to be loved by someone she could trust—someone she could give her heart to.

And she had given her heart to him, though he now tossed it aside.

"Because I must," he said.

"What about last night?" She felt her cheeks warming at the reference to their lovemaking, when he'd cried her name and given her such pleasure. "How could you send me away after what we did, what we shared?"

"It was a necessity," he replied. "If you find yourself with child, I can claim it as mine, as I was prepared to do with another before you. It's the least I can do after your…" He hesitated, as if unwilling to voice it.

Something snapped within her—and the sorrow at his abandonment was replaced by anger.

How *dare* he treat her so, without even listening to her account? Was she, as a woman, always to be ignored, whereas a man, however much of a libertine he might be, was always to be believed?

She'd thought him better than that. But, like all men, he'd proven to be a disappointment.

"My *betrayal*—is that what you were going to say?" she said in a cold voice.

"Beatrice, I—"

"No, my lord," she interrupted. "At least have the honor to voice what you are accusing me of."

"I accuse you of nothing," he said. "It's my fault. I have only myself to blame."

He took her hand, and a crackle of need threaded through her at his touch. He caught his breath, and she glanced up to see that his eyes were closed. He inhaled sharply, his nostrils flaring, and he curled his fingers around hers, caressing the back of her hand with his thumb.

"Beatrice…"

He lifted her hand, then dipped his head, brushing his lips against her skin.

When he opened his eyes again, they were filled with tears.

"Augustus, come with me," she said. "I love you."

He nodded. "I love you too, Beatrice," he replied. She curled her fingers around his, and a seed of hope grew within her— which his next words crushed. "That is why I must leave."

"When will I see you again?"

He shook his head. "I don't know."

He barked an order, and a footman opened the carriage door. Then he led her to the carriage, helped her inside, and shut the door behind her.

He raised his hand and touched the glass, placing his palm against it. She mirrored the gesture, placing her palm against his. Then he rapped on the carriage door, and it set off.

For a few moments, she remained still, unwilling to believe what was happening. Then she pulled the window down and leaned out.

He stood, beside the steps, body stiff and erect, unmoving, like a statue.

"Augustus, *please!*" she cried, not caring about the passersby who stopped and stared.

He continued to stare at her, his eyes filled with sadness, then he raised his hand, turned his back on her, and ascended the steps into the house. The doors closed behind him.

For all she knew, that might be the last time she set eyes on him.

CHAPTER FOURTEEN

Two years later, London, July 1817

A CITY HAD its own unique smell. Rome smelled of sunshine and dust. London, on the other hand, carried the odor of salt and smoke. As for sounds—the musicality of the Italian language was a far cry from the harsh notes of the voices of London's occupants. Here, on the docks, the harsh cries of sailors shouting to each other, traders offering their wares, and doxies propositioning the male travelers—the sounds were unmistakable. Had Augustus been blindfolded, he'd have known the moment the ship entered the Thames.

Overhead, seagulls swirled, scavengers looking for scraps, waiting to dive on the unwary. Then a sailor threw a bucket of scraps over the edge of the ship, and the seagulls descended, a cloud of wings and feathers, screeching at each other like harpies fighting over a man.

He descended the gangplank, his valet in tow, and a warm, familiar aroma invaded his nostrils.

Meat pies.

He had dined well during his travels, but there was nothing so comforting as a meat pie from one of the many purveyors at London's docks. One should not look too closely at the contents to decipher exactly what form of meat had gone into them, but each time he bit into the thick, heavy pastry and tasted the gelatinous gravy, he knew he was home.

Europe was a paradise that he'd used as an escape. But a part of England lingered in his blood, and he could never completely abandon his home country. Though the cold seeped into his bones, it was a part of him.

All men returned to their wives in the end.

And while Italy was his mistress—a warm, ripe mistress, filled with sunshine—England was his wife.

His wife...

Despite everything he had tried during the past two years, he couldn't forget her, not for a single moment. He'd seen her in the smiles of the women he encountered, and heard her laughter in the children who played in the vineyards.

And he felt her touch at night when he lay alone in his bed, dreaming of her sweet lips.

He'd traveled hundreds of miles to drive her from his mind and heart. But still she lingered, her purity and beauty giving him respite from his own loneliness.

Until, at last, after two years of trying to exorcise her from his mind, he admitted the truth.

He'd wronged her—by *God*, how he'd wronged her! How many times had he written to her, begging forgiveness, pleading for leave to come home. But each time he'd torn the letter up and thrown the remnants into the fire. Shame overcame him—shame at his treatment of her. Even if she had encouraged Mr. Moss, she regretted it, and though she'd never begged forgiveness, it was his *duty* to forgive her.

He loved her, after all. He loved her so much that he'd wanted to give her his name, to call her his countess, even if she may have looked elsewhere.

But that was mere pride, the foolish pride of a man who wanted his woman to have eyes for him, and only him.

But love was greater than pride. Pride had prevented him from being with her—from having her by his side, and indulging in the happiness of marriage to the woman he desired above all others. Love, on the other hand…

Love was what had brought him back to her.

No matter what she'd done, or how many lovers she had taken in his absence, he wanted her. And he was her husband, *damn it*. He had a right to claim her as his.

But, more than anything, he missed her sweetness. The women he'd encountered on his travels were sophisticated women of the world, predatory creatures who used their sex to control a man. He'd wanted none of them. Over the months, he'd found himself craving his sweet Beatrice, the bride he'd exiled to the country.

Her face still haunted him—the tear-stained expression in her eyes when she cried out his name, pleading for him to let her stay by his side.

Would she forgive him?

Of course she would. What had driven him on while he arranged for his return to England was the thought of her delight on seeing him again. All he need do was take her in his arms and beg forgiveness, and his sweet Beatrice would be his once more. But this time, he wouldn't let her out of his sight, nor would he forsake her.

As he reached the bottom of the gangplank, he spotted a familiar face among the crowd of onlookers.

Earl Thorpe. Beatrice's cousin and guardian.

Shit.

What the bloody hell was *he* doing here?

Their gazes met, and Thorpe's expression hardened. Then he thrust his hands into his pockets and approached.

"Hardwick," he said.

"Thorpe. I didn't expect to see you here."

"I had notice of your arrival," Thorpe said. "Your solicitor is a most obliging man." He gestured toward a pie shop. "Shall we?"

Augustus read the sign over the door. "Mrs. Moffett's," he said. "I'm glad to see she's still here."

"You'll find very little has changed in your absence," Thorpe said. "In *London*, at least."

Thorpe gave Augustus a sharp look, then led the way into the pie shop, where he sat at a table, and Augustus followed suit. A servant approached them.

"Two pies, please, and some ale," Thorpe said.

The servant, a girl barely out of childhood, bobbed a curtsey, then disappeared into the back, returning not long after with a tray laden with two plates and two tankards.

Augustus took a bite and suppressed a groan. "I know not how she does it, but Mrs. Moffatt is a veritable sorceress with her pies. I swear they're better than anything that could grace the regent's table."

Thorpe didn't respond. He bit into his pie and fixed his gaze on Augustus while he ate. Augustus found his cheeks warming under the scrutiny. There could only be one reason why Giles Thorpe would meet him at the docks.

"Is…" Augustus hesitated, shame tightening his throat. "Is my…"

"Your *wife*?" Thorpe raised an eyebrow. "I would tell you that she's well, if you cared to ask."

"And…the child?"

"Child?" Thorpe exclaimed. "There's no child. But then, considering that you abandoned her virtually as soon as you'd uttered the vows, that's not altogether surprising, is it?"

A ripple of coughs threaded through the shop as the other diners signaled their disapproval.

"Forgive me," Thorpe said, lowering his voice, and resuming his attention on the pie before him. "I'd promised myself I'd hear you out before admonishing you."

"There's little to say," Augustus said.

Thorpe let out a snort of laughter. "You're more like Beatrice than you know," he said. "She says exactly the same, each time I ask, usually followed with an instruction to mind my own business." He gestured toward Augustus. "I take it your two-year absence is related to what happened with your first wife. Perhaps you believed that your second was about to take the same path?"

How the devil could Thorpe have such insight? Was he capable of reading a man's mind?

Thorpe gave him a cold smile. "I'm no fool," he said. "You catch a young reprobate attempting to compromise my cousin, then you abandon her shortly after marrying her. It's as plain as the nose on my face what you were up to. What astonished me is how you could even have believed that sweet girl was capable of anything so treacherous."

"Thorpe, I've no wish to go over old—"

"Hear me out," Thorpe said. "Beatrice was in love with you, damn it! I've never seen her so attached. With Mr. Meredith, it was a childish infatuation. Mr. Moss she cared nothing for. But *you*..." He shook his head. "She adored you. She came to the marriage bed a maiden, and you abandoned her."

Thorpe pushed his plate aside and lifted his tankard to his lips.

Augustus squirmed in this seat. His conscience told him that Thorpe was right—he'd abandoned an innocent. But the arrogance in Thorpe's tone irritated him. This was a matter between him and Beatrice, not her meddlesome cousin who had sought to plague him as soon as he set foot on English soil.

"How was *I* to know she was untouched?" Augustus asked, ignoring the guilt at voicing such a question.

"Good heavens, man!" Thorpe said. "Any man of the world knows when the woman he lies with is not a maiden."

"I wouldn't know," Augustus replied. "I have little experience of maidens."

"I suppose you don't, given how freely your first wife spread her favors round," Thorpe said. "But therein lies your problem."

"How so?"

"Your first wife was taken from you. Perhaps you feel that she hadn't been punished enough for what she did. But Beatrice is not her. Beatrice is an innocent. You sought to punish her because you remain rooted in the past—unable to see beyond it."

"You're talking nonsense," Augustus said, his words sounding hollow.

"I'm not, and you know it," Thorpe replied. "Don't punish Beatrice for the actions of another. Your mistrust is *your* burden, not hers."

Augustus leaned back and sighed. "You're right, of course, Thorpe. I regret what I did, but nothing can change the past. I intend to make amends to Beatrice, then that'll be the end of it."

Thorpe gave a sly smile. "If you say so."

"Yes," Augustus said. "I do. I'm man enough to recognize when I'm at fault, And your cousin is a sweet enough creature to accept my apology." He smiled to himself. "You'll be pleased to know that I'll be traveling to Hardwick Hall in a few days, when I hope to be reconciled with my wife."

Thorpe's smile broadened, but Augustus found the man's predatory expression unsettling.

"Is anything amiss?" he asked.

Thorpe shook his head. "Nothing whatsoever," he said. "Everything is as it should be. But I feel it only fair to warn you that you'll find your wife much changed."

"Two years is a long time in a young woman's life," Augustus said, "but Beatrice's sweet nature will never change, I'm sure of it."

"Then I welcome you back to England," Thorpe said, "but don't say you weren't warned. We must all reap the rewards of our sins in the end."

He rose, dropped a handful of coins on the table, then tipped his hat and bade Augustus goodbye. Before Augustus could ask his meaning, Thorpe had gone.

As Augustus entered the clubroom at White's, a familiar voice cried out.

"The devil take me, it's Hardwick!" Montague FitzRoy, Duke

of Whitcombe—the old reprobate, as handsome as ever—leaped to his feet. "Come over here, old boy!" he cried. "I heard a rumor you were back in Town, and I refused to believe it. But here you are, the prodigal son returned."

Beside Whitcombe, Alexander Ffortescue raised his glass. "Come and join us, old chap. You'll find the brandy much improved in your absence."

"Where's Perry?" Augustus glanced around, but there was no sign of Marlow.

"Happily married, I'm afraid," Whitcombe said. "The noose catches us all in the end, though *I* intend to maintain my immunity."

Augustus took a seat and gestured to the approaching footman. "My usual, please."

"Very good, your lordship."

Some things never changed, and White's was one of them.

"Why have you decided to grace England with your presence once more?" Whitcombe asked. "Come to tame that wife of yours?"

"Hush!" Ffortescue gave Whitcombe a sharp nudge.

"What have you heard?" Augustus asked.

"Hardwick Hall has gained something of a reputation," Whitcombe said. "Anyone who's anyone can be seen at the countess's infamous parties—masked balls where reputations are maintained through discretion and anonymity. It's *the* place to be, and Lady Hardwick is the best hostess in the country. Or so I'm told."

Ffortescue let out a laugh. "*Or so I'm told*, indeed! You're only griping because you've yet to be invited."

"Neither have you," Whitcombe replied.

Had they not been arguing over his wife, Augustus would have smiled at the two of them. They sounded like spoiled children fighting over a toy that neither of them were permitted to play with.

"So who *is* invited?" Augustus asked.

"The brightest young bucks in Town," Ffortescue said.

"James de Bruin is a frequent visitor. Do you know him?"

"Lord de Bruin's eldest?" Augustus asked. "Last time I saw him, he was paddling in the Serpentine despite his nursemaid's pleas to the contrary."

"You'll find he's grown a bit since then," Whitcombe said. "He graduated from Cambridge last season. A rather naïve young puppy, in my opinion, but he's clearly smitten with his hostess. And, of course, there's young Edward Pennington."

"Who the devil's he?" Augustus asked.

"You won't know him. His parents are one of these *new* families. But he has a substantial fortune, which, as we all know, is a virtue indeed, when a man is hunting for a marriage partner or a mistress."

"You suspect my wife of having a lover?"

Ffortescue let out a laugh. "Heavens, no! A greenhorn such as Pennington wouldn't know one end of a woman from the other, though he's clearly smitten with the countess."

"And…de Bruin?"

"A lothario such as de Bruin couldn't maintain his interest in a woman who'd succumbed for very long. He relishes the chase too much. Had the countess yielded to his advances, he'd have stopped attending her parties."

Whitcombe gestured toward Augustus. "You'll find out for yourself soon," he said. "I presume you'll be traveling to the country as soon as possible."

"I think I should bide my time," Augustus said.

"What are you planning?" Whitcombe asked.

Masked balls where anonymity was preserved. Such an event would give him an opportunity to see his wife in action, unobserved—and discover what the devil had been going on in his absence—before he confronted her.

"Perhaps I should visit Hardwick Hall incognito," Augustus said.

"Spy on your wife behind a mask?" Ffortescue laughed. "I wouldn't like to be in your shoes when she discovers your deception. Besides, how would you procure an invitation?"

"That's simple," Whitcombe said. "Young Pennington will, I'm sure, take you as his guest." He leaned back in his chair and waved at a young man sitting in the far corner of the clubroom accompanied by two others. "I say, Pennington! Join us, won't you?"

The young man looked up in wide-eyed astonishment. Then he rose and crossed the clubroom to approach them.

"Your Grace." He inclined his head toward Whitcombe. "And Lord Ffortescue, what a pleasure. How may I be of assistance?"

"Monty and I were wondering if you'd be so kind as to do our friend here a favor," Ffortescue said.

"Certainly," came the reply. The young man eyed Augustus, his eyebrows raised. "And you are?"

Before Augustus could reply, Whitcombe interjected, "This is Lord Julian Stiles, freshly returned from the Continent, and returned home to tame his wayward wife."

"Oh, I say!" the young man said, clicking his heels together and giving a deep bow. "Edward Pennington, at your service, Lord Stiles."

Ffortescue leaned forward and lowered his voice to a conspiratorial whisper. "Stiles here has a particular fondness for the Merry Countess," he said. "He was wondering if you'd be so kind as to take him with you as your guest to her next party on Saturday."

Pennington hesitated. "I don't know…"

"The countess wouldn't object, I'm sure," Ffortescue continued, "and we'd make it worth your while. Your membership here is, I believe, only probationary. I could put in a good word for you with the secretary to see about making it more permanent."

Whitcombe leaned forward, his large body dominating the space. "Come on, man!" he said. "This is what men of distinction do all the time—they help each other out. It'll stand you in good stead. A man who's initiated into our particular set can enjoy all the privileges which come with that, such as access to the prettiest doxies in Town."

Trust Whitcombe to appeal to a man's baser instincts.

And it worked. Pennington blushed, the tips of his ears growing pink, then nodded. "Of course, it would be my pleasure. Shall I make the arrangements?"

"Yes, do," Ffortescue said. "Now, run along, there's a good chap."

Pennington bowed, then scuttled off to rejoin his party.

"That was underhanded," Augustus said.

"It secured you an invite, didn't it?" Whitcombe said. "Pennington's so desperate for recognition, he'll do almost anything for it. I have no objection to recommending him to one or two of the more...*vibrant* ladies of my acquaintance. By the look of him, he needs breaking in. I only hope he'll not bore you rigid on the journey to Hardwick Hall."

"What will he do when he learns that Julian Stiles doesn't exist?" Augustus asked.

Whitcombe laughed. "You worry too much! It must be your age. I daresay that if he discovers our ruse, Pennington will be so overwhelmed to be in the presence of the *real* Earl Hardwick that he'll accede to your every whim."

"You'll have to visit your tailor," Ffortescue said, gesturing to Augustus's jacket. "You'll be recognized instantly in that old thing. One does not turn up to the countess's parties dressed inappropriately. Fashions have moved on in the last twenty years."

"I've only been away two years," Augustus said.

"Yes, but that particular style of jacket went out of fashion last century," Whitcombe said. "Your little countess will spot you a mile off, and most likely have you run out of the house—that is, if she doesn't set the dogs on you!"

The footman appeared with a glass of brandy, and Augustus took it and swallowed a mouthful.

What had he got himself into?

And, more to the point, what the devil would he find waiting for him at Hardwick Hall?

CHAPTER FIFTEEN

T HE CARRIAGE TURNED into the familiar drive, and Augustus's stomach clenched with apprehension, which overshadowed the sense of relief he'd always felt on returning home.

Though he'd abandoned it after his first marriage, and again after his second, Hardwick Hall was in his bones. Steeped in ancestry, the main building was filled with portraits of his ancestors.

And they were ancestors to be proud of. The first Earl Hardwick had earned his title in the sixteenth century from a grateful monarch after thwarting a campaign against the king's life. A shrewd tactician with a sharp understanding of court intrigue, he then declined the king's invitation to reside at court and managed to keep his head in the process. Preferring country life and honest work to political intrigue, he'd married an honest woman of low birth, and toiled on the estate such that it prospered.

His successors had enjoyed limited prosperity, and the estate, though it had not yet fallen into ruin, could only be described as suffering a distinct loss of luster, which had been exacerbated by Augustus's absences. His steward had struggled to maintain the estate on the dwindling income from the tenants. It only took an occasional failed crop, or disease among the livestock, to deplete the estate's coffers.

And you exiled Beatrice there.

The guilt that had been gnawing away at his conscience

throughout his absence had, on his return to London, begun to burn throughout his body. But now, as he returned to his ancestral home, like an absent father who'd abandoned his duty, the guilt manifested itself in an intense ache that strangled his heart and constricted his breathing.

"Are you quite well, Lord Stiles?"

He continued to stare out of the window, relishing the view of the oak trees lining the driveway—trees rumored to be over a thousand years old and that would, no doubt, still preside over the estate centuries after he was interred in the family crypt.

"Lord Stiles!"

A hand touched his elbow, and he jerked back.

The young man—Pennington, was that his name?—recoiled. "Forgive me, Lord Stiles," he said. "You seemed out of sorts. There's nothing to fear. You're assured of a warm welcome at Hardwick Hall. And your wife would be welcome too, should you wish to bring her."

Augustus fought to hide his smile. If only the young fool knew that a warm welcome was the last thing he'd receive once the lady of the manor set eyes on him.

He resumed his attention on the landscape.

Then he saw it.

His heart fluttered at the sight of the beloved building, nestled among tall trees, fashioned from rust-red stone, which seemed to glow in the light of the evening sun. The windows formed a neat row running along the first and second stories, like sentinels standing to attention to welcome him home, and the light of the sun reflected off them, as if the building had been watching, waiting, for his return.

Stretching out before the building was a lush green lawn, flanked by box hedges that had been neatly clipped into soft, undulating shapes, and in front of the lawn was the lake. The sunlight danced across the surface, glittering with the ripples in the water. As he watched, a water bird burst out from the reeds, flapping its wings, running along the surface, forming a trail of ripples behind it. Then it settled on the water's surface and glided along toward the bank opposite.

It was even more beautiful that he'd remembered. The building, which had long ago taken on a forlorn look, as if to reflect the sorrow he'd accumulated over the years, now seemed to vibrate with warmth and life.

He continued to stare at the building—his home—until the carriage turned a corner and the trees obscured it once more. Then the driver steered them through the huge iron gates decorated with the Hardwick crest. Lining the driveway at either side were enormous torches, flames flickering in the evening air, to welcome the guests.

Pennington pulled a mask out of his pocket and nodded toward Augustus.

"Lady Hardwick's rules," he said. "During the ball, all guests must be masked at all times."

"For what purpose?" Augustus asked.

"To maintain discretion, and an air of mystery. Or so the countess says." The young man, clearly smitten with the countess, let out a wistful sigh.

Augustus curled his hands into fists.

Damn you, Pennington. She's not just "the countess"—she's my wife.

"Lord Stiles?"

Uncurling his fingers, Augustus reached into his jacket pocket and pulled out his mask, fashioned from pale blue silk to match his waistcoat.

An unnecessary, and frivolous, indulgence, but Whitcombe had been right in his assessment at the club. Beatrice would have recognized him instantly had he worn his usual attire. And, he had to admit, he rather enjoyed the indulgence of procuring new suits, not to mention the looks of admiration from his valet, who'd been trying to persuade him to modernize his wardrobe for the past two years.

"You look very fine," the young man rattled on. "Might I ask who your tailor is?"

Augustus smiled to himself. Pennington's frank appraisal was charming, if a little artless. He almost pitied the poor, eager young pup. Any predatory woman would devour him.

"Hawkes, on Piccadilly," he said. "Mr. Hawkes encouraged me to try a slightly more *flamboyant* style to that which I'm used to."

"It's certain to catch the eye of our hostess," Pennington said. "She pays particular attention to fashion, and is always exquisitely dressed. Though she has a rather peculiar habit of wearing gloves at all times."

Augustus secured his mask in place as the carriage drew to a halt outside the main entrance, next to a carriage bearing the de Bruin crest. Augustus saw a party of four—two men and two ladies—approaching the main doors.

A footman approached the carriage and opened the doors, and Pennington climbed out, Augustus following. Then the carriage rolled away.

He had reached the point of no return.

The two men approached the main doors, side by side. Augustus didn't recognize the footman at the door, who seemed barely out of childhood.

He gave a deep bow. "Welcome, Mister…?"

"Pennington," Augustus's companion said.

"Ah, Mr. Pennington, welcome back. And your friend?"

Pennington gestured toward Augustus. "This is Lord Julian Stiles."

The footman arched an eyebrow. "He's not on the guestlist."

"He's *my* guest," Pennington said. "I can vouch for him."

"Very good, sir," the footman said. "But I'll have to tell her ladyship."

"I'm well acquainted with your mistress," Augustus said. "We've known each other for two years."

That, at least, was true.

The footman bowed, and the two men entered the building.

Augustus caught his breath as his gaze wandered over the main hall. A hundred candles adorned the walls, filling the hall with light. The hall was much as he'd last seen it, save for two marble statues guarding the main staircase, which swept up then split in two and curled around to the upper floor. He lifted his gaze to the chandelier dominating the ceiling. Light refracted off the crystals, as if each crystal had been individually polished, forming tiny rainbows that shimmered and danced in the air. The ceiling arched above, depicting celestial beings in bright colors—brighter than he'd remembered.

"It's wonderful, isn't it?" Pennington whispered. "They say the countess spent months restoring the hall after the earl abandoned the place."

"Oh, they do, do they?" Augustus winced at the bitterness in his voice.

But Pennington couldn't be blamed for speaking the truth. The earl *had* abandoned the place. And he'd abandoned his wife.

The young man led the way to the ballroom, where the sounds of music and laughter indicated that the party was already in full swing.

Augustus entered the ballroom and drew in a sharp breath.

The room had been transformed.

The once-dull ceiling now glittered and shone, much like the one in the hall. The wooden floor that had succumbed to the ravages of time had been replaced with solid oak floorboards. The mirrors had been polished until they shone, and the gilt decorating the walls gleamed. The gallery overlooking the ballroom had been decorated with trailing vines and deep red ribbons, giving the room an air of decadence.

The orchestra sat on a raised platform at the far end of the ballroom, and footmen lined the walls, brandishing trays laden with champagne, while others wandered about the room, ensuring that no guest was let unattended.

As for the guests…

The dancers, dressed in a rainbow of bright silks, moved

about the floor in a fluid motion to the music. Clearly, this was an event where the guests made every effort to appear as elegant and fashionable as possible. As the ladies glided about the room in time to the music, their feathered headdresses formed a pattern as they turned their heads. Augustus's own suit—that he had, at first, thought overly bright—paled in comparison to some of the men's attire. All the guests were masked, though Augustus recognized some of them. The Duke of Westbury and his wife glided past, the duchess's unmistakable green eyes glittering behind her bright red mask.

He glanced about the room, his heart rate increasing with the anticipation of coming face to face with his wife, but there was no sign of her.

"Where's our hostess?" he asked.

"She likes to make an entrance once the party has begun," Pennington said. "A pity, I've always thought, for she misses much of the dancing. In all the times I've been here, I've never managed to secure a dance with her."

Pennington sounded disappointed.

The two of them strolled around the perimeter of the ballroom, then Pennington caught Augustus's arm.

"That's Miss Manford," he whispered. "I'd recognize her anywhere. Isn't she charming?"

The young lady he pointed out seemed like any other—blonde hair curled in an elaborate style, bright blue eyes glittering behind her mask, and a gown of deep pink silk.

"Do you intend to dance with her?" Augustus asked.

"I suspect she's already engaged," Pennington replied. "She has a sharp wit, and they say she has a fortune of forty thousand. Her father's rumored to own half of Yorkshire, or, at least, half the mills in the county. She's the catch of the Season—or she would be, had she been born with a title."

"What's she doing here?"

"The Manfords have been snubbed in London. Mr. Manford made his fortune in trade, and, if that's not shocking enough, Mrs.

Manford was a scullery maid, and their daughter was born only two months after they wed. But they're just the sort of family that the Merry Countess delights in welcoming into her home. And, free from the constraints of London, the young men have no qualms about flocking round Miss Manford."

"I thought the idea was that the guests were anonymous," Augustus said.

"During the ball, certainly," Pennington replied, "but we're not expected to wear our masks the morning after. Besides, some men, and women, are so unmistakable that even with a mask, one would recognize them anywhere."

Augustus glanced around the room. "The countess has a most unusual arrangement here."

Pennington gave a sigh of admiration. "She's formed her own court here, where the young and vibrant come to pay homage and to entertain each other for her amusement. I have always found the traditions of the *ton* somewhat daunting. At least here, I'm forgiven if I commit a faux pas."

"Does the countess have no rules of propriety here?"

Pennington laughed. "The countess requires her guests to do two things. The first is to treat their fellow guests with respect."

"And the second?"

"To enjoy themselves." Pennington approached a footman holding a tray of glasses. He took two and handed one to Augustus. "Drink up," he said, already tipping his glass back. "Nothing but the best here."

Augustus took a sip. How the devil could his wife afford such luxury on the stipend he gave her? She'd need to employ economy just to keep the household running.

Perhaps she had a rich lover. After all, married women were not averse to spreading their favors. Was that why she wasn't in the ballroom tonight? If he went to the lady's chamber, would he find her with another?

Jealousy joined the anger, and he tightened his grip on the glass to stop his hands from shaking.

The dance concluded, and the musicians bowed as applause rippled throughout the room. The buzz of conversation filled the atmosphere—not the monotonous sounds of the men at White's discussing their business, nor the clipped, harsh tones of the ladies at a Society party in Mayfair. No—the tone of the conversation was rich and warm—the easy conversation of men and women enjoying each other's company at an event they'd attended for the pursuit of nothing more than pleasure.

Then a hush descended over the room.

Pennington reached for another glass of champagne from a passing footman, then nudged Augustus's elbow. "I believe our hostess is about to make an entrance."

Augustus glanced about the room, but there was no sign of anyone resembling his wife.

Then he looked up toward the gallery and caught his breath.

Standing on the balcony, her gloved hands on the balustrade, was a woman dressed in a gown of deep purple silk, trimmed with gold lace. The cut of the gown spoke of elegance. The neckline was low enough to make a man's mouth water at the promise of what lay beneath, but not quite so low as to be deemed scandalous. Her mask matched her dress, and was trimmed with what looked like gold pearls. Her hair had been piled on her head in a mass of tightly coiled curls, dotted with pearls, giving her the air of a Roman goddess. An enormous plume of purple ostrich feathers, fashioned into the shape of a bird, completed the ensemble. She was already statuesque, but the style of her hair meant that she would tower over even the tallest man.

For a moment, he didn't recognize her.

Then he saw it. On her head, fashioned with diamonds and amethysts that emphasized the color of her gown, was the Hardwick family tiara—the same tiara she had worn the day they married.

The day before he'd cast her aside.

Sweet Lord! Was this elegant, sophisticated goddess the same as the innocent young girl he'd married?

The crowd remained silent, as if enraptured by her appearance.

"Lady Hardwick!" someone cried. "A pleasure to see you."

She nodded, gave a regal wave, then spoke, and Augustus drew in a sharp breath at the sound of her voice—something he'd both longed, and dreaded, to hear again.

"I trust you're all enjoying the evening?"

A chorus of assent rippled through the party, and she nodded again, her lips curling into a smile.

"I'm so glad," she said, "otherwise, an entire flock of ostriches will have sacrificed their ability to fly for no good reason." She patted her hairstyle, then gestured to the plume of feathers in her hair. "I was most disconcerted when the plumassier arrived yesterday with my purple friend here," she said. "I told him that my friend was best suited to be in London at this time of year, rather than exiled to the country. And do you know why?"

"No!" a voice cried. "Do tell us."

She gave a saucy grin and cocked her head to one side; the feathers bobbed in the air as she moved. "I rather fancy that my friend fulfils the requirements to become a lady patroness at Almack's, at least in terms of complexion and intellectual capacity."

A ripple of laughter threaded through the guests, followed by a loud exclamation: "I'll be damned, the lass is right!"

Augustus craned his neck to see who'd spoken.

"That'll be Mr. Manford," Pennington whispered. "Lady Fairchild, who aspired to become a lady patroness at Almack's, gave Miss Manford the cut direct during her first ball, and was overheard insulting her mother."

"Lady Fairchild." Augustus wrinkled his nose. "A most unpleasant woman."

"By all accounts, she said some pretty cruel things to Mrs. Manford."

"How did you hear that?"

"Miss Manford told me," Pennington said. "But our delightful countess told her not to worry about the featherbrained creature, and to relish the fact that she'd turn purple with rage at the mere notion of the Manfords being sought-after guests at Hardwick Hall. She's quite taken Miss Manford under her wing."

Augustus glanced up at his wife again. She continued to address the party, her voice filled with confidence—a complete contrast to the softly spoken bride he'd abandoned.

Then, after an instruction to the guests to continue to indulge in her hospitality, she waved to the musicians and they began to play once more. The guests soon formed pairs and busied themselves with lining up for the next dance. But Augustus kept his gaze focused on the woman in the gallery. Her gaze swept over the room, like a searchlight, focusing on each guest in turn.

Augustus froze as she glanced toward him, but he saw no recognition in the liquid brown eyes behind the purple silk mask.

Then she looked away, and he caught a glimpse of something—an alertness, like a hunted animal that disguises its fear to show bravado to its predators. Then she blinked, and the hunted look was gone, as if she wore a shield.

But the brief flash of vulnerability…

It was the look Beatrice used to give him—a look that reassured him, now, that the gentle woman he'd married hadn't been completely replaced by the glittering creature presiding over the evening.

She descended the stairs toward the dance floor and circulated around the room, greeting each guest she passed with the easy elegance of the practiced hostess. With a dainty flick of her hand, she summoned a footman to refresh the guests' glasses, and with an air of affected elegance, she held out her hand to the male guests, smiling regally as they bent over and kissed it. Then she swept past them, on to the next guest. Occasionally, a male guest would gesture toward the dance floor, but each time, she dismissed him with a shake of her head.

She looked every part the Society hostess, and nothing like

the malleable wife he'd originally sought. The woman before him now seemed immovable, and as hard as a diamond. No longer his broken angel, she was a siren.

As she moved closer, Augustus's stomach twisted with anticipation, and his heart hammered in his chest. Surely she would recognize him. Since he'd made love to her—and despite what he'd said and done, the act had, for him, been one of love—he'd not even been tempted by another woman. He had lain in bed, alone at night, dreaming of her, and of what might have been. Until, that was, he'd come to his senses and returned home.

But the wife he'd come home to had been transformed. No longer a girl, she was a sophisticated woman. Whom had *she* dreamed of during the past two years? A woman as vibrant as her would not have been in want of suitors.

Or lovers…

The urge to flee threatened to overcome him—the urge to run out of the room, drive back to London, and take the first ship bound for the Continent. Where before he'd been the more worldly-wise of the two, tonight she was the one with all the power.

And *sweet Lord*, she was coming straight toward him!

Pennington straightened and puffed out his chest in the manner of a stag displaying his prowess to the females. A slight smile curled her lips, and she held out a gloved hand.

"Mr. Pennington, if I'm not mistaken," she said. "So good to see you. I trust you're keeping well, and you've managed to broaden your acquaintance in London since your last visit here?"

Pennington took her hand and kissed it, his lips lingering a little too long, and Augustus suppressed the urge to pull him back.

"Lady Hardwick, I'm most obliged," he said. "I'm pleased to report that I've made several new friends at White's. His Grace the Duke of Whitcombe, for one."

Her gaze hardened for a moment, before her smile resumed. Then she turned to Augustus. He caught his breath. Surely she'd know him—recognize the guilt in his eyes?

"And you are?"

I'm your husband!

Before he could blurt out the words, Pennington spoke.

"This is my latest acquaintance, recently returned to London, and my guest for tonight. Lord Julian Stiles." He turned to Augustus. "Stiles, may I present Lady Hardwick, our hostess."

Augustus took her hand and ran his finger along the soft fabric of her gloves. Her eyes widened behind her mask, and the hunted expression returned. Then she blinked and it disappeared.

"Stiles," she said. "Are you perhaps a relation to Earl Stiles, the magistrate?"

"We're cousins."

The benefit of a masked ball was that the majority of one's face was concealed, enabling him to lie successfully.

"He's never mentioned a cousin," she said.

Shit.

It'd be just his luck to bump into Earl Stiles and be caught out.

Then she smiled. "Never mind—the earl is a somewhat private person. He rarely rattles on about his relatives and acquaintances"—she gave Pennington a sidelong glance—"unlike *some* I could mention."

Pennington flushed behind his mask, though whether it was embarrassment or the influence of the champagne—he was on his fourth glass—it wasn't clear.

"What brings you to Hampshire, Lord Stiles?" she asked.

"The promise of a good party," Augustus said.

She narrowed her eyes. "And what brought you to London?"

"His wayward wife!" Pennington laughed, then hiccoughed.

Which cleared up the previous conundrum. Pennington was under the influence of the champagne.

Her expression hardened behind her mask. "And what has your wife done to be granted such a label?"

"Forgive me; my friend spoke out of turn," Augustus said.

"We were merely jesting over the fickleness of women."

He regretted the words almost before he'd completed the sentence.

"In my opinion, wayward husbands are far more prolific than wayward wives," she said. "But wayward husbands have one great advantage."

"Which is?"

"Their sex, Lord Stiles. A husband can commit all manner of transgressions with the permission, and blessing, of his peers, without having to shoulder the burden of conscience or retribution."

"Lady Hardwick, I did not intend—"

"Your *intention* is immaterial, Lord Stiles. A woman will always have to bear the burden of her transgressions, however small. And, on many occasions, she must also bear the burden of the transgressions of men."

Most likely Pennington didn't see it, but hurt shone in her eyes—the hurt that Augustus himself had placed there two years ago.

"Forgive me, Lady Hardwick. It was wrong of me to say such things."

Her eyes widened, then she nodded, and the gracious smile returned.

"It's of little matter," she said. "We must never sink under the burden of our sins. We must rise above and move forward, having fashioned a slightly thicker armor with which to protect our hearts. And now, if you'll excuse me, I must see to my other guests."

She withdrew her hand, then swept past, dismissing him as she had her other guests.

Augustus didn't know whether to be disappointed, or relieved, that she hadn't recognized him.

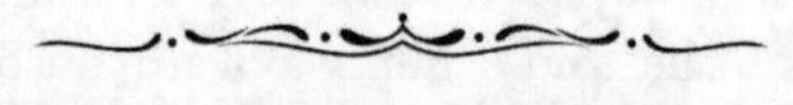

CHAPTER SIXTEEN

ESPITE THE DARKNESS, Augustus had no need of a candle. He
knew the layout of the house as if it were imprinted on his
mind, and the slivers of moonlight coming from behind the
curtains illuminated his path.

The house was quiet. The party guests had either retired for
the night, or left for home. Though tired from the journey and
the effort of concealing his identity, Augustus hadn't been able to
sleep. For one thing, Pennington's snores were enough to wake
his long-dead ancestors buried in the family crypt outside. For
another, his mind, and body, had burned with need from the
moment he set eyes on his wife.

Now that the house was quiet, he had to see her, and before
breakfast tomorrow. He had no wish to give her pain, or
humiliate her, by revealing his identity over a plate of kedgeree in
front of the other guests.

The ball had been one of the most lavish he'd ever attended.
Though the atmosphere lacked the artifice of a Society ball, he
couldn't deny the air of decadence that shimmered beneath the
surface. Whether it was because the guests were masked, he did
not know, but the anonymity fostered a greater forwardness of
manner, as if the donning of physical masks had broken down the
emotional and psychological barriers. The murmur of conversation and ripples of laughter were more spirited, and more
genuine, than anything he'd heard in London. Or, for that matter,

in Rome.

But their hostess remained detached from it all. His mouth had watered at the sight of her, as had the mouths of every other male guest, if their rapt attention on her was anything to go by. But rather than indulge in their adoration, she'd spent the majority of the evening in the gallery, watching the party from above, only occasionally taking a turn with a favored guest. When he'd inquired, one of the guests, a Lord James de Bruin, told him that the Merry Countess had always declared that she wished to dance with no man save one, though she'd refused to divulge his name.

Her lover, perhaps?

He gritted his teeth. Jealousy was an ugly trait. Kathleen had laughed at his jealousy over her many lovers. But he'd not abandoned her a few hours after their marriage. He'd remained faithful. Could he really expect Beatrice to have lived the life of a nun after he left?

But how else could she afford such lavish parties? She must have a protector, and he was determined to find out who it was.

Perhaps she was with him now. Earlier in the evening she had disappeared, leaving the guests to disperse of their own accord. Another habit of hers, according to Pennington.

And what the devil had happened to the staff? He hadn't recognized a single servant in the place. There was no sign of Miss Wood. True, housekeepers rarely attended balls, but there ought to have been at least one familiar face other than his wife's.

What the devil had his wife been up to these past two years? If nothing else, he was determined to find out the state she'd left his estate in, if only to ascertain the extent of the damage.

Curse her!

He tripped on the carpet and stumbled against the wall. Bloody champagne! He shouldn't have had that third glass. He was unused to liquor, having abstained for most of his travels.

Liquor was a great leveler. It brought every man to the floor eventually. It was known to bring out the worst in a man. Or, perhaps, it merely brought out feelings that were best kept hidden?

Such as jealousy.

He neared the end of the corridor and arrived at the door to the lord's chamber. His father's chamber, and *his* father's before him. Over the centuries, despite the improvements and changes made to Hardwick Hall, one part of it had remained unchangeable—the one constant in an ever-shifting world.

And it was this room.

But what would he find in there tonight? Would he find it destroyed, its treasures removed?

Or worse…would it be occupied by another man?

He heard a soft footstep, and he darted behind a curtain.

Just in time. The figure of a man emerged from the shadows.

Was she indulging in midnight trysts?

The man moved along the corridor, walking at a steady pace. He paused outside the door to the lady's chamber, then resumed walking. As the man drew closer, Augustus caught a glimpse of gold brocade, and he recognized the livery of the Hardwick footmen.

The man continued along the corridor at a steady pace, disappearing into the darkness at the far end.

Augustus glanced up and down the corridor, then stepped out from behind the curtain, approached the door leading to the lord's chamber, and tested the handle.

It turned with a creak that sounded overly loud in the darkness. He pushed the door forward, but it didn't budge.

It was locked.

But he'd come prepared. He reached into his pocket, drew out a key, and placed it in the keyhole. It turned with a click, and the door opened. Slowly, he pushed the door ajar, wincing at the groaning of the hinges—then, placing the key back in his pocket, he slipped through the gap and shut the door behind him.

The room was in total darkness, save for a sliver of moonlight at the window where the curtains met, and he wrinkled his nose at the musty odor and cold in the air.

He blinked while his eyes adjusted to the darkness, and blurred shapes came into view, picked up by the diffused light from the window.

The enormous four-poster bed that dominated the room was still there, and he could pick out the white pillows and the pattern of the blanket.

But the bed was empty.

The room looked identical to the last time he'd seen it—the deep leather armchair by the fireplace and the chest of drawers on the opposite wall, the moonlight picking out the edges of the gilt handles.

A soft ticking sound came from the fireplace. As he moved toward it, he caught sight of the ormolu clock on the mantelshelf—the clock his grandmother had brought back from Paris as a gift for his grandfather as a token of her love. He ran his fingertips over the glass dome covering the timepiece. Grandfather had cherished it until the day he died, tending to it with care and love, as a reminder of the wife he adored, and who adored him in turn.

He let out a sigh, fighting the melancholy that always lurked in the recesses of his mind. How he'd wished for a love as great as that which they'd shared!

A slight breeze came from the fireplace—cold, damp air from the chimney. Though the fireplace was filled with logs, it was plain that it wasn't in use. There was no sign of the residual heat one would expect, and the odor of damp from the chimney told him that the fire couldn't have been lit for some time.

It was as if the room had been frozen in time—the bed made, and the fire laid, and the clock wound—waiting for its occupant to return.

The room clearly belonged to someone.

But whom?

He approached the chest of drawers then opened the top one, and the sound of wood scraping against wood echoed through the room.

The drawer was filled with cravats, folded into identical shapes and set out in an array. He reached out and touched them, running his fingertips through the soft silk.

The cravats were far more sumptuous than anything he'd owned himself.

Which could mean only one thing.

Another man had taken possession of his room.

He gritted his teeth to suppress the wave of indignation and jealousy. He pulled the drawer fully open. It slipped out of the chest and fell to the floor with a crash, landing on his foot.

"Damn!"

He caught his breath and froze. But the only sounds were the ticking of the clock and his heartbeat whooshing in his ears. After a moment, he picked up the drawer and placed it back in the chest. It creaked and groaned as he slid it back into place.

Why the bloody hell did sounds have to carry so much at night?

He waited again, but there was no sign anyone had heard.

It was time to return to the guest chamber. He had the evidence he needed of his wife's misbehavior. It only remained to confront her in the morning, send her guests packing, and decide what to do with her.

Then a voice cried out.

"Who's there?"

He froze.

It was a voice he recognized. An angry voice, with an undertone of fear. And it was coming from the adjoining room.

"Come out, you coward!" the voice cried. "Show yourself!"

Coward, was he? How dare she make such an accusation after what she'd been doing in his absence!

The time for confronting his wayward wife was now.

He approached the adjoining door and turned the handle, half expecting it to be locked. But it swung open.

"Wh-who's there?"

There was no mistaking the fear in her voice.

He stepped into the room and saw her—the silhouette of a woman sitting up in her bed, her arms stretched toward him.

"Stop! Or I'll shoot!"

Foolish girl! Did she think he was an intruder, easily fooled by false threats?

Then he heard the unmistakable click of a gun cocking.

Shit.

He froze.

"That's right," she said, the confidence returning to her voice. "I'm armed, and am not afraid to shoot. Stay where you are! I demand you tell me who you are. You've no right to enter a lady's chamber uninvited."

Uninvited? No right? It was time his wife was taught a sharp lesson.

He approached the bed, and the trembling in her arms increased.

"Oh. You're wrong, my dear," he said. "I have every right to enter your chamber, invited or not."

She gave a low hiss. *"Good God—no…"*

At last, she recognized him. He could hear it in her voice.

"Oh yes, my dear," he said, moving closer, until he almost touched her. The trembling in her body grew more violent, and she let out a low cry.

"It's *you…*"

With a slow, deliberate movement, he reached forward and gripped the pistol by the barrel. She made no attempt to resist as he removed it from her grasp and placed it on the table beside the bed.

"Your husband has returned," he said. "Did you miss me?"

She drew in a sharp breath, then she shook her head. Perhaps she thought him an apparition.

But he was real. And he would show her how real he was.

He sat on the bed, and the mattress dipped beneath his weight. A faint aroma of rose caressed his senses, and he closed his eyes, relishing the sweet scent.

He could almost have believed that his sweet Beatrice was before him—not the hardened diamond who had flitted about the ballroom like a queen among her courtiers.

He only had to lean forward, and their lips would meet. The urge to kiss her, to claim that sweet mouth, became almost unbearable.

"Augustus…"

She spoke his name so softly that he could almost have imagined it.

"Beatrice…" He leaned forward and brushed his lips against hers. She lifted her hands to his face, and a soft whimper escaped her lips, the plaintive sound of a loving heart, yearning to be loved in return…

Then he recalled what he'd seen tonight, and what he had seen the night of Lady Moss's ball two years ago. His heart was shredded as he was assaulted, once more, by the image of her splayed out on that table, her legs parted, with another man bent over her.

He jerked free and pushed her back.

"No," he rasped. "I'll not be taken for a fool again."

She stiffened and snatched her arms free. "Why have you come, Augustus?"

"I have every right to return to my home without being subjected to questioning," he said.

She flinched, and her eyes glistened in the moonlight. Then she wiped them with an angry gesture.

"What the devil are you doing with a pistol?" he asked. "Don't you know they're dangerous?"

She let out a bitter laugh. "Only when you're on the wrong end of one. Are you perhaps perturbed that the prey has now become the predator?"

"Oh, *predator*, are you?"

"What if I am?" she cried. "A woman on her own has nothing but her instincts to survive on in this world."

"Oh, *surviving*, is it?" He laughed. "From what I've seen of your behavior tonight—and, no doubt, what you've been indulging in these past two years—I'll wager that you've been doing a lot more than *surviving*."

"How dare you mock me?" she said. "You know nothing of what I've been doing these past two years."

"No, my dear, but I know what you were doing in the days leading up to our marriage."

It was a childish riposte, and he regretted it as soon as he'd spoken.

She flinched, and he caught sight of a tear in the moonlight. A sob escaped her throat, and the pain in her voice tore at his heart.

"Beatrice, I..." He reached for her, and she lashed out.

"You're despicable!" she cried. She drew her hand back, and before he could move, a sharp sting exploded on his face where she struck him. He leaned back, rubbing his cheek. She raised her hand again, and he caught her wrist and pulled her close, until they were against each other, chest to chest, her body heaving.

Sweet Lord, how could he have forgotten the power she had over him? The flame of desire that had lain dormant for two years reignited the moment he saw her tonight, then exploded into a burning inferno as he held her in his arms...

Unable to contain the need coursing through his body, he grasped her shoulders, pulled her close, and crashed his mouth against hers. She responded instantly, and a low growl of need reverberated throughout her body. She parted her lips in invitation, and he slipped his tongue inside, his soul burning with the need to taste her. He ran the tip of his tongue across her mouth, yielding to the pure bliss of kissing a woman. She mirrored the gesture, moving her own tongue against the roof of his mouth, claiming ownership of him in turn. He deepened the kiss, and their tongues curled around each other in a slow dance of seduction.

A spark of desire rippled through his body, which had grown hard and ready for her, and the dance grew more frenzied, each one devouring the other as if their lives depended on it. It was as if, after a lifetime in the desert, they had both reached their oasis—a paradise to be savored and indulged.

Gripping his shoulders, she lay back on the bed and pulled him on top of her.

"Augustus," she panted, "sweet Lord!"

She squirmed beneath him, and he let out a groan as his manhood strained against his breeches, in desperation for the sweet release that only she could elicit.

He fumbled at his breeches while she continued to kiss him, and his manhood sprang free. Then she reached down, and he almost lost control as her hand, with its long, lean fingers, circled his length. Her skin lacked the smoothness he'd expected, but the delicious friction sent him into a spiral of madness, and his body tightened in readiness. He gritted his teeth in a desperate attempt to hold back, but he couldn't stop the wave of pleasure that threatened to burst.

She parted her thighs, and he surged forward and plunged himself inside her. A cry escaped her lips, and he withdrew then thrust in again. She arched her back, meeting each thrust with the eager response of a woman starved, and their twin cries echoed around the chamber. Then, at the moment of dissolution, he plunged into her, and her body rippled and clenched around him, bringing forth such sweet release that he thought he might die of it.

La petite mort.

"Beatrice, oh, my Beatrice!" His voice cracked as he cried her name and collapsed on top of her, relishing the feel of her sweet body beneath him, closing his eyes to savor the sweet sensation of being inside her. Then he rolled to one side, taking her with him, their bodies fused as if they were one.

Fused as their hearts had once been.

He fought to calm his breath, inhaling and exhaling slowly, to tempter the erratic beating of his heart.

He could just imagine what Whitcombe would say now.

Careful, old man—you can't be shagging with such vigor now you're in your dotage.

But this wasn't just shagging—it wasn't the mere physical release of his body. Tonight, he'd claimed the woman whom, despite his efforts, he loved. Tonight he had fed the needs of his soul, as well as his body.

"Augustus…" The soft whisper from her lips was not filled with horror, or anger, but love.

He pulled the bedsheet over them both, then relaxed into her arms and smiled.

He had finally come home.

After a moment, the woman in his arms moved and pushed him away.

"Beatrice?"

She snatched the bedsheet, and he shivered at the cold air on his skin.

His stomach clenched in shame. He was lying on the bed, fully clothed, his breeches around his ankles like he was a client at a brothel. He climbed out of the bed, then kicked off his breeches.

"What are you doing?" she asked.

"Undressing."

"For what purpose?"

"So I can join you."

She shook her head. "No. You must go."

"After what we just did?"

"That was a mistake," she said. "A mistake I've no intention of repeating."

He let out a laugh. "You jest, surely?"

"I'm perfectly serious."

"You're *evicting* me?"

"Why not?" she replied, her voice hardening. "Isn't that what you did to me the morning after our wedding?"

So that was it. He'd hurt her pride.

"Fair enough," he said. "You've had your revenge."

"This isn't about revenge!"

"Then what is it about?" he demanded. "This is my estate, and you're my wife. You'll find that the law is on my side."

"The law can go to hell," she said. "What did the law ever do to help *me*, when you sent me away to a strange place, all on my own, with no one to turn to?"

"You know perfectly well why I sent you away."

"Oh yes," she said, her eyes glittering. "You did it because of your childish insecurities over your first marriage, that you chose to punish me for. You did it because you were weak, and chose to run away rather than face your insecurities like a real man."

"And is that what you indulged in, while I was gone—a *real man?*"

"Curse you!" she cried. "I don't have to explain myself to you, or to any man. I've managed perfectly well here on my own."

"*Managed*, have you?" he said. "Don't delude yourself. Lavish parties held every other month…none of the staff who've served my family for years have stayed on…" He shook his head. "It's just as well I returned when I did, so I can put a stop to the decadence and prevent you from driving the estate into ruination."

"Damn you!" she said. "So quick to judge others, yet you fail to turn the insight you claim to have onto yourself. If you must know, the majority of the staff had left by the time I arrived—remember, after you forced me out of your London house and had me transported here like a convict? Your housekeeper was unable to maintain her position."

"So, you kicked her out?"

"No. I set her free. If you must know, she lives in the village, on a stipend paid from the estate, with her husband."

Augustus recoiled in surprise. "Her *husband*? She's unmarried, and in her thirties!"

"Which, in your eyes, renders her beyond marriageable age, I suppose. It seems that she and Mr. Evers have been in love for some years. They married last year, and have a baby."

"She married my *steward*?" Augustus said. "And had a child, at *her* age? What the devil has been going on in my absence?"

Her voice grew tight, as if she gritted her teeth. "Two people, very much in love, but constrained by their positions, have finally been united," she said.

"And has *he* left my employ also?"

She shook her head. "I gave him the opportunity, but he wished to remain."

"Why was I not informed?"

"Because it's none of your business!" she cried. "You left me on my own. Should I have waited for you to return while the estate crumbled around me? I'm sure they'll be delighted to see you. Perhaps they'll give you a bed for the night, because you're no longer welcome here. This is *my* home. I've worked hard to make it what it is, and I'll not have you swooping in on a whim to destroy everything I've built."

"And what about what *you* destroyed?" he asked, approaching the bed.

She put out a hand to fend him off. "Don't come any closer! I did nothing, Augustus—nothing! Yet you saw fit to accuse me. You listened to a man's account of what happened over the account of the woman you claimed to love."

"I did love you," he said.

"And I loved *you*!" she replied. "You were everything to me! The difference between a man and a woman is that the woman's love is real—it can weather doubt and fear. And it can weather mistrust and abandonment."

His heart twitched at the pain in her voice—and her words...

Did she still love him, as he loved her?

"Beatrice, I..." He reached for her hand, but she pushed him away.

"I don't want to hear it," she said. "Just go. Please."

"No," he said. "I'm here to stay. You're my wife. You belong to me—as much as I belong in this house, and in your bed."

Before he could stop her, she picked up the pistol and aimed it at him.

"Damn you, Augustus! Why did you have to come back?"

"Because this is my home," he said, "and I intend to claim it, as much as I intend to take my place as your husband. There's nothing you can do to stop me."

"Oh, isn't there?"

The calmness with which she spoke should have warned him of the danger—but he ignored it. He moved toward her.

"Beatrice, stop acting the fool. If you brandish a weapon, you must be prepared to—"

A loud explosion rang out.

Augustus let out a cry and took a step back. A sharp pain tore through his arm, as if someone had driven a hot spike through his flesh. He looked down and saw a dark stain spreading across the sleeve of his shirt.

The world slipped sideways, and the lights in his mind pulsed in and out. Then a roaring sound grew in his mind, like a great waterfall threatening to tear him down. His legs buckled, and he found himself falling through the air, plunging toward oblivion.

His wife had shot him.

CHAPTER SEVENTEEN

B EATRICE HADN'T EXPECTED the recoil to be so strong. Her arm jerked back, and she dropped the pistol, which clattered to the floor. Through the puff of smoke that made her eyes sting, she saw her husband crumple to the floor.

Dear God, what had she done?

She leaped out of the bed and kneeled beside him. "Augustus," she said. "Augustus!"

He let out a groan and opened his eyes. "What the devil?" He lifted his head, then groaned again. "Good grief, woman, you *shot* me!"

"Where did I hit you?" She forced the tremor from her voice, fighting the terror that swelled in the back of her mind.

"My arm," he said. He moved his left arm, then cried out. "*Fuck!* That hurts."

"Then I'd advise you to keep it still."

She rose to her feet, and he reached for her ankle.

"I *said*—don't move!" she hissed. "I must light a candle so I can check your wound. Though, judging by your complaining, I'd say you've not been hurt too badly. Those who complain the loudest are almost always the better off."

"What's happened to you, Beatrice?" he asked. "Since when did you become so hard?"

Since the day you abandoned me.

Choosing not to respond, she reached for the silver tinder box she kept on the mantelshelf and struck it twice, until a spark ignited its contents. Then she blew on the embers until a small flame appeared, and held a candle to it. Once lit, she placed the candle in a holder and returned to her husband.

"Can you stand?" she asked. "I need to look at your arm."

He looked up at her, his silver eyes glittering in the candle-light.

She should have recognized those eyes as soon as she saw them tonight, behind his mask. Lord Julian Stiles—the mysterious man Edward Pennington had brought as his guest—did not exist.

She held the candle up and gave a sigh of relief as she caught sight of a bullet hole in the door. It must have passed cleanly through the flesh. Some of her fear receded, though her heart still thudded at the notion of what might have been…

He struggled to his feet, and she caught his uninjured arm to steady him, then led him to the armchair by the fireplace.

"Thank you."

His quiet words threatened to release the tears pooling in her eyes. But now was not the time for sentiment. Sentiment led to weakness—the past two years had taught her that. Action was the only way to survive.

She placed the candle beside the chair, then took hold of his left wrist.

"Stay still," she said, "so I can look at the wound."

He sat back, like an obedient child, while she peeled back his sleeve until the wound came into view.

A shallow groove ran along the flesh of his arm, but, though the sleeve was soaked with blood, the bleeding seemed to be stopping.

She rose and approached the dressing table where she kept a decanter of brandy, then she opened the drawer and pulled out a petticoat. Grasping it between her teeth, she tore off several strips, then returned to the chair. She placed the remains of the petticoat at the mouth of the decanter and upended it.

"What are you doing?" he asked.

"Sterilizing the wound."

"You're—*what?*"

"Keep still, and let me get on with it," she snapped. "And try not to cry like a baby."

She pressed the soaked cloth against his arm, and he let out a strangled groan. Ignoring his whimpers, she wound the strips of silk around the wound, then secured the makeshift bandage with a knot.

"I'll have to send for the physician," she said, "but that'll do for the moment. At least you won't bleed all over my floor."

Footsteps approached from outside, and she jumped as someone knocked on her door.

"Your ladyship, are you in there?"

It was the footman.

"Come in, Charles."

The door swung open to reveal the footman, flanked by two of the guests—Lord James de Bruin and Mr. Manford.

"Bloody hell," Manford said, his Yorkshire accent prominent. "I thought I heard shooting. Have you apprehended an intruder?"

"Yes," she said, "but he's no ordinary intruder."

"That I'm not." The man on the chair rose to his feet, and the newcomers stepped back, eyes widening.

Augustus was half-naked…

The *lower* half.

Beatrice fought a wicked urge to giggle. She'd always made it clear to her guests—especially the tenacious Lord de Bruin—that while she permitted a soupçon of decadence at her parties, she was there as hostess rather than participant. What the devil must they be thinking now, coming upon a man sitting in her bedchamber, as bold as brass, and devoid of his breeches?

"I happen to be her husband."

"Good God!" de Bruin exclaimed. "You mean…*you're* Earl Hardwick? I thought you'd long since abandoned your estate, never to return."

"Perhaps that's what you were led to believe," Augustus said.

"Not by any account of *mine* on the matter, I assure you," Beatrice said, "but, rather, the irrefutable evidence placed in front of all who have visited Hardwick Hall over the past two years."

To his credit, Augustus averted his eyes in shame.

"Now, I believe my husband is in need of his rest," Beatrice said. "Lord de Bruin, Mr. Manford, I thank you both for your concern, but as you can see, I'm not in danger. Charles, would you be so good as to escort my guests to their chambers, please?"

The footman bowed with an air of nonchalance, as if nighttime shootings were a regular occurrence, then he steered the two men back into the corridor and closed the door behind him.

Beatrice glanced back at her husband, who was lowering himself into the chair, his body shaking. Even in the candlelight, she could see that his face had grown pale.

"Would you like a brandy?" she asked.

He shook his head. "I've drunk enough for one night. But I have one request—nay, a demand. I want your guests out of the house by tomorrow."

Even in pain, his arrogance didn't abate.

"Who are you to dictate what I do with my guests?" she asked.

"I'm your husband."

"You need to have been present to claim that title."

"I'm here *now*, aren't I?"

"To do what?" she cried. "Claim ownership of me and expect me to fade into the background like the obedient little ingénue you'd intended to mold into the perfect little wife?"

He had the grace to look guilty. "How did you know *that*?"

"You mean other than deducing it for myself based on your behavior?" she said. "Men gossip as much as women—more so, for *they* have nothing to fear from the consequences. Lord Ffortescue's cousin has a loose tongue, especially when indulging in my champagne. I believe your friends planned to find you a biddable little woman to service your every whim—at least, that's what the young fool said."

He shook his head. "I-I don't know what to say."

"There's little *to* say," she replied. "But if you're expecting a submissive little puppet, then I'll be delighted to disappoint you. Your biddable Beatrice is no more."

"Has she gone forever?" he asked, his voice softening.

"What did you expect after what you did?" she replied. "You left me to deal with an estate in ruins, on my own, in a world I was unprepared for. What does a woman do when she's tossed into a stormy ocean? Does she succumb to the waters and drown, while she waits to be rescued by a man who'll never come? No—she swims. Inelegantly at first, but swim she does, until she's no longer in need of rescue. She learns to be far stronger than the man who threw her into the waters in the first place."

He leaned back in the chair. "Forgive me," he said.

"There's nothing left to forgive," she said. "The days of waiting for your return have long gone."

"Then what can I do?" he asked. "Where should I go?"

Though she wanted him gone—wanted to never see him again, lest she succumb to her desire—she was no fool. Like it or not, Hardwick Hall was his home.

She wiped her hands, then returned to the bed and slipped under the sheets. "I suppose you should remain here," she said.

Hope ignited in his eyes, and he rose and approached the bed. "Oh, Beatrice! You don't know how much—"

She held up her hand. "You'll have seen that your room was just as you left it," she said. "I ensured it was maintained and ready for you should you return."

"For two years?" he asked, hope in his voice.

She nodded, fighting against the childish hope that had lingered within her since the day she arrived here.

"Yes," she said softly. "For two years."

He reached for the bedsheet and lifted it, but she snatched it back.

"What are you doing?" she asked. "You're not welcome *here.*

Your room is next door."

"But I thought—"

"You thought wrong."

He nodded and backed away. "I'll return to the guest room," he said. "It seems a shame to disturb the lord's chamber when you've gone to such lengths to preserve it exactly as it was."

She flinched at the bitterness in his tone. He picked up his breeches and slipped them on. Then he bowed and exited her chamber through the door leading to the corridor.

She lay back on the bed, watching the flickering light of the candle. In her dreams—childish dreams they might have been— she'd pictured a tearful reunion, with the both of them declaring their regrets and professing their love. But her anger and indignation at what he'd done had cut her too deep. Some wounds never fully healed. Two years was a long time for a scar to form over her heart—thick, hard, and resilient—to protect her from the despair that had almost consumed her during those first few months, alone, in an isolated country mansion.

It was only right that he accede to her demands and leave, but as she turned onto her side, the pillow cool against her fevered skin, the sense of loss, of being alone in a huge, empty bed, threatened to overwhelm her once more.

Her husband had returned, and though she was determined to hate him, she couldn't.

She loved him, and she always would. But he must never know how deeply she loved him, for though she had withstood poverty and toil over the years, she knew that she would never be able to withstand having her heart broken.

Not again.

CHAPTER EIGHTEEN

B Y THE TIME dawn had broken, Augustus was already up, having struggled to sleep during the night. After leaving his wife's chamber, he'd fought the urge to claim her once more. The sweet ecstasy of holding her in his arms was greater than he could have imagined.

But the hard outer shell he'd seen during the ball, which had dissolved when they made love, had returned. And despite what he'd said—despite the fact that, by law, she belonged to him—he wanted her willing.

He winced as he dressed, his arm throbbing with pain. He'd left his valet in London, giving him leave to visit his family. The poor man had been in Europe tending to his master's needs for two years without any vacation. But Augustus was in need of him now.

The bandage had held firm during the night. Wrapped around his arm with precision and neatly finished with a secure knot, it was the work of an expert.

How had she learned such a skill? Most women would have fainted at the sight of blood. But Beatrice had taken control and dealt with his wound as expertly as any surgeon.

Perhaps she'd spoken the truth when she said that she had learned to swim stronger than any man.

That was the difference between the Beatrice he'd seen last night and the young woman he'd married.

She had grown up—transformed into a strong, independent woman.

By the time he'd finished dressing, a beam of sunlight shone through the window. Tying his cravat as best he could, he stepped outside the guest chamber and came face to face with Edward Pennington. At the far end of the corridor he could see a number of other guests milling about.

"Ah, Stiles. Good morning."

Augustus acknowledged his companion with a nod. "Pennington."

"Breakfast should be ready soon," Pennington said. "I hope you're hungry. The Merry Countess's cook provides the best kedgeree in England. You'll now have a chance to get a good look at the other guests, without their masks. Though, of course, they'll also get a good look at *you*." Augustus didn't respond, and Pennington frowned. "Stiles, is something amiss?" he asked. "You look a little unwell."

"I'm afraid I must make a confession," Augustus replied. "My name's not Julian Stiles."

"Who are you?"

"My name is Augustus. Augustus Hardwick."

Pennington let out a low hiss. "So you're..."

Augustus nodded. "That's right. I'm the master of this house."

"And"—Pennington shook his head—"that means you're the husband of..."

"Our hostess, yes."

"Does she know?" Pennington asked. "She said nothing last night." Then he frowned. "Was it some jape that the two of you planned?"

"No," Augustus said. "It's entirely my doing. I deceived both her and you, and for that I must ask your forgiveness. Rest assured, my friends spoke the truth when they said they'd sponsor your membership of White's. In that, at least, you were not deceived."

He offered his hand, and the young man took it.

"*My* forgiveness you have, Hardwick," he said, "but what about your wife?"

"I spoke with her last night, after the ball."

Pennington shook his head. "I can't begin to understand why you did it."

Before Augustus could reply, the gong for breakfast rang, and more guests appeared. The two men followed the rest of the party toward the dining room.

Their hostess was not there.

Augustus helped himself to a plate of kedgeree and took a seat at one end of the table. Pennington raised his eyebrows, then nodded and sat beside him. He glanced around the table, and recognized the family Pennington had pointed out last night, Miss Manford and her parents. The father had been one of the two men who burst in on him and Beatrice shortly after she'd shot him, the other being James de Bruin. De Bruin himself sat near the center of the table, already eating.

A faint aroma of spices filled the air, and he took a mouthful of kedgeree.

Pennington was right: it tasted exquisite.

Breakfast seemed an informal affair, with guests helping themselves, then dispersing once they'd had their fill. A buzz of activity could be heard outside, as the carriages had begun to gather to take their owners home.

By the time Beatrice arrived, breakfast was in full swing. The men rose to their feet and bowed. She smiled at the company, glanced toward Augustus, then crossed the floor to help herself to kedgeree and took the seat at the other end of the table.

"Good morning, countess," Mr. Manford said. "I trust ye slept well?" He gave a pointed glance at Augustus before continuing eating.

"I did, thank you," she replied. "Do sit down." Then she raised her voice. "Do you know my husband?" A hush descended over the room, and she gestured toward Augustus. "The earl has returned," she said. "As you see, he's taken his place at the head of the table."

Several pairs of eyes stared at Augustus, but he ignored them and finished his meal.

When breakfast was over, Beatrice steered the party into the main hall, bidding them farewell. Augustus followed her and took her arm. To his relief, she made no attempt to resist.

One by one the guests climbed into their carriages and set off, until one carriage remained, and they stood on the gravel drive—alone, save for Edward Pennington.

Augustus turned to the young man. "I must thank you for your hospitality, Pennington, but I'll be staying here from now on."

"What shall I tell His Grace, and Lord Marlow?" Pennington asked.

"Tell them that I have been reunited with my wife."

Pennington approached Beatrice, and she held out her hand. He took it, bowed, and lifted it to his lips.

"I must thank you, once more, for your hospitality, countess."

Her lips curled into a soft smile. "And I must thank you, Mr. Pennington, for bringing my husband home." Her eyes twinkled with mischief. "Though I understand that you did so unwittingly, and were the victim of deception."

Pennington bowed once more, then climbed into his carriage. As it set off and rolled down the drive, Augustus's wife pulled herself free from his grasp. He winced at the stab of pain in his arm.

"You may be my husband," she said, "but I'd rather you didn't touch me."

"I beg your pardon?"

"You lost the right to touch me two years ago."

"Are we not equal now?" he asked. "Seeing as you shot me last night."

"I didn't mean to shoot you."

"Did you mean to compromise yourself with Heath Moss?"

She let out a sharp sigh. "I won't dignify that with a response when you're set upon believing the worst. Nothing I say, or do, will change your mind. If you don't believe me, that's *your* problem, not mine."

"And the parties?" he asked. "Do you want a reputation for decadence?"

"Whom I invite into my house is my business," she said.

"No, it's *my* business, as master of the house," he replied. "The parties must stop now I have returned."

"You can't tell me what to do!"

"With the estate in the state it's in—" he began, but she interrupted him.

"You know nothing about the estate!" she cried. "I've run it single-handed for two years, and it's been making a profit for months now. If I wish to indulge in a little pleasure, why should I be denied? You said that we should reap the rewards of our sins, and you've striven to ensure that I reaped the rewards for sins I did not commit. Why should I not reap the reward of my toil? Or do you perhaps feel that I should never be rewarded for my actions—only punished?"

A stab of guilt needled at him. "The world will expect me to take charge of the estate now I'm returned," he said.

"The world can go to hell," she said. "What has the world ever done for me?"

"Beatrice…" He reached for her hand and caught her wrist.

"Let me go!" She tried to struggle free, then he turned her hand upward and drew in a sharp breath.

Unlike the smooth skin of a lady, the skin on her palms was rough, like that of a laborer's wife. She tried to pull free, but he held her wrist firmly with one hand while, with the other, he traced a line across her palm, running his fingertips over the callouses.

He met her gaze. She stared back with an air of defiance, but she couldn't completely disguise the pain in her eyes. Eventually, he relaxed his hold, and she withdrew her hand and curled it into a fist. A faint flush of rose spread across her cheeks, and she averted her gaze, as if in shame.

What had she said?

Why should I not reap the reward of my toil?

What toil had it been to leave such evidence on her skin—her perfect skin, which had once been smooth and unblemished?

And she was ashamed.

Yet she was not the one who had cause to be ashamed. He had left her, a naïve girl, on her own, with an unbearable burden that many a stronger person would have crumpled beneath. But if what she said was true, she had triumphed over the adversity of her circumstances, circumstances that *he'd* thrust upon her, and prevailed.

She blinked, and a tear threatened to form. His heart ached to see it—he couldn't bear the thought of her sorrow.

He'd been a fool, or, as Marlow would have said, a complete and utter arse. His only hope was that she'd forgive him, but the barrier of steel surrounding her would not be so easily penetrated.

"Very well," he said. "If you wish the parties to continue, then I've no objection. If the estate is as prosperous as you claim, then I see no reason not to permit the occasional extravagance."

He smiled at her, waiting for her gratitude. After all, it was the sort of indulgence his grandfather had bestowed on his grandmother.

But her expression hardened. She dipped into a curtsey and curled her lip into a sneer.

"His lordship is *most* gracious," she said. "And now, if you'll excuse me, I have much to do." She set off toward the house.

"Such as?" he called out.

She stopped and turned. "Believe it or not, Augustus, the house does not run itself, and nor does the estate. Not that I'd expect *you* to understand, seeing as you saw fit to abandon both."

Her arrow hit home.

She cocked her head to one side, as if sizing him up. "I take it I have your permission to continue with my duties?" she asked.

He winced at the bitterness in her voice. "Of course," he said. "There's no need to ask."

She curtseyed again, then turned her back and disappeared into the house.

Bloody hell…

His conscience, which had been pricking at him all day, now sought to hammer at his skull, demanding to be heard.

Had he misjudged her? She'd accused him of succumbing to the suspicion born from his late wife's infidelities, and she was, in all likelihood, justified in her accusation. Kathleen had shattered his trust such that after their doomed marriage, he'd looked upon all women with suspicion, whether they deserved it or not.

His conscience, and his heart, told him that Beatrice most definitely did *not* deserve it.

But rather than listen to reason, he'd avoided the issue and run away like a coward, leaving her alone.

How in the name of the Almighty would he ever begin to make it up to her?

How would she ever find it in her heart to forgive him?

And would he ever forgive himself?

CHAPTER NINETEEN

A s Beatrice approached the farmer's cottage, a basket over her arm, spatters of rain splashed onto her face. Not long after breakfast, clouds had obscured the sun, rendering the day cold and melancholy—to match her temper.

Despite the weather, the cottage was an oasis of color. A climbing rose surrounded the doorway, and in the garden beyond, a rainbow of colors shimmered in the breeze. Mrs. Atkin was a miracle worker with her flower garden, and her blooms often adorned Beatrice's bedchamber, their sweet scent lifting her spirits even on the darkest day.

Beatrice lifted her hand and knocked on the door. Then she glanced at her knuckles, covered in scrapes from yesterday's toil when she was helping the farrier, and felt the heat rise in her cheeks once more.

Her husband had noticed the state of her hands. No longer the hands of a lady, they were the hands of a laborer. She viewed the marks with fondness. They were evidence of the love she bore for the estate she'd hated at first, but now called home. But others would not understand. The guests at her parties, the friends she'd left behind in London, even Giles and Henrietta, would see her blemishes as marks of shame, evidence that she had been reduced in circumstances.

Half of her acquaintance would look down on her, and the other half would pity her.

And she had long since lost any appetite for the pity of others.

The door opened to reveal a plump, red-faced, smiling woman with iron-gray hair tucked neatly beneath a frilled cap. Her face broke into a smile of welcome.

"Your ladyship, what a pleasure to see you! Do come in."

"Thank you, Mrs. Atkin." Beatrice followed the woman inside.

"Daniel's out in the fields today, your ladyship, with our Kit. But he should be home soon. He'll be ever so disappointed if he misses you."

"I've brought some of Cook's oatcakes," Beatrice said. "Though you must tell him to *share* them this time." She handed the basket over. "I trust Annie's keeping well today?"

"Thank you ever so much for asking, ma'am," Mrs. Atkin said. "Our Annie is in good health today. She had a little turn yesterday, but Dr. Pegg said it was nothing to worry about."

"Good," Beatrice said. "The doctor still visits every day?"

"Aye, though I've said there's no need for you to go to the expense."

"It's my pleasure," Beatrice said.

Given poor Annie's circumstances, there was *every* need for Beatrice to take care of her. Annie, Mrs. Atkin's eldest, was nearing her confinement. The poor girl had been compromised by a young man from the neighboring village, who abandoned her as soon as she quickened with child. With no husband to support her, and her parents struggling to make ends meet, Annie's situation was one to be pitied.

Beatrice understood Annie's desperation. While she might have steeped herself in self-pity when she first arrived at Hardwick Hall, she at least had respectability, a roof over her head, and the means to improve her lot. Poor Annie had nothing.

Perhaps Augustus's abandonment had been necessary, in order to teach her a lesson. Only through adversity did a man, or a woman, grow stronger. And the past two years had made her stronger.

Augustus…

A hand touched her arm.

"Are you well, Lady Hardwick? You look distressed."

Unwilling as she was to voice her distress, news of Augustus's return would soon be all over the estate. Beatrice owed Mrs. Atkin the truth before she heard it from the village gossips. Given her daughter's ruination, the farmer's wife had heard enough gossip.

But before Beatrice could reply, footsteps approached from the back of the house, and a voice called out.

"Are ye there, Betty, love? Kit and me would like a cup of tea, if you wouldn't mind. I've fixed that fence, but it's right thirsty work. Or perhaps ye have time for a bit of a cuddle first?"

Mrs. Atkin flushed scarlet. "Daniel!" she cried.

"Oh, stow it, woman! Our Kit's courting now. It's about time he learned what goes where."

"Lady Hardwick is here."

The footsteps stopped, and Beatrice heard a sharp intake of breath, followed by a curse. Then the farmer emerged from the back of the house, wiping his hands on a cloth. His deep brown eyes twinkled as he ran a hand through a mop of blond hair. He was accompanied by a youth who was the spitting image of him, save for his eyes, which were a clear blue, and the fact that he was several inches taller, and had to bend his head to fit through the doorway.

"Mr. Atkin," Beatrice said, "and Christopher. I trust my visit is not inconvenient?"

"Of course not, Lady Hardwick—it's a pleasure, as always," the farmer said. "Begging yer pardon; I trust ye didn't hear what I said just then."

His son flushed scarlet, and Beatrice couldn't help smiling. "I heard nothing untoward, I assure you," she said. "Of course, my definition of *untoward* may differ from that of others. I applaud your stamina." She winked at his wife. "Mrs. Atkin, I suspect you're a fortunate woman."

The farmer's eyes widened and he looked at his wife, alarm in his expression. Mrs. Atkin burst out laughing, then she approached her husband and they embraced.

The laughter died on Beatrice's lips at the sight of a couple so devoted to each other. Though she should be happy for them, it only served to remind her of the ache in her own heart—an ache that had intensified now that the object of her melancholy had returned.

Mrs. Atkin freed herself from her husband's embrace and took Beatrice's hand. "What's wrong, your ladyship?"

Only then did Beatrice notice the tears rolling down her cheeks. Ashamed, she wiped them away.

"My husband has returned."

"Mercy me!" Mrs. Atkin cried.

"The earl has returned?" the farmer asked.

Beatrice nodded.

"Is he back for good?"

"I-I believe so."

"Well, if that isn't a bit of good news!" Mr. Atkin said. "What do you say, Betty?"

Mrs. Atkin slapped her husband's arm. "I say you're a great oaf with a head full of straw!" she cried. She turned to Beatrice. "Begging your pardon, your ladyship, but your husband abandoned you, just like that young Ian did to my Annie."

"You forget the troubles the earl had over the first Lady Hardwick, God rest her soul," Mr. Atkin said. "He was ever so upset when she passed. And then losing that poor child fair broke his heart. I've never seen a man so lost."

"Oh, be quiet!" Mrs. Atkin said. She took Beatrice's hand. "Everyone here knows you're nothing like the first Lady Hardwick, and the earl's a fool if he doesn't appreciate what you've done for the place."

"Lord Hardwick's no fool, Betty," Mr. Atkin said. "Begging your pardon, your ladyship, but I'm sure all will be well now he's returned. Pay no attention to my wife."

Mrs. Atkin let out a huff, then a broad grin stretched across her face. "Oh, your ladyship! Now the earl's returned, there'll be babies! A baby makes everything all right, doesn't it? I told my Annie that no matter what's happened before, she'll have the greatest treasure the Almighty can bestow upon a woman. Once you're with child, you'll think differently, I'm sure."

A child…

A secret voice whispered in the back of Beatrice's mind of her dream: a child to nurture, and to love.

After Augustus had left two years ago, she fell into melancholy, but she had climbed out and forged a life for herself, without him. But the one thing she yearned for was a child of her own. And she'd struggled to conquer the pain of knowing that she'd never be a mother.

But now her husband was back, her hope had been reignited. Perhaps, even now, given what happened last night, she was carrying his child.

But if she weren't…

She was determined to hate him—to keep him at a distance lest he hurt her again, to safeguard her heart.

But with him in her home, and demanding his place in her bed, how would she ever be able to withstand the temptation?

"So you see, Lord Hardwick, the estate's finances are in a considerably stronger position than they were when you last inspected the ledgers."

Augustus looked up from the paper in front of him and fixed his gaze on the steward. The man seemed to have grown younger in the years since Augustus saw him last, whereas Augustus felt the years as if each one had been etched into his bones.

The man positively glowed with the flush of youth, though he must be fifty, at least.

"How do you account for such a transformation in the estate's fortunes, Mr. Evers?"

"That's simple," came the reply. "An addition to our income, and an extra pair of hands."

"You mean more tenants? Some of the empty cottages have been let?"

"They have," the steward replied, "and the Johnsons' old farm is working again now a new family has taken it over. But I was referring to Lady Hardwick."

"My *wife*? What could she have possibly done?"

The steward frowned, disapproval gleaming in his eyes, and leaned back. Though Augustus occupied the seat behind the desk, he felt as if *he* were the one being interviewed.

"Her ladyship has worked hard for the benefit of the estate and all its occupants," he said. "It was plain to see when she arrived that she understood little about running a home, and even less about running an estate. But she was eager to learn, and she insisted that both Fanny and I teach her everything we did."

Augustus shook his head in disbelief. "She did?"

The steward's frown deepened. "The poor lass was like a lost lamb when she first stepped out of the carriage. Fanny took to her right away. And seeing as her ladyship was an orphan, Fanny treated the child like the daughter she'd always wanted."

"My wife's no child," Augustus said.

"Not now," the steward replied. "She weathered the rapid rise to adulthood with aplomb. But my Fanny will always love her like a daughter."

"Fanny?"

"Miss Wood, as she was."

Augustus found himself blushing. How many years had his housekeeper been in his employ, yet not once had he bothered to find out her first name? Or, for that matter, had he bothered to notice whether she was in love and wanted a home, and family, of her own?

Beatrice had noticed. Most likely, her tender heart had melted at the thought of the couple being in love, and she'd helped them.

However, that didn't explain how the estate now prospered.

The steward arched his eyebrow as if he read Augustus's mind. "Her ladyship put her annuity, and her hands, to good use," he continued. "After Fanny and I married, she undertook the housekeeper's role, with Fanny's help, before hiring a replacement, and filling the vacant positions among the staff."

"Vacant positions? Did she evict the rest of the staff, then?"

The steward shook his head. "No, you mistake me, your lordship. We had to let many of the staff go on account of the finances, save the stable master and the cook. Lady Hardwick saw to it that the positions were filled again when she had the funds to do so. But the greatest change she implemented was overseeing the repairs to the tenants' cottages, in particular, restoring the Johnson farm—or I should say the Wilton farm, seeing as Mr. Wilton is the present occupant."

The Johnson farm had always been less than prosperous. Mr. Johnson struggled to pay his rent, and after he died, his widow had moved back to her family in Kent and taken the children with her. The farm had fallen into disrepair, and Augustus, still bitter from his wife's betrayal and the loss of her child, had ignored his steward's pleas to restore it and escaped to the Continent.

Beatrice, it seemed, had not ignored the place.

But then, she, unlike him, had no means to escape. Rather than run away from the problem at hand, she had taken it to heart and worked to resolve it.

"Is the farm working to its full capacity?" he asked.

The steward nodded. "The first year was difficult, but with economies around the house, Lady Hardwick was able to provide the capital needed to repair the buildings and replenish the livestock." He pushed the ledger under Augustus's nose. "The figures don't lie, Lord Hardwick," he said. "Though we weathered a deficit last year, the estate prospers."

"How did you fund the deficit? And how did my wife fund the extra staff?"

The steward colored. "Perhaps you should speak to her ladyship."

His discomfort could only mean one thing: Beatrice had procured the funds through nefarious means. Perhaps she'd sold some of the estate's assets.

Dear Lord! Had she dispensed with family heirlooms that she had no business to touch?

He fisted his hands to control his temper. "What did she sell?"

The steward opened his mouth to reply, then hesitated.

"Damn it, man!" Augustus cried. "If she's been stripping my family's heritage and selling it to the highest bidder, I have every right to know."

The steward set his mouth into a straight line and flicked through the ledger, until he reached a page where he ran his finger over the entries and stopped halfway down the page.

"There," he said.

Augustus leaned forward and read the entries. "One white silk gown, worn once. Three muslin day dresses. One pair of teardrop earrings, sapphires set in diamonds. One ruby necklace. One pearl necklace. One Thomas Mudge detached lever escapement pocket watch bearing the engraving *To my beloved Anthony. Love is as eternal as time itself.*" He glanced up. "Anthony?"

"Her ladyship's late father, I believe."

Augustus stared at the entry. As he'd suspected, his wife had sold family heirlooms to restore his estate. But she hadn't sold his heirlooms.

She'd sold *hers.*

"And—the parties?" he asked, aware of the tremor in his voice.

"Paid for from the profits from the estate. The food is sourced locally—the beef and pork from the Wiltons' farm, mutton from the Atkins' farm, and the wine comes courtesy of a merchant with whom her ladyship entered into a deal to recommend him to her guests, in exchange for a small percentage of his profits."

Augustus did not like the disapproval in the steward's voice.

Damn the man, he was speaking to Augustus as if *he* were the wayward one! "I meant to ask, how often do they take place?"

"Every two months or so."

"And my wife plays the glittering hostess at each and every one?"

"Of course."

"And"—Augustus hesitated—"does she entertain her lover when the parties take place?"

He winced at the petulance in his tone, but he'd found himself unable to resist asking the question. He needed to know, once and for all, and the only man he trusted to use discretion on such a delicate matter was a paid subordinate in a position of authority. Chambermaids and footmen were wont to gossip. As to his friends, they could not be trusted on such a delicate matter. Imagine how Whitcombe would laugh!

But his steward, he could trust.

The steward remained silent, and Augustus averted his gaze, his cheeks warming with shame. It was one thing to suspect his wife, but a different matter entirely to voice it to another. Once spoken, words could not be unspoken. Nor could they be forgotten.

The silence continued, and he became aware of the ambient sounds in the room—the solid, regular ticking of the longcase clock in the hallway outside, his and the steward's steady breathing, and the rapid ticking of his pocket watch…

…the watch, which had belonged to his father, he kept close to his heart. A family heirloom that he would never part with willingly—that he would only ever sell if his fortune had been stripped down to the clothes on his back.

What have I said?

He shook his head.

Dear God, forgive me, what have I done?

He lifted his gaze, his palms growing slick with anticipation of what he would see.

The steward had fixed his gaze on him, his eyes dark with

disapproval. The neat, efficient man who had deferred to Augustus since he'd inherited the earldom now looked at him with an expression of disappointment.

It was as if his father, and grandfather, were looking at him now, with all the expectations of decency and honor that came with his rank...

...and they both fond him wanting.

Augustus had never felt so ashamed.

"Forgive me, Mr. Evers," he said. "I should not have asked such a question."

"A man must always voice his suspicions if he has them," the steward replied, "for in not speaking of our fears, we risk being overpowered by them. It is therefore not my place to criticize the question you've asked. But, in turn, I would ask you one thing."

"Which is?"

"What reason has Lady Hardwick given to arouse such suspicions?"

None at all.

"I had, at one time, thought..."

His voice trailed away under the steward's calm scrutiny, and he shook his head. He couldn't disgrace Beatrice by relating what had happened at Lady Moss's ball.

"You must admit that my wife presents a rather predatory persona to her guests."

Mr. Evers rolled his eyes in the manner of a nursemaid trying to explain the difference between right and wrong to a child. "If I may be so bold, the lady who hosts parties is a different creature to the young woman who takes care of the estate and every living thing within it."

Sweet heaven, it seemed that the steward was half in love with Beatrice, as half of the party guests were.

And how the devil had the usually taciturn steward gained such eloquence?

"You seemed to have gained a talent for observing human nature, Mr. Evers," Augustus said.

"For which I credit my wife," came the reply. "A man may possess clarity of thought and be unencumbered by emotion when it comes to making decisions, but a woman understands the hearts and motivations of others with an insight that those of our sex can only dream of possessing."

"Has marriage turned you into a milksop, Mr. Evers?"

The steward shook his head. "No, your lordship. Marriage has given me the fulfilment in life that I didn't know I craved. I have a life partner who stands beside me, who supports me, and who challenges me when I am in need of it. Marriage has given me immeasurable happiness, such that I thank the Almighty for each day that I wake up with my wife in my arms."

The heat rose in Augustus's cheeks. Had he been standing, he would have shuffled from one foot to another, as he'd once done at Eton after he was caught truanting and was sent to the housemaster for a thrashing.

But no thrashing could have assuaged the guilt that burned inside him at this moment.

The steward's expression showed no anger, only contentment. "In short," he continued, "marriage has given me the missing half of my soul."

Augustus rose to his feet, and the steward followed. He offered his hand. "Mr. Evers," he said, "forgive me. And, though it is overdue, let me congratulate you on your marriage."

A warm hand took his and clasped it firmly. The skin was roughened, like the skin of Beatrice's hand. It was the hand of a worker.

While Augustus had been languishing on the Continent, living off his own annuity, his wife, and all at his estate, had been undertaking the duties he'd abandoned.

No wonder she wanted nothing to do with him.

More than anything, he wanted to make amends—to win her back.

What had the steward said? *The missing half of my soul.*

Fine words, but they were the truth. Augustus's soul had

always been incomplete. Even when he'd thought himself in love with Kathleen, there was something missing—something he couldn't quite fathom. Only when Beatrice entered his life had he begun to feel whole.

Beatrice was the key. But a voice whispered to him that the damage he'd done to her was irreparable, and that any effort he might make to atone would be too little, too late.

But he had to try.

Chapter Twenty

BEATRICE HEARD A knock and looked up from her writing desk.

"Come in!"

The door opened and the housekeeper slipped in. Miss Hinde was younger even than Beatrice, but she was an intelligent and capable woman. And kind, as Miss Wood—now Mrs. Evers—had been. She handled the female staff with tact and kindness that elicited far more enthusiasm and efficiency than a stern hand might have. The young woman had pledged to take young Annie Atkin into employment after her confinement, to enable her to support her child, and Beatrice looked forward to the prospect of having a child about the place—two children, given that dear Mrs. Evers was nearing her time.

Though her heart gladdened at the thought of having children bringing life into the house, she couldn't help the melancholy that afflicted her over the prospect of having a child of her own.

For in order to conceive a child, she'd have to be willing to let Augustus into her bed again. And the prospect of sharing such intimacies with a man she could no longer trust was not something she could bear.

When they made love the night of their wedding, she had given him her heart. Then, last night, when they succumbed to their passions, their twin cries echoing around the walls of

Hardwick Hall, she had exposed her heart once more.

How could she take him into her bed and keep her heart at bay? It would make her no better than a harlot, a woman who traded her body for her own ends, in order to take, rather than to give.

"Lady Hardwick?"

The young woman's inquiry returned Beatrice to the present, and she rose from her chair, rang the bell for tea, then crossed the floor to the two-seater sofa beside the window.

Miss Hinde had helped stave off some of Beatrice's loneliness, and she looked forward to the daily ritual of taking tea with her housekeeper—a treat to look forward to at the end of a long day, especially during the summer months when there always seemed to be so many things needing doing around the estate. No doubt the sharp-tongued debutantes she'd known in London would laugh at the notion of enjoying the company of subordinates, but Miss Hinde had a ready wit and a kind heart—something most Society ladies lacked.

The housekeeper sat next to Beatrice, drew out a pocket-book, opened it, then held it out. "I think you'll approve of the menus I've devised for the next week."

Beatrice took the book and read over it, running her forefinger down the page. "Very good," she said. "Ah! Pork on Monday. Excellent. Mr. Wilton is to be commended on his produce this year. Have you remembered to send a hindquarter to Dr. Pegg?"

"Already done, Lady Hardwick. Mrs. Pegg conveys her thanks."

"And"—Beatrice hesitated—"my request for supper tonight?"

The housekeeper nodded. "The arrangements have been made," she said. "Artichoke soup, roast goose, apple pie, and we had enough ice for sorbet."

"And are they…"

"All his lordship's favorites, yes," the housekeeper said. "Just as you asked. Mrs. White said he was always pestering her for sorbet as a boy, and that every time she served goose, he'd often be caught slipping into the kitchen at night when the household was asleep to pick at the remains."

"And it was no trouble?" Beatrice asked. "I'd hate to disrupt Mrs. White's schedule."

"Mercy, no!" the housekeeper said. "She told me it would be a pleasure to cook for him now he's returned. The artichokes are a little past their best, but she's found them sufficient to make a passable soup, and there's enough apples in storage to last us until the next crop."

As they continued to discuss the menus, a maid appeared with the tea tray. She placed it on the table in front of the sofa, bobbed a curtsey, and exited the parlor.

Beatrice poured a cup, dropped a spoonful of sugar in, and handed it to the housekeeper before pouring a cup for herself. Then she leaned back in her chair.

She might not trust Augustus enough to give herself to him totally, but she could, at least, make him feel at home at Hardwick Hall. It was, after all, his home.

And despite her determination to never bare her heart to her husband, she still loved him.

BEATRICE DESCENDED THE staircase, and the longcase clock in the hall chimed seven times as soon as she stepped onto the hallway floor, as if it wished to herald her arrival. Dispensing with the tradition of taking a drink in the parlor before dinner, she went straight to the dining room.

She opened the door and froze.

Her husband, whom she'd not seen all day, was already there.

Despite her pretense at nonchalance, her heart fluttered as she caught sight of him. Dressed in a dark green jacket that fitted his broad chest to perfection and, if she were not mistaken, one of the cravats she'd procured during his absence, he still possessed the ability to render her weak at the knees.

He rose to his feet, and, for the first time since his return, she had the opportunity to look at him—*really* look at him.

In many aspects he looked as he ever had, save for the silver threads in his hair being a little more prominent. The kindness that had first drawn her to him still lingered in his eyes, but his face seemed lined with weariness. For a moment, she felt a twinge of sympathy for him. Then she recalled her own sorrow. His misery of years past had been brought about by the betrayal of his late wife, but any misery he might feel now was brought about by his own hand.

The same hand that had caused her own misery.

On no account must she let herself be taken in by him.

Be strong. Protect your heart at all cost!

"Beatrice—" he began, his voice thick with emotion, but she raised her hand and interrupted.

"Good evening, husband," she said.

He hesitated, then nodded, waiting for her to sit, after which he resumed his seat.

A formal ritual, perhaps, for a supper between husband and wife in the intimacy of their own home. But formality was the fortress behind which she intended to protect her heart.

She glanced toward the footman at the door and gave a slight nod. He bowed, clicking his heels together, and shortly after, the door opened and another footman appeared with a tureen of soup. He glanced toward Beatrice, eyebrows raised, and she nodded toward her husband.

Augustus was the head of the house now he'd returned, and therefore he must be served first.

After helping himself to soup, her husband waited for her to do the same, then they began eating.

"Have you been visiting the estate today?" he asked.

"I have." She dipped her spoon into the soup, then lifted it to her lips. The taste was exquisite. Mrs. White had outdone herself, but, given that she'd made no secret of her adoration for the earl she'd indulged with sweetmeats and treats since boyhood, it was not unexpected.

"Good," he replied. "The weather was very fine today."

The weather? Since when had he shown interest in the weather?

It was as if they were strangers, meeting each other for the first time. And perhaps it would be better if they were. The chasm that separated them now was born of years of hurt. A few pleasantries about the day would not be enough to span it.

They continued the meal in silence, and though Beatrice focused her attention on the food in front of her, her skin burned as if she could feel his gaze on her. But each time she looked up, he averted his eyes, paying attention to one of the many paintings that adorned the walls.

When the main course was served, the discomfort in his eyes disappeared, morphing into joy when the footman placed the goose in front of him.

Picking up the carving knife, he glanced up at Beatrice and smiled. It was a smile of unbridled joy.

Her heart fluttered, and she took a sip of wine to steady her nerves. If he continued to look at her like that, her resolve would crumble.

"I've not had goose for…" He shook his head. "It must be seven years, at least."

"I asked the cook to…" Beatrice began, then she stopped herself.

His eyes widened, and the urge to drown in their silver depths threatened to overcome her. How she had longed to see him smile at her like that, as he once had! Then she looked away and continued to sip her wine, her hand trembling so violently that she was in danger of spilling her drink.

The table was large enough to prevent conversation, unless they wished to shout at each other from the opposite ends of the room. And with the footmen in attendance, Beatrice had no wish to exert herself. There was so much to be said, but nothing either of them could say to the other.

The table represented the chasm between them—each taking comfort from the privacy of the little realm they occupied in their places at the table.

But she saw the delight in his eyes as each dish was placed before him—the wonder as he tasted the sorbet, and finally, the joy as he tasted the dessert.

"I swear," he said, "even after months of storage, the Hardwick apples taste better than any other." His eyes shone with pride. "I've always said, my estate produces the finest apples in all the country."

My estate.

All it took was two words to confirm her place in the world as nothing more than a possession. The estate she'd worked so hard on to ensure its survival—with land, buildings, and people she had grown to love with her body and soul…

…it did not belong to her, and never would.

It belonged to him.

She set her spoon down and pushed her plate away. A footman appeared at her side and removed the plate.

She rose to her feet. "With your permission, husband, I shall retire. I find myself somewhat tired."

AUGUSTUS LEAPED TO his feet.

Bugger.

He'd said the wrong thing.

Again.

But, truth be told, he had no idea what to say to her—the woman who had sacrificed so much for his estate.

No, not his estate. *Their* estate.

For the past two years, it had been wholly hers. Though it was his by right of birth, she had earned the right in the eyes of a higher authority—that of decency and fairness—to call it her own. For what sacrifices had *he* ever made for his home? He'd loved it, but that love had only manifested itself in a fondness, like what a man had for his favorite mistress—a thin, superficial fondness that might begin with adoration and a pledge of undying loyalty, but was only ever demonstrated by tossing a coin at it in the hope that cash would remove the necessity to make any real effort.

And it was no coincidence that tonight's meal consisted of all his favorites. His wife had as good as confessed it herself. Or she would have, had she not stopped herself.

She still cared for him. Whether it mirrored the indulgent fondness that the cook used to bestow on him as a boy, or the love that he craved, he did not know.

Then she pushed her plate away and rose to her feet, her body trembling as if with the desire to flee.

"Beatrice, I—"

"There's no need for you to retire," she said. "You're at liberty to smoke, if you wish, and take a brandy." She gestured to the footman. "Victor here will oblige you. And there will be coffee in the drawing room if you wish."

"Won't you join me?" he asked.

For a moment, he thought she'd say yes, and he caught his breath, acknowledging the hope that had leaped to the fore.

Then she shook her head. "I am very tired, Augustus," she said. "Today has been…" She made an aimless gesture in front of her, then sighed. "I wish to be excused."

For a moment, vulnerability shone in her eyes, and he caught a glimpse of the young woman who had captured his heart—the broken angel he'd fallen in love almost from the moment he set eyes on her. Then her expression changed. She straightened her stance, as if steeling herself for battle, and the hardness returned.

"I have no wish to detain you against your will," he said, willing the softness to return.

But it did not. She merely gave him a quick, tight smile, then swept out of the room.

But he wasn't ready to admit defeat. The campaign to win her back had only just begun. And, unwittingly, she had conceded one battle tonight, in selecting his favorite dishes. If nothing else, it proved that her heart was still for the taking.

With a renewed sense of hope, he waved the footman over. A brandy was in order. To celebrate his victory, however small, and to fortify him for the battles to come.

❦

CHAPTER TWENTY-ONE

AFTER KITTY HELPED her out of her gown, Beatrice dismissed her maid, then climbed into bed. The sheets were cool against her skin, which burned as if she'd caught a fever.

It was no fever of the body—but of the heart.

How would she bear it, having him so near? Her senses quivered at the mere thought of him, and her body had come alive when she caught the faint scent of wood and musk in her nostrils—the scent she first noticed when he took her into his arms and kissed her for the first time.

It was the scent that had set her ablaze with desire the night he'd first made love to her.

And then he abandoned you.

Gritting her teeth, she focused her mind on the morning that he'd sent her away, recalling the bitter hurt. She must not surrender to him again. She needed to be cold, rational—to weigh up her situation as a man would, with calculated logic rather than the irrational needs of the heart.

She'd been unprepared for his return. That was why he'd discomposed her so much. The pain she'd kept suppressed for two years had resurfaced, as raw as it was the day he sent her away. But the pain would lessen over time. All she need do was weather the first turbulent days, and weeks, as she had done when she arrived at Hardwick Hall.

She had survived his abandonment. Surely she'd be able to

survive his return.

The sounds of activity that she'd grown used to—the servants bustling about, clearing away dinner, tidying the parlors, and laying the fires for tomorrow, and, in the case of Mrs. White, setting the bones to boil—soon faded, and was replaced by another sound.

Voices in the room next door. Her husband's, and another man's.

Shortly before Beatrice retired, she'd heard the sound of a coach outside. Kitty had told her that the master's valet had arrived—somewhat disheveled, she said with a giggle.

Was it the same valet who'd prepared her husband for their wedding night?

Her cheeks warmed with shame. Though the staff and tenants at Hardwick Hall knew that Augustus had sent her here alone, they didn't know why. Her husband's valet, though, like her personal maid, would know the full story. And though Kitty was the model of discretion and had never breathed a word about it since, could she trust the valet to be equally discreet?

Might he view her with the same contempt that Augustus had, perhaps thinking her a harlot?

She fisted her hands and rolled onto her side.

She was *not* a harlot.

Over the years, apparitions had visited her in her dreams—the haughty Lady Irma, the spiteful Juliette Howard—branding her a whore, and though she'd woken in the morning with her heart hammering against her chest in despair, she had since conquered her fears. She'd be damned if the arrival of a manservant would bring those fears to the fore again.

The voices stopped, and the house grew quiet, save for the sound of her breathing.

She blew out the candle and blinked, her eyes growing accustomed to the dark until she could pick out the sliver of moonlight from behind the curtain.

As sleep began to claim her, she heard a creak, followed by a click and a soft footstep.

"Bea?"

Was she dreaming? The voice, filled with love, had called her Bea. A sign of familiarity and affection.

She sat up.

He stood in the center of the room, his face illuminated by the candle in his hand.

"May…" He blinked and hesitated, and she saw uncertainty in his expression. "May I join you?"

Her resolve crumbled, her weakened soul hearing the call of his heart, and she nodded, slowly, unwilling to speak her assent, for fear her voice would betray her desire.

He set the candle aside, and the bed dipped under his weight as he sat beside her.

He lifted his hand and placed his palm against her cheek, and a soft cry escaped her lips. Such a tender gesture, so light that she could almost have believed she'd imagined it. Yet it seared her body, warming her blood and stirring the blaze of desire that had ignited the moment she heard his voice.

Then, with a gentle, tender gesture, he traced the outline of her face with his fingertips, and the light touch sent shivers down her spine. Though last night she'd been overcome with passion at the way he claimed her, thoroughly and completely, the delicate motion of his fingertips against her skin was a far more powerful weapon than anything else he could have wielded. Last night he'd answered the needs of her body. Tonight he threatened to answer the needs of her heart.

He ran his fingertip down her cheek until he reached the corner of her mouth. Then he traced the outline of her lips and sighed.

"Oh, Beatrice," he whispered. "Every night I lay alone, dreaming of your sweet lips. You have no idea how long I've waited to taste them again."

He dipped his head, and she shivered as his hot breath caressed her skin. A shudder of need coursed through her body, pooling at her center, where the secret ache began to pulse—the ache that, to her shame, she had often attempted to ease by her own hand, her cheeks aflame with shame at her wantonness, which had only ever left her partly fulfilled.

He took her hand and lifted it to his lips. Then he brushed his lips against her knuckles, flicking his tongue out and dipping it between her fingers; the soft, velvety weapon caressed her skin, sending shivers through her body.

Gently, he turned her hand over and traced a line across her palm. Then he kissed her hand, running his tongue over the surface where the skin had hardened over the years.

She shifted her thighs, squeezing them together to ease the ache, and he drew in a deep breath.

"Ah, my love," he whispered, "is it too bold of me to hope that the delicious scent is that of your need for me?"

She inhaled, and the soft scent of the roses in her chamber caressed her senses—but this time, another, deeper aroma joined the sweetness.

The sharp, primal scent of desire.

"How I have longed for that sweet scent," he said. "Better than any perfume, for it is the primal scent of a woman's need when she's readying herself for pleasure."

His words sent a fizz of desire through her veins, and she caught her breath.

A low chuckle reverberated through his body, and he held her close, their chests rising and falling in unison, as if they had been fashioned for each other.

"That sweet scent…" he breathed. "Do you know how deeply I have longed to know whether your taste is as sweet?"

Beatrice caught her breath at his wicked words. Her defenses almost gone, she willed herself to resist the primal urge within her…the need to have him inside her—the need to surrender herself wholly to him.

The need to be loved and cared for, such that she might, even for a moment, let her mind slip sideways and shed the responsibilities that had been thrust upon her.

Then he placed his hand at the back of her head and pulled her close until their mouths met.

He kissed her—gently at first, as a horse master might tame a nervous filly. He peppered the corner of her mouth with tiny kisses, then he swept his tongue along the seam of her lips, stroking, then nudging, as if quietly asking for admittance.

Unable to resist, she parted her lips, and his tongue slipped inside, probing gently against hers, then he withdrew, as if coaxing her to respond.

"Oh Beatrice," he said. "Kathleen was…"

She stiffened, her passion doused as if he'd thrown her into the lake.

Kathleen.

His former wife. The woman he'd compared her to while attempting to justify his abandonment of her.

"Beatrice?"

He moved to kiss her again, and she pushed him back.

"No!" she cried. "Why must you always return to *her*? Do you value me so little that I can only ever be seen as her replacement?"

"Beatrice, I'm sorry," he said, "I—"

"I don't want to hear it!" she said. "I am *not* her, do you understand?" Her voice rose in pitch as she struggled to contain her emotions. "And I never will be!"

She shook her head to dispel the fog of need. What the devil had she done, succumbing to him like a weak-willed creature with no mind of her own, nor any self-respect?

"I know you're not her," he said. "*Sweet Lord*, you're *nothing* like her! That's why I love you!"

She drew her knees up and wrapped the blanket around herself to protect herself from his gaze. "You have no understanding of the word," she said. "Not when you're still in love with her. Perhaps that's why you made love to me last night. Because you were pretending I was *her*!"

He recoiled, his eyes widening. "How could you say such a thing after knowing what she did?"

"Because it's her name on your lips tonight!"

"I only meant—"

"I care not what you meant!" she cried. "I was resolved not to let you into my bed again, yet you used your wiles to seduce me. But no more! You may wish to live with the ghost of your first wife, but don't expect *me* to!"

"Beatrice, don't be a fool."

"Oh, a fool, am I?" she replied. "If that's what you think, then why don't you find another woman to bed—one to match your superior intellect?"

"Beatrice, I'm your husband."

"You may be my husband according to the law of the land, and that of the church," she said, "but I care nothing for such laws. They've caused me nothing but misery. You have lost the right to call yourself my husband in every other sense of the word."

He recoiled, and she caught a flash of pain in his eyes, but she gritted her teeth to maintain her resolve.

His shoulders slumped, as if in defeat, and, without a word, he withdrew, climbed off the bed, and slipped through the adjoining door, taking the candle with him.

Were it not for the need pulsing through her body, or the tears stinging her eyes, she'd have believed that their encounter had been another bad dream.

CHAPTER TWENTY-TWO

AUGUSTUS SPURRED HIS horse into a gallop, relishing the feel of the air on his face.

With the estate running smoothly, he found he had much more leisure time than he'd expected. Mr. Evers managed the estate with efficiency, and even the little housekeeper, who seemed barely older than a child, saw to the household such that his needs were all met.

Even Simon had declared that his life was distinctly less arduous than it had been while they languished in Italy—a world steeped in culture and light, but lacking the freshness that could only be found in the English countryside.

And the valet, curse him, had become the latest soul to fall for Beatrice's charms.

It had been barely two months since Augustus's return, and Beatrice had already invited Simon's family to spend a week on the estate, in a cottage that had been restored in Augustus's absence but was as yet unlet. The valet, who had missed his family during their travels on the Continent, could not contain his joy on seeing his mother and younger sister again.

And to cap it all, Beatrice had offered both women a position in the household. It transpired that Simon's mother had a talent for growing vegetables, but had been unable to find employment since she'd been widowed, on account of her sex. Beatrice, who seemed to consider herself a champion of womanhood, had promptly demanded that the head gardener at Hardwick Hall hand over supervision of the kitchen garden to Mrs. Hever, and the milksop of a man agreed.

Augustus had even caught his valet singing while pressing his cravats. Singing! As if things weren't bad enough.

But he couldn't begrudge Simon a little happiness. He clearly doted on his family, and to see him wandering the rose garden with his sister, neatly dressed in her maid's uniform, gave Augustus a sense of pride.

But *he* was not the one who had right to be proud. It was Beatrice who had brought the family together.

Since the night he'd almost made love to her again—that disastrous night when he was foolish enough to mention his late wife—a fresh barrier had arisen between them.

Beatrice was all civility and deference to his position as lord of Hardwick Hall, and he found nothing to criticize in the manner in which she performed her duties. In fact, he could not have wanted for a better countess, who ran the household with efficiency, visited the tenants with genuine affection, and received visitors with grace.

To any outsider, they must have looked the perfect couple.

Except for the fact that her civility toward him was steeped in coldness.

In a few stolen moments, he'd spied her in the garden picking a rose, or in her parlor seeing to her correspondence. When unobserved, the coldly civil wife disappeared, as did the gracious hostess, and he saw the woman he'd fallen in love with.

To the untrained eye, she looked no different to the elegant countess she presented to the world. But Augustus recognized signs of melancholy—a plaintive sigh, the casual gesture when she tucked a stray tendril of hair behind her ear, and the moisture that occasionally glistened in her eyes—before she caught him looking and turned from him.

On his arrival at the stable yard, he called out. A groom rushed out to meet him and held the reins while he dismounted.

"Give him a good rubdown, will you?" he said. "I'm afraid I rode him rather hard today."

"Of course, your lordship," came the reply, "and you needn't worry about Heracles. He loves a hard ride. Her ladyship has been known to ride him all the way to Highcroft and back."

Of course she would. Beatrice could handle the estate as well as any man. There was no doubting that she'd be able to handle a powerful animal such as Heracles with the same skill.

He set off for the main house. Already he could see a carriage at the front door. The first of tonight's guests had arrived.

The first of many, most likely, now the news had circulated about England that the Merry Countess's husband had returned. Doubtless the gossips were eager to find out whether the earl took equal pleasure in the decadence.

Though this time he understood the economy and efficiency that had gone into the preparation for tonight's ball. The mutton for the pie for supper had come from the Atkins' farm, and Augustus had seen for himself the contract his shrewd wife had negotiated with the wine merchant.

As he entered the house, he saw his wife overseeing the final touches to the decorations, talking to one of the footmen.

She looked up and met his gaze, and he caught his breath at the sight of her. She wore a dress of vivid blue, the color of a deep summer's sky, that shimmered in the light, with shades of violet, as she moved.

He approached her and smiled, but she glanced toward the longcase clock and frowned. "Our guests are due any minute," she said. "The Harwoods are here already."

"Where are they?"

"Resting in their chamber," she said. "I trust that meets with your approval?"

He flinched at the edge to her voice. "Of course," he said. "Forgive my tardiness. I'll be ready forthwith."

He ascended the stairs two at a time in his eagerness to please her. Perhaps tonight, once she saw that he intended to be at her side and support—rather than oppose—her, the frost in her heart might begin to melt.

As he entered his chamber, he glanced at the clothes Simon had set out—a dark blue jacket and a cravat of a brighter blue, together with a matching mask.

It was the same color as his wife's dress. Simon was, indeed, a clever man.

As Augustus removed his riding jacket, the valet entered his chamber. Silently he removed his master's necktie and shirt, then led him toward the tin bath that dominated the chamber, from which plumes of steam rose.

Augustus stepped inside and settled into the hot water, relishing the heat seeping into his aching bones. He'd not had the opportunity to ride during his travels, preferring to walk everywhere, and he'd forgotten that the muscles required for riding were a very different set to those needed for walking. But now, those muscles were giving him a harsh reminder of their existence.

By the time his bath was finished, he lay back while Simon tipped a final jug of water over his head, then rose from the bath, stepping onto the thick carpet while Simon draped a gown over him. There was much to be said for a bath. It washed away not only the grime of the day, but the tension both in the body and mind. The aroma of sandalwood from the soap still lingered in his nostrils, and as he stood patiently while Simon dressed him, he let himself relax, with a sense of hope that tonight, though he might not entirely breach the barrier his wife had placed between them, he would, at least, begin to weaken her defenses.

BY THE TIME Beatrice stepped onto the gallery overlooking the ballroom, most of the guests had arrived and were milling about the ballroom, chattering to each other while soft music played in the background. She'd already spotted Mr. Manford with his wife and their delightful daughter. Mr. Manford's portly physique was unmistakable, despite the mask, as was his habit of shaking the hand of everyone he came into contact with. At the far end of the ballroom, she spotted the rakish Lord de Bruin. It was primarily due to him that she'd resolved never to dance at her parties. The young man thought a good deal too much of himself. Handsome he might be—rich, he certainly was—but he was all too aware of his attributes.

She glanced over the ballroom at the men and women who sought a little pleasure and entertainment away from the Society parties of London. The boyish figure of Mr. Pennington was nowhere to be seen. Perhaps he dared not return to the fortress into which he'd unwittingly admitted the marauder.

"Beatrice."

The marauder himself appeared at the other end of the gallery and approached her.

Her breath caught at the silver of his eyes gleaming behind his mask—a mask of pale blue to match her gown. He offered his hand, and, on instinct, she took it before she could stop herself. He lifted it to his lips, and she shivered at the warmth of the breath that caressed her skin.

"You look beautiful tonight, Beatrice."

She nodded in acknowledgement, then freed her hand. She leaned on the gallery balcony and motioned to the lead musician.

The music stopped, and the crowd fell silent and turned to face her.

She could never stem the overwhelming sense of pride on seeing the host of upturned faces in brightly colored masks glittering in the candlelight, looking directly at her. Over the past year, the attention and interest of her guests had helped ease some of the pain of her loneliness.

Out of the corner of her eye, she caught sight of a dark blue sleeve and a pair of hands gripping the gallery rail beside her. Her husband moved closer, until she felt his body heat.

"My friends!" she cried. "You are most welcome! Tonight we have a particular cause for celebration, as you see."

She gestured toward the man beside her. Augustus glanced at her, then bowed his head to acknowledge the crowd.

"Where's your ostrich plume, Lady Hardwick?"

She recognized James De Bruin's voice, somewhat slurred. Clearly he'd already been indulging in her hospitality.

"I'm in no need of decoration tonight," she said. "And my feathered friend is, I believe, contemplating securing a dance for herself with a partner with whom she can converse at an equal level of intellect. Perhaps you might oblige, good sir, for I'll wager you have all the attributes."

A ripple of laughter echoed through the room, punctuated by Mr. Manford's guffaws.

"And now," Beatrice continued, "you must not let me keep you, when you can be more agreeably entertained tonight."

She gestured to the lead musician, and the music resumed, signaling the start of the first dance. A number of couples lined up on the floor, and a handful of the men disappeared into the adjoining room in search of the card tables, Mr. Manford among them.

Beatrice smiled to herself. Manford was frowned upon by most, including some of her guests. A sharp intellect and business acumen was, in the eyes of some, not enough to atone for humble beginnings. But those who sought to humiliate him at the card tables were invariably taught a lesson in humility themselves.

"You approve of gaming tables?"

Beatrice turned to face her husband. "Why not?" she asked. "Isn't that what you play in your gentlemen's clubs? My guests know to abide by the rules, of which there are but two. The first is that the stakes must be in cash—no promissory notes or trinkets—with a maximum stake of twenty guineas. I'm not an advocate for ruination of men."

"And the second?"

"Fair play, Augustus," she said. "If a player is caught cheating, he is evicted. After his punishment, of course."

He stiffened. "*Punishment?*"

She suppressed a smile. "At the second party I held, one of my guests—Mr. Shorthouse, a rather arrogant man whose hands were inclined to wander—considered himself above the law and saw fit to conceal aces up his sleeve."

"What happened?"

"He denied it, at first, though given the number of witnesses, he had no defense. I had him evicted on account of the cheating, and stripped of his breeches on account of the denial."

"H-his *breeches*? Beatrice, what the devil were you playing at?"

"I'm not an unreasonable woman, Augustus," she said. "I gave him a choice. Either remove his mask, so that all might identify him, and submit himself to the magistrate in the morning, or parade across the dance floor without his breeches, never to be seen again. He, rather sensibly, chose the latter."

"He chose to remove his breeches?"

She shrugged. "With a little help from the footman, yes. It was the lesser of two evils. His mask was left in place, to preserve his anonymity, if not his modesty."

He grimaced, and she braced herself for a tirade of disapproval. Then he made a sound like a strangled cough. His hand flew to his mouth, and his whole body shook.

Then he threw back his head and laughed.

"Husband?"

"Oh, Beatrice!" he cried. "Woe betide any creature who tries to best you! There's no woman in England like you. What have I done to deserve such a clever wife?"

The sincerity with which he spoke warmed her heart. He was proud of her! Did he know how long she had prayed for the day to come when he showed his pride in her—that he valued her?

Or did he merely seek to flatter, in order to ingratiate himself?

His laughter died, and he took her hand. "Forgive me," he said. "I shouldn't make light of such matters. I take it you've had no trouble from the man since?"

She shook her head. "He dares not mention the incident for fear of exposing himself." She suppressed a giggle at the notion of the lecherous Mr. Shorthouse *exposing* himself. "And I'm hardly in danger of encountering him again. I've not been in London since…"

She caught her breath, but there was no need to finish the sentence. He gave her hand a gentle squeeze.

"Beatrice, I—"

"We're neglecting our guests," she said. "Tonight is your entrée into my corner of Society. I would not have my guests say that they're missing out on their host. Shall we?"

He hesitated, then nodded and offered his elbow. She took it, and they descended the stairs into the ballroom to greet the guests.

⤚⟫⟩⟨⟨⤙

AS THE PARTY drew to a close, a dull ache began to spread in Beatrice's head. It started earlier in the day, and she'd attributed it to the hot weather, but the ache had intensified during the party. The curious stares from the guests took their toll. Rumors had circulated far and wide as to what had happened when her husband abandoned her. But she'd stemmed the tide of gossip, playing the role of the Merry Countess.

Now her husband had returned, the guests positively vibrated with eagerness to learn the details. Though for a moment she relished the feel of his warm, solid body beside hers, as if she were the same as any other wife being escorted by her doting husband, the knowledge that she'd always be overshadowed by the ghost of his late wife sat in the back of her mind like a dark, festering shadow.

His presence, which she craved, soon grew unbearable. Sensing her discomfort, he'd left her to join the card tables, and she didn't see him again until supper was served.

But her fickle heart craved his nearness almost as soon as he'd gone. That burning need fizzed inside her.

Curse it! Had the past two years meant nothing? Despite all she'd experienced on her own, was she still the same love-struck child who wanted nothing more than to be loved by him?

The sight of the couples dancing—some of whom were, most likely, in love—that used to bring her joy at her parties now filled her with envy. She skirted the edge of the ballroom until she reached the corridor leading to the kitchen. The noise abated, and she slipped into the darkness. A moment's respite and a strong cup of tea would restore her spirits. Her guests were fully occupied with enjoying themselves. Nobody would miss her.

"Is the Merry Countess not dancing?"

She turned to see a tall man in a striped blue and white jacket and wrinkled her nose at his cologne. "Lord de Bruin." She grimaced at the odor of wine on his breath. "Aren't you enjoying the evening?"

"Oh, I am very much," he said, "but I'd enjoy it a lot more if I could join in the dancing."

"There are plenty of young ladies willing to dance, if you'll ask them."

"There's only one lady I wish to dance with tonight." He took her hand. She tried to snatch it free, but he gripped it tighter. "Will the Merry Countess favor her humble servant with the final dance of the evening?"

"I thought I made it clear, Lord de Bruin," she said. "I have always said that I would only dance with my husband."

He shook his head. "If I remember right, you said that you would always give your husband first refusal. Given that he's clearly not inclined to dance with his delicious wife, it behooves me to make amends on behalf of my sex, lest you think all men are ungallant."

"Do you impugn my husband's gallantry?"

"I do no such thing, Lady Hardwick," he replied, "but I do ask myself why, when your guests are making merry on the dance floor, you skulk in dark corners looking miserable."

"Lord de Bruin!" she cried. "How dare you—"

He tightened his grip and drew her close. "My dear Lady Hardwick, it can't have escaped your notice that everyone is gossiping about what the earl has been up to during his two-year absence."

"What the devil are you implying?"

His grin broadened, giving him a predatory look. "Come now, don't be so coy. All I'm saying is that you're as much entitled to indulge as he is. How does the old proverb go? *What's sauce for the goose is also sauce for the gander.* If the earl continues to neglect his delectable wife, you'll find plenty of others willing to make up for his shortcomings." He tightened his grip.

"Unhand me, sir," she said. "Now."

"You can't tell me you don't wish for a little attention," he said. "After all, isn't that why you hold these lavish parties? To compensate for the emptiness in your life?"

"How dare you?" she cried. "My life is none of your concern. The earl is my husband, and I have pledged to be faithful to him, and him *only*. I shall dance with no other. Not tonight, nor any other night."

"Even if he's been unfaithful?" de Bruin sneered. "I hear the Italian doxies are even harder to resist than those in London."

"Yes!" she said. "Even if he's taken multiple lovers, and I daresay he has! I made a vow, which I view as sacred, no matter what *he* thinks."

"Well, that's a damned waste of a good woman," he said. "But you'll permit me a little kiss for my troubles, will you not?"

"I'll do no such thing."

He released her hand and grasped her shoulders. Seizing the opportunity, she gripped his arms and pushed him back.

He advanced on her again, then froze as an angry voice roared.

"What the devil are you doing with my wife?"

De Bruin swirled around to face the newcomer. Augustus stood at the end of the passageway, illuminated in the candlelight.

With de Bruin's back to her, Beatrice took his wrist and twisted his arm behind his back. Then, with her free hand, she gripped the back of his neck and squeezed until he moaned in pain.

"Ouch!" he cried. "What the devil are you doing?"

"Ridding my home of vermin," she said. "Now, are you going to go quietly?"

"But—"

"I'll make arrangements for your carriage to be brought round as soon as possible. Meanwhile, you can wait for it outside."

"I say, you can't leave a chap on the doorstep, waiting like a lemon."

"I can and I will," she said. "I made it perfectly clear that any act of dishonesty or dishonor will be dealt with severely. Of course, if you wish to protest further, I can ensure that you exit the building in the same style as the unfortunate Mr. Shorthouse. My guests might appreciate a little extra entertainment." She glanced toward his breeches. "And," she added, "I suspect it would be *very little indeed*."

She turned to her husband. "Augustus, please ask one of the footmen to make the necessary arrangements while I escort Lord de Bruin out of the building."

For a moment, she expected him to protest at her unladylike behavior. Then he grinned and nodded. "It would be my pleasure."

"What kind of man are you, to be ruled by your wife?" de Bruin sneered.

"I'm more of a man than the rake she tosses out on his ear."

Beatrice tightened her grip and marched de Bruin toward the front door. The footman standing sentinel caught sight of them, and his eyes widened.

"Would you be so kind as to take care of my guest while he waits outside for his carriage?" Beatrice asked. "I'm afraid he's suffered a rather unfortunate disappointment, and must return home immediately."

The footman bowed. "This way, sir," he said.

Beatrice released de Bruin, who stumbled forward and collided with the footman.

Just as she'd thought: the excess of champagne fueled his predatory confidence, almost as much as it had incapacitated him. Doubtless he'd wake tomorrow with a sore head and little recollection of tonight's events. Though his memory might, perhaps, recover when he realized the invitations from Hardwick Hall were no longer forthcoming.

And to think, she'd once believed him to be a suitable match for Amelia Manford! But that delightful young woman deserved better. Edward Pennington, for example, for all his artlessness, was a kind enough man who cared little for social status. He was easily swayed, but that was no bad quality in a husband.

As she stood in the hallway, the music ceased. The dancing was over. Soon the guests would retire to their rooms with hot cocoa.

Hot cocoa…

If she closed her eyes, she could almost smell the aroma.

Soft footsteps approached.

"Beatrice."

Her husband appeared before her.

"What happened just then, Beatrice? With de Bruin?"

She drew in a sharp breath to stem the anger ignited by his words. Surely he didn't suspect her of having a tryst?

"I don't have to explain myself to you," she said sharply. "I tried that once before, remember? Of course, if you wish to abandon me once more as a result of the actions of others, then you know where the door is. I daresay Lord de Bruin will oblige you with a ride in his carriage."

He reached for her hand, and she snatched it free.

"Don't touch me!"

"No!" he cried. "You misunderstand me. I only meant to ask

how you managed to disarm that young man so easily."

"If you must know—my cousin, Henrietta," she said. "After…" She hesitated, unwilling to relive the memory of her elopement. "After what happened when I was younger, I asked Henrietta to teach me how to fight. I had no proficiency with a sword, but I had some skill with a pistol…"

He grimaced. "Yes," he said quietly. "I concur that you have skill with a pistol. Unless, of course, you were shooting to *kill* the night I returned here."

She drew in a sharp breath and felt her cheeks warm with shame.

"You did nothing that I didn't deserve," he said. "I-I'm ashamed to say that I overheard much of your conversation tonight with de Bruin." He paused, as if waiting for a response, before continuing. "You do not wish to ask why I followed you?"

"I have no need to ask, given your opinion of me, Augustus."

"You're wrong," he said. "Very wrong." He shook his head, his eyes glistening behind the mask. "Beatrice, I never for a moment suspected you of anything untoward with de Bruin. I merely wanted to know whether you were all right, and"—he hesitated—"to apologize. I was quite caught up in your conversation…"

A shiver ran through her. Did he trust her so little that he listened to her private conversations?

"You were *eavesdropping*?" she asked. "Did you expect to hear something a little more salacious, or perhaps you expected me to submit to de Bruin's advances?"

He shook his head.

"You do me a disservice," she said, her voice tightening with fury. "De Bruin is a mere boy. He couldn't begin to satisfy my requirements for a lover. And I would never be so vulgar as to entertain my lovers under this roof. To maintain propriety, I would venture abroad to meet my lover, as is the custom among disappointed wives."

He flinched. Her arrow had hit home.

"Do you mock me, Beatrice," he asked, "or are you speaking the truth?"

She caught her breath at the notion that he could even entertain the thought of her taking a lover. His lapse in trust in her was to be expected, but she'd feared it even as she goaded him.

Would he never wholly trust her?

Then his eyes widened, as if in understanding.

"Forgive me," he said. "You have every right to mock me. When I heard what you said about me to de Bruin—and that you would remain faithful nonetheless—I was so overcome with shame and self-pity that I quite forgot the danger you were in."

"I was in no danger," she said. "I can take care of myself."

"Your safety is my responsibility," he said, "as your husband."

She opened her mouth to deny him, to remind him of what he'd done, but the expression in his eyes prevented her. They seemed to be pleading. Not a plea for forgiveness, or understanding...or even love.

But a simple plea to not be hurt.

Then she nodded. "Thank you—Augustus."

His body relaxed, and he took her hand and lifted it to his lips.

"I think we should return to our guests," she said. "They'll be wondering where we've got to."

He offered his elbow, and she took it, letting him lead her back inside.

CHAPTER TWENTY-THREE

B Y THE TIME Augustus arrived in the breakfast room the next morning, the guests were already there. But there was no sign of his wife.

"Ah! Lord Hardwick!" a voice cried. "Splendid party, as usual. I trust the countess will be joining us later?"

Mr. Manford was already seated, working his way through an overfilled plate of kedgeree, his wife and daughter sitting to his left. He beckoned to Augustus, gesturing to the seat at the head of the table, as if he were the host and Augustus the guest.

But Augustus could not condemn the man for his lack of propriety. Manford's jovial countenance and obvious delight in everything around him had an honesty that many men lacked.

He helped himself to a plate of eggs, then sat at the head of the table, aware of the empty space at the opposite end.

"My wife was a little tired last night, Mr. Manford," he said. "I believe she wishes to take her rest this morning."

"You lucky bugger."

Manford's soft whisper was quiet enough to elude the ears of most of the guests, but Mrs. Manford blushed and let out a giggle. She looked fatigued, which most of the party might attribute to dancing, but the satisfied smile on her face, together with the exchange of heated looks between her and Mr. Manford, told a different story.

As for Beatrice, her reasons for not attending breakfast had nothing to do with Augustus. He'd wanted to visit her last night, badly. But, on the brink of knocking on her door, he'd withdrawn. The key to winning her was to elicit an invitation into her heart, and her bed, rather than claim it for himself. And last night he'd failed to prove himself worthy of her trust, because his own trust in her had wavered. It might have only been for a fleeting moment, when she'd remarked on taking a lover. But it had been enough to make her withdraw from him once more. And, as his father had taught him, the way to hook the fish was to leave the bait on the water's surface, then wait for her to take a bite.

What the devil could he do to prove himself worthy of her? Perhaps he should seek Manford's counsel. The man was brash, overly loud, bumptious, and his face several shades too ruddy to be deemed respectable. Yet he exuded a warm-hearted generosity that Augustus couldn't help but be drawn to, and his wife wore a permanent expression of a woman well pleasured. They had eyes for none but each other, and the constant loving glances and fleeting touches of the hand told him that here was a couple who adored each other, as if they were two halves of the same soul.

If only he could understand Manford's secret—the secret to a happy and fulfilling marriage.

Perhaps it began with small gestures—like pebbles cast into a lake, causing tiny ripples at first, which multiplied and amplified with each subsequent pebble, until the water had shifted.

And it was never too late to start casting the first pebble.

He beckoned to a footman, who scuttled over.

"Would you send a breakfast tray into her ladyship's chamber?" he whispered. "I can see to the guests this morning if she wishes to take her rest and enjoy a little peace and quiet."

"Very good, sir." The footman bowed and disappeared.

By the time the footman returned, breakfast was concluded, and the guests began to disperse. He approached the table and bent over Augustus to whisper in his ear.

"Her ladyship's not yet rung the bell for her maid, sir. I took the liberty of knocking on her door, but could get no response."

She must be exhausted.

"Let her rest," Augustus said. "I shall see to her myself once our guests have departed."

The footman hesitated and opened his mouth to speak, but Manford let out another laugh.

Much as Beatrice heaped praise on the man, his overly forward manner was a little trying. But Augustus merely nodded and smiled while Mrs. Manford's blush deepened.

As soon as Augustus saw the last of the carriages down the drive, he set off for his wife's chamber, but before he reached the staircase, the footman accosted him.

"Forgive me, sir, I didn't wish to say so in front of the guests, but Lady Hardwick ventured out last night."

"Perhaps that's why she wishes to remain in bed this morning."

The footman blushed, and Augustus's stomach twisted at the expression in the man's eyes.

"What are you not telling me?" he asked. "The countess is at liberty to take a midnight stroll in the gardens. She often does so, when the weather's as hot as it was last night."

"Yes, but she left in such a hurry," came the reply, "and Peg told me that she took Kitty with her."

In the middle of the night? And who the bloody hell was *Peg*?

For what purpose would his wife need her maid for a midnight stroll? Unless it were no ordinary excursion.

What had she said?

To maintain propriety, I would venture abroad to meet my lover, as is the custom among disappointed wives.

The devil that lurked in the darkest recesses of his mind rose once more, whispering, in glee, that he deserved to be cuckolded. Or perhaps it was Kathleen's ghost rearing up to mock him? She had died cursing him. And though he'd believed that the curse had manifested itself in the loss of her child—the child he'd accepted as his own—perhaps it was an eternal curse, dooming him to betrayal.

Then he shook his head.

What manner of fool am I to believe such rot?

There must be a perfectly reasonable explanation as to where his wife had gone.

But, the devil at his heels, he took the steps two at a time in desperation to see her.

By the time he'd reached the door to her chamber and knocked three times, the footman had caught up with him.

"Go and fetch her ladyship's maid," Augustus ordered him.

The footman scurried off, and Augustus knocked on the door again.

"Beatrice? May I come in?"

Silence.

He turned the handle and pushed the door open.

The room was empty.

Her gown from last night was draped over the chair by the dressing table, and the bed was neatly made.

He approached the bed. A cup filled with what looked like hot chocolate was on the table beside the bed. He lifted the cup to his lips and took a sip.

The liquid was cold.

The surface of the bed was not completely smooth. A slight bump showed about halfway down. He pulled back the coverlet to reveal his wife's nightgown, still wrapped around the warming pan that, like the cocoa, was stone cold.

His wife had gone, her bed not even slept in.

Hurried footsteps approached, and the footman returned.

"Where's her ladyship's maid?" Augustus demanded.

"She's not in her room," the footman said, panting. "They must still be out."

Augustus felt his gut twist with apprehension. Had Beatrice run off? Or perhaps had an accident? He didn't know which was worse. A dark little corner of his soul prayed that it was the latter—that at least she had not deserted him. Then shame overcame him.

Where the fuck are you, Beatrice?

The footman drew in a sharp breath.

Augustus must have cursed aloud.

Damn, that was all he needed, a lily-livered servant unable to weather a few profanities.

Then he glanced at the footman. With youthful features, face blotched with red, and the gangly, loose-limbed stature of a puppy, the servant was barely out of boyhood. Fear shone in the lad's expression, then Augustus noticed his own hands were balled into fists.

Perhaps the lad thought he was in for a beating.

"Can you tell me anything about when she left?" he asked. "Did she receive a message? What about Peg, whoever she is?"

"I-I don't know." The footman's expression belied his words.

Augustus took the boy by the shoulders. "I think you do."

The footman's blush deepened. "I-I'm not supposed to… P-Peg's one of the scullery maids, your lordship."

"And you indulge in gossip with scullery maids?" Augustus asked. "Or perhaps something a little more depraved?"

The boy's eyes widened. Ah, that was it. He was clearly sweet on the girl.

Augustus tightened his grip.

"Peg and I didn't mean any harm," the boy said. "She said her ladyship insisted she tell no one."

A knot of fury tightened in Augustus's stomach. So, his wife wished to keep secrets.

He released the footman. It wasn't the fault of the messenger.

"What exactly did Peg tell you?" he asked. "You have my word that you won't be punished, and neither will Peg. But take this as a warning: deceive me again and you'll both be dismissed. Is that clear?"

The footman nodded. "Peg told me that a boy arrived with a note for her ladyship. She passed it to Kitty, then, when she returned to the kitchen later, she saw the mistress and Kitty leaving through the side door."

"Where did they go?"

The lad shook his head. "I don't know."

"Heavens, boy, *think!*" Augustus cried. "What about the note?"

"Begging your pardon, sir, but Peg didn't read it, seeing as she's not learned her letters. But when young Jonas brought it—"

"Who the bloody hell is Jonas?"

"Farmer Atkin's youngest."

"Oh, heaven preserve me from slow-witted young men!" Augustus said. "Why didn't you tell me that at the beginning?

He shoved the young man aside and retraced his steps to the main staircase, almost losing his footing on the tiles of the hallway floor as he reached the bottom.

Then he strode toward the main doors, roaring at the waiting footman to open them. As soon as he was outside, he headed toward the lane leading to the Atkins' farm. Then, overcome by a cocktail of jealousy, fear, and fury, he broke into a sprint.

CHAPTER TWENTY-FOUR

THE SUNLIGHT CAST a warm glow on the farmhouse building, giving the roof tiles a reddish hue.

Augustus couldn't remember the last time he'd visited the Atkins' farm, though he recalled the sorry state the roof had fallen into. But now, the building looked as good as new.

The sound of female laughter rang through the air—unrestrained mirth, the sound of pure happiness.

Icy fingers squeezed at his heart.

Though he'd not heard it often, he recognized Beatrice's laugh.

Striding along the lane toward him was his wife, a bouquet of flowers in her hand. Next to her was a tall young man he didn't recognize.

With his honey-blond hair that shone like gold in the morning sun, and the clearest blue eyes imaginable, an air of earthy virility shimmered around the youth's body. He embodied all the attributes of an Adonis—strong features, an easy smile, a powerful, masculine frame…

…and, most of all, youth and vitality.

Qualities that Augustus no longer possessed.

The couple didn't notice Augustus, so engrossed were they in each other. The young man walked with ease next to Beatrice, and—*dear God*—she was clinging to his arm!

Augustus felt the bile rise in his throat as their words floated across the air.

"Those flowers will look wonderful in the bedchamber."

"Oh, they will, won't they, Christopher?"

Christopher? Who the devil was he that she spoke to him with such familiarity—and that they discussed bedchambers together?

They reached the door to the cottage, and the young man pushed it open, then bowed. "After you, my lady."

Beatrice let out a giggle, then she threw her arms around his neck. "It's been such a wonderful night!" she cried. "And, of course, the child will be happy at Hardwick Hall, and you'll be welcome to visit whenever you like."

Unable to listen to any more, Augustus strode toward them. "What the devil do you think you're doing?" he roared.

They turned, and two pairs of eyes stared at him.

"Augustus!" Beatrice cried. "What are you doing here?"

There was no trace of guilt in her voice. Her eyes still twinkled with joy, but, as he continued to glower at her, the mirth faded, replaced by fear.

"Is something amiss?" she asked.

He let out a bitter laugh. "Shouldn't I be asking *you* that?"

The young man bowed. "Lord Hardwick," he said. "To what do we owe the pleasure—"

"Your *pleasure* is the least of my concerns," Augustus snarled, "particularly as you seem to have overindulged in it. Kindly remove your hands from my wife." He held out his hand. "Beatrice, come here."

"Why are you so angry?" she asked.

Was she a simpleton, or did she deliberately set out to goad him?

"You don't *know?*"

She shook her head. "You should come inside."

"Why in the name of all that is holy would I do *that?*"

Another face appeared at the door—Mrs. Atkin. The farmer's wife looked similar to when Augustus had last seen her seven years ago, save for the gray hue of her once jet-black hair.

Her eyes widened, and she glanced at Beatrice. "Have you told his lordship?"

Beatrice shook her head. "Not yet."

"Told me what?" Augustus asked.

"Oh, my!" the woman cried. "Well, if you don't approve, your lordship, I hope there's no harm done. Begging your pardon—it was her ladyship's idea. But don't go blaming her, mind. She offered out of the kindness of her heart."

Augustus gritted his teeth and fixed his gaze on his wife. "I *said*—told me what, Beatrice?"

For a moment his wife stared at him, apprehension and confusion in her eyes. Then understanding crossed her expression, and the fear was replaced by contempt.

"Oh, for heaven's sake!" she cried. "You're determined to think the worst of me, aren't you?"

"It's not Lady Hardwick's fault," Mrs. Atkin said. "She's grown so fond of Annie, and we saw no harm in it."

"Who the hell's *Annie*?" Augustus asked.

"Annie is Mrs. Atkin's daughter," Beatrice said, her voice cold. "And *this*"—she gestured to the young man—"is their eldest son."

Augustus stared wide-eyed at the man. Was this towering youth the small boy he'd seen playing in the fields when he first took Kathleen to visit the tenants more than seven years ago? Not that his first wife had shown any interest in the tenants or the estate—or, indeed, in anything other than jewels, trinkets, and lovers.

"You're not—"

"That's right, your lordship," Mrs. Atkin interrupted, pride in her voice. "That's my Kit. All grown up now, since ye last saw him."

"Then tell me, Master Kit," Augustus said. "Perhaps you can explain my wife's familiarity toward you."

The young man blushed, and Augustus saw him for what he was: an artless boy, with a physique that belied his youth.

"Christopher deserves our congratulations on his engagement," Beatrice said. "He's been courting young Prue, the miller's youngest."

"Cause for celebration it may have been, but it doesn't explain why you abandoned your home overnight."

The young man blushed and released Beatrice's arm as if it burned him.

"Augustus!" Beatrice hissed. "You're insulting this good family, and embarrassing me." She passed the flowers to the farmer's wife. "Mrs. Atkin, do you have something I can put these in for Annie?"

At that moment, a sharp cry rose from within the cottage. Beatrice glanced around, concern in her eyes, and for the first time, Augustus noticed that they were swollen and dark-rimmed with fatigue, and her complexion was pale.

Mrs. Atkin placed a hand on Beatrice's arm. "Hush, child, all is well now," she said. "Why don't you take some tea in the parlor?" She nudged her son. "Kit! Stop making the place look untidy. Go and find your father while I make the tea. Hurry, lad!"

The young man nodded, slipped into the cottage, and disappeared, as if he couldn't get away from Augustus quickly enough.

"Mrs. Atkin, there's no need," Beatrice said.

"There's every need, lass, after what ye've done for our Annie. We've plenty of hot water on the range. It's no trouble. Come on, now."

Augustus watched as his usually single-minded wife let herself be ushered into a side room, then he followed.

Once alone with his wife, Augustus reached for her hand, but she snatched it free.

"Beatrice?"

Ignoring him, she crossed the floor and stood at the window, staring outside.

"You can't blame me for leaping to conclusions," he said. "First, you tell our servants to keep secrets from me while you disappear, then you don't send word when, for all you know, I could have been searching for you through the night."

"Were you?" she asked.

"Was I what?"

"Searching through the night?"

"I discovered this morning that you had gone out and not returned."

"Then at least you were spared the trouble of searching for me during the night," she said. "And now you've found me."

Why the devil was she acting so strangely?

"You can't blame me for coming to the wrong conclusion, given what I saw," he said, "or that you wished to keep your excursion a secret."

Had she not glanced at him before resuming her attention on the view outside the window, he'd have thought she hadn't heard him.

"Do you even want to know what I thought?" he asked.

She turned to face him then, her eyes dark. For a moment, he thought she was going to scream at him, to release the rage she must feel at his suspicions. But instead, she gave a sigh of resignation.

"I find that I no longer care."

"Why won't you tell me what happened? Don't I deserve honesty from you?"

Her eyes flared for a moment, then she suppressed the anger and nodded.

"As my husband, you're entitled to the truth, though I would remind you that I have never been anything but honest with you. Asking a trusted servant to maintain a confidence is not an act of dishonesty, when it's done to protect another."

Why did she constantly speak in riddles? Why did all women speak in bloody riddles?

Would he *ever* understand her?

The door opened, and Mrs. Atkin entered, carrying a wooden tray with a thick stoneware teapot and two cups. She placed it on the table.

"Thank you, Mrs. Atkin," Beatrice said, giving a smile, which disappeared as soon as Mrs. Atkin exited the parlor.

"Would you like some tea?" Augustus asked.

She shook her head. "I fancy Mrs. Atkin only offered it in order to remove us from her doorstep so you could make your accusations in private."

He winced at the edge to her voice, opened his mouth to reply, then closed it again. Given his inability to say anything to appease her, perhaps silence was the best defense.

At length, she sighed. "Mrs. Atkin's daughter had a fall last night, and her birthing pains started early," she said. "I told Mrs. Atkin to send for me should she, or Dr. Pegg, be in need of assistance, and…" She hesitated and averted her gaze, and he caught a glimpse of moisture in her eyes. "The poor girl was in so much pain. Her pains lasted through the night. But the child was born healthy, if a little small."

"Their daughter's had a child?"

She nodded. "A boy." Her lips lifted into a smile. "The most beautiful little boy…"

He shook his head. "I can't understand the secrecy. Why is the girl not with her husband?"

His wife let out a sharp sigh of derision. "Why do you *think*?"

He shrugged. "How should I know?"

"Annie was taken advantage of by her young man, who abandoned her shortly after she fell pregnant. She's luckier than most in that her parents didn't cast her out. They know, as I do, that the blame for any liaison always falls on the woman. But Mr. Atkin is a better man than most. He loves his daughter enough that he has never doubted her honesty, or chastised her for her folly. As soon as Annie has recovered, I have promised her a position at Hardwick Hall, where her child can join her if she wishes."

There was no need to ask why Beatrice had made such an offer, or gone to such lengths to help the young woman. Beatrice had a kind heart, and the girl's plight must have moved her.

Perhaps she wished to help protect a young woman from the accusations and gossip to which she herself had once been subjected.

"To think," Beatrice continued in a whisper, as if to herself, "Annie's barely fifteen—*fifteen*! In her short life she's weathered more than most of us can possibly imagine."

Before he could respond, the there was a knock and Mrs. Atkin appeared. She glanced from Beatrice, to Augustus, and back.

"Begging your pardon, your ladyship," she said. "Will you be wanting more tea?"

Beatrice rose to her feet and lost her balance. Augustus leaped up and reached out to steady her.

"No thank you, Mrs. Atkin," he said. "I think it's time my wife went home."

Beatrice glared at him. "I can answer for myself."

The woman's eyes widened, and she glanced at Augustus, apprehension in her expression.

"You mistake me, my love," he said. "I'm only concerned for your welfare. You look exhausted."

"But Annie…"

"You've done all you can for Annie, and more, yer ladyship," Mrs. Atkin said. "She's resting, and your Kitty's with her. You should take care of yourself now. Or, perhaps, let your husband do the caring." She turned to Augustus. "Your lordship, shall I send Kit to Hardwick Hall with word to fetch the carriage?"

"No, Mrs. Atkin, it's barely half a mile," Beatrice said. "I can walk."

"If you're sure?"

Beatrice nodded, but when Augustus took her arm, she leaned against him for support as he led her out of the cottage.

She turned to Mrs. Atkin, and the two women embraced. "Tell Annie I'll see her when I can," Beatrice said.

"Aye, lass, I will."

Beatrice shivered, and Augustus removed his jacket and

placed it over her shoulders. She leaned against him, and they set off at a slow pace toward Hardwick Hall.

Shame prevented him from speaking to her. What could he say? He'd acted abominably and, once again, come to false conclusions. Beatrice's taunt from last night about taking a lover had hit home. And later that night, his first wife had visited him in his dreams, cackling in triumph like a harpy, telling him that her curse would blacken his life forever.

It might be a reason for his behavior. But it was not an excuse.

And as he looked at the exhausted figure of his wife walking beside him, the guilt threatened to crush his chest. She'd spoken of what Annie Atkin had endured. But what about her own suffering?

As they crossed the threshold of Hardwick Hall, watched by an open-mouthed footman, his wife removed the jacket and handed it back to him. On impulse, he caught her hand.

"You were wrong about that young girl, Beatrice," he said. "I know one woman who's weathered more heartache than she." He squeezed her hand, and she at least made no attempt to withdraw it.

"It matters not," she said.

"It does matter, Beatrice," he replied. "It matters very much. That young girl has been fortunate enough to find a champion in you—someone she can trust without fear of abandonment. You have endured far more than that young girl, and you had nobody to take care of you—nobody to trust."

He lifted her hand to his lips and kissed it, but she did not react.

"I swear to you, Beatrice, that from now on, you will have someone to take care of you should you need it. Someone you can trust, who will never doubt you again. You're the most wonderful woman I have ever known, and I consider myself the luckiest man alive to be your husband."

She slipped her hand free and approached the stairs. "If you'll excuse me, I'd like to retire now."

"Did you not hear what I said?" He flinched at the desperation in his voice. Why didn't she show any emotion? At the very least he expected anger from her—tears, even frustration.

Not this cold indifference.

"Beatrice!" he cried.

She turned, fatigue in her eyes.

He spread his hands. "What would you have me do?"

She closed her eyes, and her chest rose and fell in a sigh. Then she opened them again. "Augustus," she said, "you may do and say what you like. For I find that I no longer care."

Her words, delivered in a quiet, toneless voice, cut through his heart with more pain than any angry tirade he might have expected.

Unable to respond, he watched her turn her back and ascend the staircase with slow, weary steps, until she disappeared out of sight.

CHAPTER TWENTY-FIVE

T HE CARRIAGE DREW to a halt, and Beatrice held her hands to her breast as her cousin climbed out, followed by his wife and a toddler.

All summer she'd been looking forward to their visit, but Henrietta had suffered a chill, and Giles had insisted she rest. Now, with autumn almost upon them, they had come to stay for a fortnight.

"Oh, Henrietta!" Beatrice cried. "You have no idea how glad I am to see you! And little Diana, how you've grown!"

She ran forward, arms outstretched, while the little girl stuck her thumb in her mouth and hid behind her mother's skirts.

"Diana is a little tired," Henrietta said. "She became overexcited in the carriage at the prospect of seeing her godmother again."

Unable to stem the tears, Beatrice embraced Henrietta, holding her tight and closing her eyes, relishing the scent of fresh air and lavender that had always reminded her of Thorpe Hall, her former home.

A small hand tugged at her skirts, and she reached down and clasped it, her heart swelling as the little girl entwined their fingers together.

"Don't I get a greeting, cousin?" a deep voice asked.

Beatrice relaxed her hold on Henrietta and turned toward her cousin. "Of course, Giles," she said. "You are most welcome."

"Hardwick Hall is looking as delightful as ever, I see," Giles said, taking her hand then kissing her on both cheeks. "And you're looking well. Might it be due to your husband's return?"

Still holding the little girl's hand, Beatrice glanced toward the main entrance, where her husband stood waiting. Though he was lord of the estate, he hung back like a nervous child.

Then he strode forward, the gravel crunching under his boots.

"Thorpe, how wonderful to see you and your charming wife. Welcome to Hardwick Hall. I'm so glad you accepted our invitation, and I know Beatrice has been looking forward to your visit." He gestured toward the building. "What do you think of the place?"

"It's not the first time Giles and Henrietta have visited," Beatrice said, aware of the sharpness in her tone.

Augustus offered his hand to Giles. For a moment, uncertainty showed in his expression. Giles, ever the stickler for propriety and honor, hesitated and stared at the proffered hand.

When Augustus had abandoned Beatrice, Giles's anger was only surpassed by her own sorrow. Over the months, his anger had abated, but Beatrice found herself wanting to avoid a confrontation between the two men. Giles, after all, had himself acted like a savage after Beatrice's elopement, and were it not for Henrietta's persuasion, heaven knew how he might have punished her for her folly. In that respect, he and Augustus were very much alike.

"I saw your husband, all too briefly, on his arrival in London," Giles said. Then he took Augustus's hand and clasped it. "I trust you find England in a better state than when you left?"

"England itself I cannot comment on," Augustus said. "As to Hardwick Hall, the place is transformed. The credit, of course, goes entirely to Beatrice. I cannot say how proud I am of my wife. But then, as her cousin, you must already be well aware of her qualities."

Giles opened his mouth to respond, but Henrietta spoke up.

"Lord Hardwick," she said, holding out her hand. "I trust you're taking good care of dear Beatrice?"

Augustus colored, then took her hand and kissed it. "As much as any man can take care of such a capable woman." Then his gaze shifted to the little girl beside Beatrice, and his expression softened. "And who is the delightful young lady we have here?" He approached Diana, then bowed and offered his hand.

The little girl looked up at him, her expressive eyes wide. Then she let out a giggle.

"I'm Augustus," he said, "but you can call me Uncle Gus, if you prefer. I'm very pleased to meet you."

The child released Beatrice's hand and stumbled over to him, arms outstretched. His eyes lit up with astonished delight, and he lifted the child into his arms. She placed her arms around his neck and buried her head in his chest.

"Would you credit that?" Henrietta said. "Diana rarely warms to strangers."

Augustus frowned, and a flicker of pain crossed his expression. "Then I consider myself fortunate to hold this precious child in my arms." He glanced at the sky. "I fear rain is coming. Let me show you inside, Lady Thorpe."

Henrietta nodded, and the two of them entered the building side by side.

"Cousin?" Giles appeared at Beatrice's elbow. "Your husband looks well," he said. "You *both* look well. I trust you find his presence agreeable?"

She opened her mouth to respond, to release the bitter hurt that had been festering since his latest show of mistrust. But her conscience prevented it.

Her conscience—and the expression in his eyes when he'd held the child in his arms.

In his eyes she saw the deep longing that she shared, which called to her at a visceral level. But she also saw the grief he'd been harboring for seven years—grief at losing the child he'd called his own.

Her husband had a heart the size of an ocean, and today, as on other days, she'd caught a glimpse of it.

"You've not forgiven him, Beatrice, have you?"

"What makes you think that?" she asked.

"I'm no fool," came the reply, "and I know you too well. I can see the anger that still lingers in your eyes, and the pain in his."

"Giles, he abandoned me…"

"Aye, he did, but that was two years ago. Then he returned, and you shot him." She opened her mouth to protest, but he raised his hand. "Permit me to finish," he said. "Yes, Henrietta reads me your letters. But don't fear; your aunt Euphramia doesn't know. And just as well—her heart wouldn't be able to take the knowledge that her beloved niece has turned into some sort of brigand."

"Giles…"

"Lord Hardwick is here now, and he's your husband."

"I have honored my marriage vows these past two years."

"There's more to a marriage than the upholding of vows," he said. "Much more. I only hope you'll come to realize that before it's too late."

"I'm thirsty, cousin," she said. "Aren't you?"

"Not particularly."

"I'll have tea sent to your chamber. I'm sure Henrietta would like some after the journey. Supper's not for hours yet."

He let out a sigh. "Have it your own way, Beatrice," he said. "I'll not plague you over your husband anymore. You're a grown woman and must find your own happiness."

He gave her hand an affectionate squeeze, then they followed their spouses into the building.

BEATRICE POURED COFFEE into two cups, and handed one to Henrietta. Then she crossed the drawing room floor and perched herself on a two-seater sofa. Her cousin and his wife had been at Hardwick Hall for two days but, unlike the party guests, were never in danger of outstaying their welcome. Giles and Henrietta were the sort of guests who reduced the burden on their hostess, and, when in their company, Beatrice could fall into a companionable silence, without feeling the need to fill the void with inane chatter.

Henrietta sipped her coffee. "Supper was delicious, Beatrice, thank you. Your Mr. Wilton is to be commended on the quality of his beef. And, of course, the company made for an excellent evening."

"I'm so happy you're here," Beatrice replied. "I've grown used to the solitude, and find much to occupy myself with in the evening, but I know Augustus misses male company. He gets on well enough with the steward, of course, but he must miss the company of his peers. I'm afraid he'll drive Giles to distraction with all manner of dull topics of conversation."

Silence fell, save for the crackling of the fire, and Beatrice sipped her coffee, relaxing back into the chair.

"He's a good man, Beatrice."

She glanced up to see Henrietta staring directly at her. "I've always known Giles is a good man," Beatrice replied, "even if he was overly harsh with you at first."

"I didn't mean Giles."

Beatrice felt her cheeks warm. "Oh."

"Your husband is a kind and considerate man. Kinder than most."

"How would you know?" Beatrice asked. "You've been here, what—two days?"

"I see much," Henrietta replied. "We both do, Giles and me. Did you know that your husband has offered to climb onto the roof of one of the farm buildings in order to help with the repairs?"

Beatrice let out a snort. "Told you that himself, did he?"

"No, I overheard him discussing the matter with the farmer.

They were in his study when I happened to pass by on returning from my walk yesterday. Augustus introduced me to the man—a Mr. Wilton, is it? A little young to be running a farm on his own, but Augustus is helping him in every way that he can."

"*I* was the one who ensured the Wiltons were established on the estate," Beatrice said, aware of the petulance in her voice.

Henrietta frowned. "Would you take credit for your husband's efforts as well? Nobody is denying how hard you've worked, Beatrice. But you must acknowledge that your husband is doing much to prove his worth to you. Not many husbands would do the same."

"Then why does he still not trust me?" Beatrice asked. "He even accused me of having an affair with one of the tenants!"

"Did he say as much?"

Beatrice hesitated, then shook her head. "Not in words. But I saw it in his eyes."

"Could his behavior have stemmed from a misunderstanding?"

Beatrice sipped her coffee, aware of Henrietta's gaze on her. Augustus had jumped to conclusions the morning Annie Atkin had her baby. But she'd had time to reflect on what he must have seen. Had she seen him embracing another woman after having been out all night without sending her word, she would have struggled to contain her jealousy. And her anger.

Even now, as she continued to reject his offers of friendship, she couldn't contemplate the notion of him being with another.

Not because she viewed him as a possession—but because she loved him.

Perhaps he loved her, and it was love that had driven his anger.

And what had he done since then? He'd given Beatrice leave to visit Annie Atkin and her baby as often as she liked. And he had made a pledge to the family that he would settle a sum on Annie should she wish to marry, and that he hoped she would marry a hardworking man of good character.

Henrietta moved to sit beside Beatrice. "I'll not deny that your husband behaved badly toward you," she said, "but shall I tell you why you should give him a chance?"

"I daresay I'll not be able to stop you."

Henrietta let out a laugh. "You know me well enough to understand that I'll say my piece regardless." She took Beatrice's hand. "There are two reasons why you must give him a chance. The first is for *his* sake. Men are, by their nature, weak when it comes to matters of the heart. They don't understand emotions, any more than we understand *their* need to always be outdoing each other and proving their prowess. They must always be fighting, looking for enemies around every corner. And so we, as women in a marriage, must summon enough mettle for the both of us, and take the higher path."

"What if Augustus is not a good man?"

Henrietta frowned. "Do you believe that?"

Beatrice felt her cheeks warm with shame, then shook her head. "No," she whispered. "He's a good man, a kind man. But I cannot forgive his mistrust when I did nothing to earn it." She bit her lip to stem the tears, but she couldn't stop her hands from shaking.

"Ah, my dear Beatrice, that is where we come to my second reason."

"Which is?"

"You must give him a chance for *your* sake."

"For mine?"

"Yes." Henrietta nodded. "Augustus might have his faults, but he loves you—it's plain to see that. And I believe that you also love him. Do you wish to deny yourself a life of love for the sake of your pride? Would you deny yourself, and him, a family, children of your own?"

Beatrice flushed and looked away.

"Or...does he visit you at night?"

Beatrice shook her head.

"Is that why you're melancholy?"

"I told him to leave me alone," Beatrice said.

"And he respected your wish, even though his longing for a child is so acute you can see the pain of it in his eyes?" Henrietta let out a sigh. "What husband would make such a sacrifice for his wife if he did not love her?"

A child…

The ache in Beatrice's heart for a child, which had grown over the years, had been only partially eased by the arrival of Henrietta's daughter—a goddaughter to dote on. Little Diana brought life and laughter to Hardwick Hall when they visited.

But to Beatrice, the little girl's presence was like an opiate. With each of Henrietta's visits, Beatrice craved more of the child's time, and each time she waved them off as they departed for home cut a little deeper than the last.

"Perhaps I should invite him into my chamber." She sighed. "A child is what we both want."

"Don't take him back unless you're willing to give everything of yourself," Henrietta said.

"I cannot risk my heart again."

"Neither can you risk your soul."

The door opened, and the men entered.

"Ah!" Henrietta cried. "I trust you've put the world of men to rights rather than putting each other to sleep?"

Giles let out a laugh. "Hardwick is an excellent conversationalist, my love," he said. "I must say, I didn't know he'd visited so many exotic locations while in Europe. Did you know he heard the great Czerny play in Rome? Imagine a world of music and art so far removed from the staid entertainment one finds in England. I swear I am quite in love with Italy, and intend to take you there on vacation."

He glanced at Beatrice. "Cousin, you never told me what a wealth of entertainment your husband is. His journals are filled with the most delightful tales of the history he experienced on his travels—from undiscovered coves on the coast, to unspoiled villages high up in the mountains. Why the devil have you not been encouraging him to publish his memoirs?"

Beatrice felt the heat rise in her cheeks. Augustus had tried to tell her of his travels and show her his journals. He'd even suggested they take a vacation in Italy. But, each time, she had refused, telling him that the very last thing she wanted was to be the obedient little wife at his side while he retraced his steps through the places he indulged in after he'd deserted her.

The pain in his expression at the time was mirrored by the pain in his eyes now.

She exchanged a glance with her husband, and her eyes misted over. He had every right to condemn her in front of their guests.

But he did not.

"We have been planning a vacation for some time, Thorpe," he said. "Beatrice has taken a great interest in my travels, and encourages my writing, as she encourages me in everything else. But I have to admit being somewhat selfish in wanting to keep my tales to myself. For if I were to encourage half of society to trample all over the unspoiled places I discovered on my travels, they would cease to be unspoiled, and their tranquility would be smothered."

Without waiting for a response, he helped himself to a coffee, then wandered over to his regular chair by the fireplace.

Henrietta chattered on, asking him about his travels, while Beatrice listened, ashamed that she had never bothered to ask him herself, when he'd always shown a marked interest in everything she did and said.

Shame threatened to engulf her again as she listened to his animated conversation. He'd never looked this joyful.

And it was all due to a little consideration from another.

But her shame was for the knowledge that her husband, who had always upheld himself as a man of honesty, had told a lie.

Not to benefit himself—but to portray her as a better woman than she was.

Chapter Twenty-Six

"Oh, your lordship. We weren't expecting you." The plump woman stood in the doorway and dipped into a curtsey.

"Mrs. Atkin, is my wife here?"

Before she could answer, a male voice rose from inside the cottage. "Who is it, Betty?"

"It's his lordship!" she cried, astonishment in her voice.

"Then let him in, woman! Bloody hell, what are ye doing letting the earl dawdle on our doorstep?"

She colored and ushered Augustus inside. "Her ladyship's in the parlor with Annie and the baby. Is something amiss?"

"No," he said, "but my wife was due back for dinner an hour ago."

"She must have lost track of time—she's so taken with the little one. I-I assure you, nothing's amiss."

A stab of guilt needled at him. The last time he was here, he'd stormed into the cottage making all kinds of accusations against his wife, and the woman's eldest son, who was now, according to Beatrice, married to his sweetheart with a baby on the way.

Good God, he'd acted like a complete arse that day! And he'd paid for it since with his wife's mistrust—and her indifference.

But ever since her family had come to stay, she seemed to have softened toward him. Lord Thorpe was a stern man, but also a fair one. And Beatrice looked up to Lady Thorpe as a mother figure. Augustus could only hope that they had persuaded his wife to give him a chance, particularly given that they were leaving at first light.

"My apologies, Mrs. Atkin, I didn't mean to distress you," he said, "but our visitors are leaving tomorrow, and will be retiring soon on account of their early start in the morning. I know Lady Hardwick will want to spend her last few moments with her family tonight."

The woman nodded and ushered him toward the parlor, from where he could hear a soft voice singing.

The room looked much the same as the last time he'd seen it, save for the fire that burned brightly, giving it a homey, comforting atmosphere.

Raising his hand to prevent Mrs. Atkin from announcing his presence, he stood at the threshold watching its occupants.

A young woman lay reclined on a sofa, wrapped in a blanket, eyes closed, her pale face illuminated by the fire.

On the chair beside her sat his wife, cradling a baby in her arms, a blue silk shawl draped over her knees.

A soft smile shone in Beatrice's eyes as she rocked gently to and fro, her lips moving.

"To sleep, to sleep, little soul…"

The singing he'd heard earlier was his wife's.

The purity of her tone almost tore his heart in two, and he caught a breath as a deep ache in his chest mirrored the longing in her voice.

The baby in her arms stirred, and a small pink fist appeared from within the blanket. Augustus watched as his wife lifted her hand and stroked the little fist with her finger. Then the baby curled his fingers around hers, and she let out a soft cry.

"Oh, you sweet, precious thing!"

The tender moment where she bared her soul, oblivious to the onlookers, almost broke his heart. He stepped back, unwilling to intrude on so precious a moment, and a warm hand clasped his.

"There's no need to be ashamed of your feelings, your lordship," Mrs. Atkin whispered.

He glanced toward her and blinked. Only then did he notice the moisture in his eyes.

"If I may be so bold, her ladyship was born to be a mother. You've only to look at her to see that. She's been a wonder with my Annie, who still suffers from melancholy. And she's quite taken with the young'un. She'll love your children even more, have no fear. She's loyal, kind, and a natural mother. She's nothing like…" She hesitated. "I mean, she's quite unlike most fine ladies."

He nodded and patted her hand.

Mrs. Atkin was a good woman. Not only because she understood his fears and wished to reassure him, but because she'd refrained from mentioning his first wife—the root cause of his insecurities and doubts.

And looking at the picture of his wife, his Beatrice, cradling the child in her arms as one day she might cradle *their* child, the specter of his first wife—that had been simmering in the back of his mind—faded into nothingness.

He let out a sigh, and the singing stopped. Beatrice glanced up, and the serenity in her eyes was replaced by apprehension.

"Beatrice, your cousin awaits you at home. Henrietta will be retiring immediately after supper, and I didn't want you to miss her." He stepped forward, giving her a smile of reassurance. "Forgive me for disturbing your visit, but I know how fond you are of Henrietta. I can walk you back here tomorrow, if you like?"

"I'm able to walk by myself."

"Of course," he replied. "But the offer is there. I am at your disposal, whenever you have need of me."

The two of them stared at each other, like uncertain adolescents on their first meeting. Then the farmer's wife bustled into the room and took charge.

"Here, give baby Danny to me," she said. "I'll keep an eye on him till Annie wakes."

Beatrice let Mrs. Atkin pluck the baby from her arms, then rose to her feet, smoothed down the front of her gown, and slipped her shawl around her shoulders. She leaned over the sleeping Annie and placed a kiss on her forehead.

Augustus offered his arm, and, to his relief, she took it and let him lead her out of the cottage.

The sun had already slipped below the horizon before they reached Hardwick Hall, and Beatrice shivered. He drew her close. She stiffened, then relaxed against him as they continued along the path.

The main building came into view—a tall silhouette against the evening sky, surrounded with a soft pink halo. Wisps of clouds hung in the sky, their undersides illuminated a bright orange to reflect the last rays of the dying sun.

"The weather should be fair tomorrow for the harvest," he said. "Look at the sky!"

"Yes," she replied. "Mrs. Atkin taught me that a pink sky heralded good weather the next day. I am hopeful for a good harvest, perhaps even better than last year's."

"The estate is prospering," he said. "I have you to thank for that."

She gave no reply.

"I daresay you'll be making plans for the next party." Though he tried to speak casually, he couldn't disguise the tightness in his voice. He wanted his wife happy, but he had no desire to see the hard diamond make an appearance once more.

"I'll be too occupied with the harvest supper," she said. "The tenants expect it as a tradition at Hardwick Hall."

"I'm not aware of such a tradition," he said.

"It's a tradition *now*."

By this time, they'd reached the main entrance. Augustus placed his hand over hers. "It's a good tradition," he said. "One I hope to see continue for many years to come. I very much look forward to welcoming our tenants into our home."

She glanced at him, the evening light reflected in her eyes, giving them a golden hue. "You don't mind?"

"No," he whispered. "It's wonderful, truly wonderful."

On impulse, he dipped his head and caught her lips in a kiss. Her eyes widened, but she made no attempt to resist.

"My love…"

He flicked his tongue against her mouth, and she parted her lips, her breath forming a warm sigh against his skin. A low whimper escaped her lips, and he claimed her mouth, relishing the sweet taste he'd been denied for so long. She opened her eyes, and his heart ached at the love in her expression.

They were made for each other, bound by something deeper than a mere marriage contract—a pagan spell that had cleaved them together from the moment they met.

She was his, and none other's. His Beatrice…

"Beatrice!" a voice cried.

She froze in his arms.

"*There* you are!" Lord Thorpe stood in the doorway, his features illuminated by the candle in his hand, a footman next to him. "I was beginning to get worried. Henrietta's half-asleep and supper's grown cold."

The spell was broken. Beatrice broke free and, mumbling an apology to her cousin, entered the building, Augustus in her wake.

SUPPER CONCLUDED, THEIR guests safely retired, Augustus lay in his bed, staring upward. Lights danced across the ceiling as the candles flickered in the air, together with the last of the flames from the fire.

Beatrice had, as usual, played the hostess to perfection. Supper had been an informal affair, a family supper rather than a dinner for guests, and he'd relished the easy conversation.

And Thorpe and his wife had been joined by their child—the

delightful Diana, who was the spitting image of her mother, save for the expression around her eyes, which mirrored her father's—especially when she stared at Augustus from beneath a furrowed brow.

How he'd relished bouncing the child on his lap! Having always been addressed so formally since inheriting the earldom, to hear himself described as "Uncle Gus" made him realize the full extent of what he'd been missing. Children were not merely vehicles through which the ancestral line was preserved. They were little souls in their own right, sent to complete a family and to rekindle the fading youth of the old.

Not for the first time did his friends' jibes of old return to haunt him—the comments about his age, his lessening virility.

Had he left it too late to have children of his own?

His wife had warmed to him on their return from the Atkins' farm. Had Thorpe not interrupted him, he might have discovered exactly how much. Her merest touch still had the ability to send fire racing through his blood.

Even now, as he lay in his empty bed, thinking of her, his manhood swelled with need. Earlier, after Simon folded his garments and left, he'd paced about the room, moving ever closer to the door separating their chambers.

Would she have welcomed a visit?

Would she welcome one now?

He closed his eyes, letting the sounds of the night envelop him—the crackling of the dying fire, the ticking of the clock on the mantelshelf, and the occasional screech of an owl outside.

Click.

Augustus remained still, his senses alert, hoping against hope.

His prayers were answered.

Another click—and a long, drawn-out creak of hinges. Someone had opened the door.

He heard a soft rustle of silk.

"Husband..."

The voice, low and husky, was a seductive drawl, as if a siren had risen from the sea and come into his chamber to tempt him.

He opened his eyes and sat up.

His wife stood before him, wearing a thin night rail, her face glowing in the candlelight, a smile on her lips.

"Beatrice?"

"Hush…" she whispered, so quietly that he almost believed he imagined it.

Her eyes were so dark they looked black. Fixing her gaze on him, she unlaced the front of her nightgown, then let it slip off her shoulders until she stood before him, completely naked.

Sweet Lord! His manhood surged at the sight before him—her creamy flesh glowing in the firelight, the long-limbed body with its tempting curves, and the full, pert breasts, already beaded with desire.

She glided toward the bed and took his hand. Then she lifted it and placed it on her breast.

Compelled by a need he could no longer control, he caressed the soft skin, and she arched her back in offering, pressing her breast against the palm of his hand. He flicked the nipple, and she let out a low growl as the little bud stiffened against his skin.

Then she grasped his wrist and moved his hand lower, along her chest, then down her stomach, until she reached the thatch of curls at the top of her thighs.

A primal need coursed through him, and his cock stiffened, poking insistently against the bedsheet. She lowered her gaze, and her smile broadened, showing even white teeth that seemed to lengthen in dim light, as if she were a predator come to devour him.

And he would willingly be devoured.

"My love…" he said.

"Hush!" she said, baring her teeth.

A seed of doubt sprouted in his mind. What was she about?

She pulled back the bedsheet and climbed in, pushing him back until he lay flat. He reached up to caress her face, and she grasped his wrist and shook her head. She crawled until she straddled him, then she lifted his nightshirt, her smile broadening as his manhood sprang free, ready and waiting.

A shiver rippled through him. The seductive creature straddling him was not the gentle woman he'd married.

"Beatrice…" he panted, forcing himself to control the powerful lust that had gripped him the moment she removed her nightgown. "Beatrice, I don't—"

"Oh, husband, I think you *do*," she purred.

Her long, lean fingers circled his cock, and his body jerked at the surge of lust as he let out an involuntary growl of pleasure. She caressed his length, in the manner of an inexperienced doxy practicing her craft, and he shifted his body to increase the delicious friction, chasing the nugget of pleasure.

Then she eased herself on top of him and enveloped him in her tight warmth. She let out a low gasp, and fear and uncertainty flashed in her eyes.

Then the seductress returned, and she shifted her hips back and forth to create a delicious rhythm. He reached up and took her face in his hands, pulling her down until their mouths met.

"No!" she cried, snapping her head back. Placing her palms on his chest, she straightened her arms and continued to rock back and forth, her breathing coming out in ragged gasps in time with each hard movement. She dug her fingers into the skin of his chest. The frisson of pain ignited a fire within him, and he cried out.

"That's it…"

She increased the pace, thrusting her hips back and forth, while he mirrored the gesture, relishing the rhythm. Then her body began to ripple around him, drawing him in deeper, clenching him in an iron grip, claiming mastery over his body.

And he was a willing slave. He threw back his head and shouted her name at the moment of completion, as he yielded to the glorious ecstasy and poured his life into her.

She continued to move against him, her breathing echoing in the night—strong, hard puffs of exertion as she rocked her body back and forth, as if in desperation to draw every last drop from him.

Then she grew still, with him inside her, spine straight, her chest heaving. Her breasts moved up and down with each breath, and tiny beads of sweat glistened on her skin. Her distended nipples, hard and erect, were silhouetted against the firelight.

The urge to taste them overcame him, and he stretched out his hands like a starving man pleading for his first meal.

But she slapped his hands away.

Slowly, she climbed off him. Then she picked up her night rail and slipped it over her head, smoothing her hair as if she'd been on a midnight stroll. Without a word, she padded toward the adjoining door.

"B-Beatrice?"

She froze and turned toward him. Her face was shrouded in darkness, but her eyes glittered like two cold stars in the midnight sky.

"My love…" he began, and she flinched. "Won't you stay?"

She shook her head. "I've done what I came here to do, and have no further use for you tonight."

The delicious warmth in his body drained, replaced by icy fingers clawing at his gut, and he sat up. "What do you mean?"

"You need an heir. I want a child."

"Y-yes, but…"

"Ah, I see," she said, returning to the bed. "Are you ready for me again so soon?"

She reached toward him, but this time it was he who pushed her back.

"No," he whispered, bile rising in his throat. "I'll not make love to you like this."

"It's not making love," she said, her voice bitter. "It's just sex, with one objective. Isn't that the purpose of marriage?"

Her voice wavered, and for a moment, he thought she would burst into tears. Then she stepped back.

"Until tomorrow, *husband*."

He watched her, open-mouthed, as she slipped back through the adjoining door and pulled it shut. Then he lay back, his heart thudding against his chest.

At length, his breathing eased, and he blinked, watching the lights dancing across the ceiling.

Had it been a dream, born out of his need for her?

No. The sharp scent of female need still lingered in the chamber.

He rolled onto his side, praying for sleep to come, and for the night to be over. But as he lay waiting for oblivion to claim him, another sound penetrated his senses above the crackling of the dying fire.

The faint, soft sound of a woman crying.

Chapter Twenty-Seven

"Goodbye, darling Beatrice!"

Henrietta took Beatrice in her arms, and Beatrice clung tightly, as if by strength of will she could persuade her beloved friend to stay forever.

"Bea? Is anything the matter?"

Beatrice shook her head, though she couldn't stem the tears that dripped onto Henrietta's shoulder. But Henrietta showed no sign she'd noticed them.

How could she explain to Henrietta what was wrong? Or what she had done?

Last night she had acted like a whore. She had seduced a man for her own ends. It didn't matter that he was her husband. She'd behaved like a wanton, nonetheless.

He might have thought her a harlot before—though he had never been so vulgar as to call her such—but what must he think of her now? Last night she had well and truly earned the label, in her voice, manner, and deed. She had donned the mask of the soulless seductress and ignored the plea in his eyes. Then she'd taken what she wanted from him, returning to the safety of her chamber. Only then had the mask slipped.

Giles crossed the gravel drive and joined them beside the carriage. "You'll see us at Christmas, Beatrice," he said, his breath coming out in puffs in the dawn air. "Now, where the devil has our little Lady Harridan got to? I want to get to Thorpe Hall before dark."

"Dada!" a voice cried.

Beatrice turned, and her heart fluttered at the sight of her husband in the doorway, little Diana in his arms.

"Where have you been, young lady?" Giles asked, his voice stern.

"I've been hiding!" the little girl said proudly. "But Uncle Gus found me."

Augustus strode toward Giles and deposited the child in his arms.

She reached out, and Augustus took her hand. "Goodbye, little Diana," he said. "But it's not forever. I'll see you at Christmas."

"Ooh yes!" came the reply, and Diana bounced up and down in her father's arms so violently that he nearly lost his grip.

"Steady, Miss Bounce," Augustus said, laughing. "Remember your promise?"

Diana stopped moving immediately, her eyes filled with adoration as she beamed at Augustus. "I do, Uncle Gus."

Giles let out a laugh. "She's her mother's daughter, the little minx," he said. "What has she promised you?"

Augustus smiled and caressed the child's cheek. "You've promised to be on your best behavior on the ride home, haven't you, sweet one?"

Diana nodded.

"Ah, but what does my daughter expect in return?" Henrietta asked. "She's not one to make a poor bargain."

"Only the biggest Christmas gift in all of England!" Augustus said. He leaned forward to kiss the child on the forehead, and she flung her arms around him again.

Beatrice stood back, watching their exchange, her heart melting. What a wonderful father he'd make! Her hand moved to her stomach. Perhaps, even now, she had a child on the way.

Then she lowered her hand, consumed by guilt. Little Diana was conceived in love. Whereas last night…

A footman opened the carriage door, and Henrietta climbed inside. After helping Diana in, Giles followed. Then they set off, the wheels crunching on the gravel, and disappeared down the drive, where the morning mist was beginning to clear.

Beatrice sensed, rather than saw, her husband standing beside her. But shame prevented her from meeting his gaze.

"Beatrice?"

Her cheeks flaming, she glanced up and blinked the moisture from her eyes. He reached out to take her hand, and her heart sank as he hesitated, then withdrew it.

"There's no reason to be sad," he said, kindness in his voice.

She shook her head. There was every reason. She'd behaved cruelly toward him. And though she longed to beg for his forgiveness, shame—and cowardice—prevented her.

He nodded toward the departing carriage. "You'll see them again, soon. Christmas is less than three months away."

"It's not because—" she began, but he interrupted her.

"It matters not," he said. "There's much to do today with the harvest."

"Yes, of course," she said. The sun was already creeping over the horizon. Soon the church bells would be ringing to herald the harvest, and the tenants and villagers would emerge from their cottages, eager to work together. "I must see if Mrs. White is making progress. There's much to do today to keep the tenants fed."

"Isn't that the housekeeper's responsibility?" he asked.

"It's all hands together at harvest time. Miss Hinde will be busy with her own tasks."

He gave her a soft smile. "All hands together. I like that." He hesitated, as if about to say something, then nodded. "If you have no further use for me today, I'll leave you to go about your duties undisturbed."

No further use…

She flinched at the echo of the words she'd used last night. In the cold light of day they sounded callous—heartless.

He gave a stiff bow and returned to the house.

CHAPTER TWENTY-EIGHT

B Y THE TIME the food was ready, and the baskets packed, Beatrice's arms ached and sweat dripped down her back. But their toil had been fruitful. The kitchen table was laden with baskets of bread, cheese, and cake, and bottles of lemonade. Though it was made of solid wood, Beatrice swore she could see it bowing under the weight.

"We've surpassed last year, I think," she said. "What say you, Mrs. White?"

"Oh yes, ma'am!" the ruddy-cheeked cook said, placing a fruitcake into a basket. "The tenants will be right grateful."

"They have earned it with their hard work," Beatrice said. "I trust the ale is on its way?"

"Aye," the cook said. "Not too much, mind. That Mr. Atkin is rather too fond of a drop."

"I wouldn't worry about that." Beatrice laughed. "He's too afraid of his wife to take more than one mug."

"Oh yes!" The cook let out a deep laugh, her chin wobbling. "A right royal clout over the head, she gave him last year! Folk say he had a lump on his forehead the size of a goose egg for the next fortnight." She glanced around the kitchen, hands on hips, while a number of servants gathered. "Right, you lot!" she said brightly. "Time to load up and be off."

Beatrice picked up a basket, and the servants followed suit. All the staff took part in the harvest. Even her husband's valet took a basket, following his mother and sister out of the kitchen and loading their baskets onto Farmer Wilton's cart.

After the last of the baskets were loaded, Beatrice climbed on, together with Mrs. White and Mrs. Hever, and they set off for the fields, the rest of the servants following in their wake, holding hands and singing. It was already well past noon, and the workers would be hungry and thirsty.

As the cart rolled through the gate at the top of the field, Beatrice's heart soared as she caught sight of the laborers cutting the wheat, their scythes shining in the sunlight. The men swung the blades with effortless grace, as if engaging in a dance. Beatrice knew how heavy the instruments were, having tried, and failed, to cut wheat herself last year. She'd lost her balance and fallen flat on her back in the field, much to the horror of the watching crowd. Then Mr. Atkin helped her up and dusted her down, politely suggesting that she might prefer a more dignified occupation, and she'd bent double laughing.

The field sloped downward and faced southwest, giving it the benefit of the sun for most of the day. It was dotted with carts already laden with wheat. Women worked beside each, tying the wheat into neat bundles and tossing them onto the carts. Children ran about, picking up stray strands of wheat and tying them together in knots, or chasing each other in circles. One child broke away from his friends and ran down the incline toward the men. A sharp female voice called out an admonishment and stopped him in his tracks, and he ran back to his mother, earning a clip around the ear.

Life and laughter filled the air, bringing with it a sense of thankfulness and hope—thanks that the land had prospered, and hope that the winter months would be comfortable.

Beatrice cast a glance over the field where the men worked. At the far end, she saw a young man, barely out of boyhood, with an older man, who must be his father. The father was teaching his son how to wield a scythe. Her eyes misted at the tender scene where the man watched over his son, set him right, and praised his efforts.

She jumped down from the cart and approached the men. Stripped to the waist, their shirts tied around the middles, they looked like pagan gods—with brutal, primal, muscular frames that could only be achieved through years of toil.

One stood out among the rest. His toned, athletic body was leaner than the others. But his muscles rippled with each sweeping movement of his arm as he swung the scythe from left to right in a fluid motion. He stopped and leaned back, rubbing his lower back and wiping sweat from his brow. Then he continued, moving forward with each sweep of the scythe—left, right, left, right—until he stopped once more and pushed his hair out of his eyes, his body heaving with exhaustion. The man next to him thumped him on the back, and they exchanged a few words, after which they both roared with laughter.

He threw his head back, his hair flicking through the air—jet black, with ripples of silver, to match the color of his eyes.

Beatrice drew in a sharp breath.

It was her husband.

"Ahoy there!" Mrs. Atkin cried out, and the laborers stopped their work and looked round. A cheer rose, and they put their scythes down and approached the cart. Squeals of delight came from the children, and they ran toward them, while the women unloaded the baskets.

As they passed Beatrice, each man bowed, and she smiled, thanking each of them for their hard work. But her eyes were for one man only—the silver-eyed man who had toiled away in the field.

Then he looked up, and their eyes met.

Her heart fluttered and her stomach somersaulted. He had never looked so handsome or virile. His physique exuded raw male power, but she also saw vulnerability—in the sweat on his brow, and the way his chest heaved with exertion.

But what claimed her heart was the expression in his eyes— the love he had for his land and the people who lived on it.

He slowed his pace, his gaze fixed on her, and she fought the urge to turn away in shame.

"Best harvest ever, your lordship!" Another man overtook him and clapped him on the back, so hard that he almost lost his balance. Then, roaring with laughter, he circled an arm around the man's shoulders, and the two of them continued together. Beatrice recognized Mr. Atkin's eldest.

They approached Beatrice, and the man bowed his head.

"Good afternoon, your ladyship," he said.

"Kit!" Mrs. Atkin cried. "Get yer lazy arse over here and help me with these baskets!"

"Coming, Ma!" He turned to Augustus. "I'll leave ye in the care of yer wife," he said. "I'm right hungry. I wonder if there's any of Mrs. White's fruitcake."

"There's plenty," Beatrice said. "Mrs. White's been boiling the fruit all week. Mind you save a slice to take home to your wife."

Augustus leaned forward, placed his hands on his knees, and drew in a deep breath. Beatrice approached him and offered her elbow.

For a moment, he stared at it, uncertainty in his expression. Would he reject the olive branch she offered? He had every right, given how she'd behaved last night. Then he smiled and took it, and they set off at a slow pace back toward the cart, where the picnic had already been set out.

"Thank you," he said. "I'm quite ashamed of myself."

"*You've* nothing to be ashamed of."

Her meaning hung in the air, but he didn't take the bait.

"I'm afraid I have," he said. "These men are far more skilled at this than I could ever be. I fear I only hindered their progress."

"Over here, your lordship!" a voice cried. "We've saved the best for you—and Lady Hardwick, of course."

Someone had set down a blanket and placed cushions on it, with plates laden with bread and cheese, and two mugs.

"Ah!" Augustus said, straightening his back, though Beatrice could see a grimace of pain. "The lord and lady's table." He placed an arm around her waist and took her hand. "Shall we?"

He led her to the blanket and helped her to sit, then he flopped down beside her with a grunt of pain. Several pairs of eyes were on them, and Beatrice felt herself blushing under their scrutiny.

Augustus pulled a knife out of his pocket, sliced off a hunk of cheese, and offered it to her. "My lady."

She took it, and a cheer rippled through the onlookers. Then, with a clatter of crockery and knives, everyone began to eat.

As the sun dipped below the horizon, its rays stretching along the field, the laborers gathered their tools and set off for home. Carts laden with wheat rolled through the gate, followed by the laborers singing in a chorus to celebrate a fruitful harvest. There was still much to do, but, according to Mrs. Atkin, the weather promised to be fine. They had made good progress today, and, barring a disastrous turn in the weather, the work would be completed in time for the harvest supper.

Augustus had insisted on Beatrice riding on one of the carts, while he walked with the rest of the men, joining in the song, his baritone adding to the chorus.

Beatrice had not heard him sing before, and her heart tugged at the rich notes of his voice. He looked utterly at peace, and happy.

And he deserved to be.

Perhaps, in time, he'd forgive her behavior as she—now she could admit it to herself—had long since forgiven him.

The cart rolled to a halt outside Hardwick Hall, and Augustus helped her down. She stumbled as her feet touched the ground, and he steadied her with his arms. She relaxed into his embrace, breathing in the scent of him—the woody, masculine aroma, together with the scent of toil and sweat. She closed her eyes and inhaled. It was the scent of a hardworking man. A good man.

Her man.

She smiled, relishing the moment, as a sense of pride filled her heart.

Then he released her, and the moment was lost.

They entered the hall together, and a footman appeared, holding a small silver tray with a letter on it.

"Pardon me for interrupting, your lordship, but this came from London."

Augustus strode across the hallway and plucked the letter from the tray before tearing it open. He read the first page, glanced at Beatrice, then addressed the footman. "Have the carriage brought round immediately, and have Simon come to my chamber and prepare my trunk."

"Very good, sir." The footman bowed and left.

"You're leaving?" Beatrice asked.

Augustus colored and stuffed the letter into his pocket. "I must."

"For London? You won't reach there tonight."

"I know," he said. "I'll break my journey at the inn at Ripley."

"When do you plan to return?"

She cursed herself as soon as she asked the question. She sounded like a jealous wife whose husband was leaving to visit his mistress.

Surely not…

He took her hand, and a shiver ran across her skin at his touch. She'd hoped he might come to her tonight, so that she might atone for last night and they could make love properly.

"I'll return as soon as I can," he said.

"Is that all you're going to tell me?"

"For the present," he said. "I have a particular reason for going and would ask that you trust me"—he hesitated—"if you're able to do that."

She winced at the undertone of bitterness in his voice. He had every right to be bitter and angry.

"Do you dislike the work?" she asked, aware of how petulant she sounded. "I understand the Wiltons' roof is yet to be attended to."

His chest rose and fell in a sigh. "Beatrice, I'm too tired to argue," he said. "I'm well aware that I've failed you on multiple occasions. Can you not trust that I'm doing everything I can to make up for it?"

"By going away?"

"Yes," he said, his voice weary. "By going away. Now, if you'll excuse me, I really must get ready if I wish to reach Ripley before midnight."

"Then do as you please, and go," she said. "There's nothing *I* can do to stop you. In fact, why don't you—"

"Ahem."

She broke off at the sound of someone clearing their throat and looked up. The steward stood at the turn in the staircase, looking distinctly uncomfortable.

"Ah, Mr. Evers. Excellent," Augustus said. "Walk with me, would you?"

He bowed to Beatrice, then climbed the staircase to join the steward, and the two men climbed together and disappeared.

Beatrice turned to the red-faced footman by the door. "Have some tea brought to my parlor, would you?"

He bowed in silence, then scuttled off, no doubt eager to spread gossip about the latest altercation between the master and mistress.

As Beatrice curled her legs up beneath her on the sofa in her parlor, she heard the sound of wheels on gravel. She leaped up and ran to the window, to see the carriage disappear down the drive.

Her husband had gone.

The last time he abandoned her, he'd told her that he loved her. This time he hadn't even said that.

But what reason had she given him to love her?

How many times had he told her in recent months that he loved her, and she'd remained silent in her determination to punish him for his earlier mistrust? Perhaps she'd meted out one punishment too many and only succeeded in hurting herself.

AUGUSTUS GLANCED OUT of the carriage window as the main façade of Hardwick Hall disappeared among the trees lining the drive.

Perhaps he ought to have told his wife the reason for his swift departure. But he had no wish to raise her hopes only to disappoint her once more. He'd weathered enough of her disappointment for a lifetime.

His steward had caught him before he left. Mr. Evers promised to take care of Beatrice during the remainder of the harvest, to make sure she did not overexert herself. She'd looked tired today—not just the physical weariness from a day working out in the open, but the mental exhaustion of one low in spirits.

Which was the reason for his journey.

Beatrice was not a woman who valued wealth or titles. Other than the parties where she played a part, she wore hardly any jewelry, compared to his first wife, who'd draped herself in diamonds at every opportunity. It was the small things that mattered to Beatrice—a vase of flowers in her chamber brought to her by Annie Atkin, promises made to a faithful tenant, and a treasured and beloved personal possession once lost but, with luck, found again.

It was through the small gestures that he intended to win her love back.

Provided he wasn't too late.

Mr. Evers had taken a great liberty tonight, taking Augustus's hand and speaking to him in the manner of a friend—perhaps knowing that Augustus sorely needed a friend.

She's a good woman, sir, if a little resolute. She'll come round in time. You just have to be patient and wait.

The carriage drove past the gates and out onto the road, and he leaned back into his seat, praying that the steward would be proven right.

CHAPTER TWENTY-NINE

BEATRICE DESCENDED THE staircase into the great hall. Candles flickered, sending dancing lights across the room, garlands decorated the banisters from top to bottom, intricate decorations fashioned from corn and wheat hung from the candle sconces, and a display of fruits and vegetables adorned the high table—rich autumnal colors that glowed in the candlelight.

The air was filled with the aroma of spices and pastry, and Beatrice's mouth watered at the prospect of Mrs. White's famous game pie.

Tonight was unlike the lavish parties she hosted during the remainder of the year. She was not the brittle hostess standing aloof from her guests, relishing in the prosperity of her home and the exclusivity of her invitations. Tonight lacked the artificiality of those events, as it was for people she genuinely loved and cared for.

Fate had looked kindly upon them this year, and the weather had held until the harvest was over. Now, a frost threatened to take a hold of the countryside, and—according to Widow Atkin, the farmer's elderly mother, rumored to be a faerie—the smell of snow was in the air.

Rather than watch the guests arrive from her lofty vantage point in the gallery, she intended to welcome each and every one of her guests with open arms—the parson and his wife, right down to Jonathan, the young footman who'd declared his intent to marry Margaret, one of the scullery maids. Mrs. Hinde had warned Beatrice of his infatuation, but in encouraging their suit, Beatrice had ensured that Jonathan treated young Margaret with respect, and he promised to court her only when he could demonstrate his ability to support her. It gladdened Beatrice's heart to be able to help the young couple.

Beatrice took her place at the entrance to the hall and waited. Though she stood alone, tonight was not a night for low spirits. She had weathered solitude for two years, and last year she had greeted her guests as she did tonight—with no one by her side.

As the guests began to arrive, a buzz of conversation filled the hallway—laughter, mingled with sighs of wonder and excited shrieks from the children at the decorations.

She greeted each guest in turn with a word of welcome and, in the case of Annie Atkin, an embrace and a kiss.

"Annie!" she cried. "How wonderful to see you so well. I'm very glad to have you here with us tonight."

Annie glanced, wide-eyed, around the hall. "It's so big!" she said. "Ma told me how big it was, but I didn't believe her."

A young man Beatrice didn't recognize stood beside Annie, shifting his weight nervously from one foot to another.

"Oh, begging your pardon, your ladyship," Annie said, dipping into a curtsey. "This is Bertie Garton. He's a friend of our Kit's, come to stay for the harvest to help Da." A note of pride resonated in her voice. "Bertie's pa owns the bakery in Sedgefield Village, over the other side of the hill."

Beatrice offered her hand, and the young man's eyes widened before he took it and bowed.

"Delighted, m'm," he mumbled, his cheeks reddening.

"You were helping out in the field this week?"

"He was, your ladyship," Annie said, glancing at the young man, whose eyes shone with adoration as he met Annie's gaze.

"The young man can answer for himself, lass," a gruff voice said.

The portly figure of Mr. Atkin stood behind Annie, arm in

arm with his wife, his son Christopher and daughter-in-law Prue beside them. Bertie's blush deepened.

"Mr. Atkin, I see you're in good form," Beatrice said, laughing.

The burly farmer drew her into a bear hug, much to the astonishment of his wife, who slapped him on the arm.

"I've told you not to be so familiar with her ladyship!" she cried. "A big lump such as yourself will crush her pretty dress."

He withdrew, a meek expression in his eyes, and Beatrice burst out laughing. A big bear of a man he might be, but the enormous farmer was completely ruled by, and besotted with, his wife.

He nodded toward Annie, who was leading Bertie deeper into the great hall. "A scrawny pup, that boy is," he said, "but he'll do well for our Annie."

Beatrice glanced at the couple. "Is he a good man?"

"Our Kit speaks very highly of him," Mrs. Atkin said, "don't you, Kit?"

Christopher Atkin nodded. "There's none finer, in my opinion, your ladyship."

"And," Mrs. Atkin continued, "my Daniel has already said he'll break every bone in the boy's body if he doesn't treat our girl right."

Beatrice laughed again. "The mark of a true gentleman, indeed."

"He's a good lad, and he's ever so taken with baby Danny."

"Where is your grandson?" Beatrice asked.

"With my mother-in-law," came the reply. She's minding all the little 'uns tonight."

"I'll have Mrs. White set aside a pie or two for her."

"Lord bless you!" Mrs. Atkin grasped Beatrice's hand and held it to her heart.

"Come along, woman," Mr. Atkin growled. "Ye're holding up the line."

They set off in Annie's wake, still grumbling at each other, as

Beatrice turned to welcome the rest of her guests.

Among the line, she saw Jonathan, the young footman, arm in arm with a young girl with a mop of unruly red curls and a face full of freckles.

They approached her, wide-eyed.

"Jonathan," she said, "and Margaret, isn't it? Welcome."

They bowed and curtseyed in unison.

"Thank you, your ladyship," the young man said. "I'm eager to try the pie that Peg here helped to bake."

"So am I," Beatrice said. She turned to the young woman. "Mrs. White has told me how helpful you've been in the kitchen, my dear."

The young maid flushed scarlet and mumbled her thanks, and Jonathan led her into the hall.

The parson and his wife were among the last to arrive, at which point the hallway was filled with guests milling about. Beatrice circulated among them, listening to their chatter and occasionally joining in. But tonight was for them, not her.

Shortly before supper was announced, she heard the sound of a carriage outside. The main doors opened and the candles flickered as a rush of air blew through the hall.

She craned her neck to catch a glimpse of the newcomer, and her heart somersaulted in her chest.

Standing in the doorway, hair disheveled, wide-eyed amazement in his expression, was her husband.

"Hurrah! His lordship is here!"

A cheer rose among the guests, and they moved back like a receding tide to form a path between him and Beatrice.

He brushed a dusting of snow off his shoulders, glanced about the hall, and settled his gaze on Beatrice.

Young Jonathan ran forward, though he was a guest tonight. "Your coat, sir?"

Augustus shed his greatcoat and draped it over the young man's waiting arm. Then he pulled something out of his pocket, handed it to the footman, and whispered something in his ear.

The footman glanced toward Beatrice, then bowed and scuttled off.

Augustus watched the young man go then resumed his attention on Beatrice, as if they were the only two people in the hallway.

He walked toward her, slowly at first, his footsteps hesitant against the stone floor, and held out his hands.

Beatrice glanced about the room at the sea of faces—the eager expressions of her guests—until her gaze settled on her husband's eyes, which were filled with a plea.

He stopped before her, hands outstretched.

"Beatrice," he said. "May I accompany you tonight?"

A ripple of whispers and murmurs threaded through the company, as if everyone held their breath waiting for her response. Perhaps they thought it a tradition that the two of them had devised. But Beatrice saw it for what it was.

A plea not to be turned away.

She reached forward and took his hands. His fingers were cold, and she caressed his skin with her thumb, letting her warmth flow into him.

"You are most welcome," she said.

A collective sigh rippled through the company. Then the gong rang for supper, and the party filed into the great hall and took their places.

Beatrice steered her husband toward the high table, where four places had been set, one for each of them and the parson and his wife. At each of the two central places was a crown, fashioned from sprigs of fir, for the harvest king and queen.

He stifled a gasp. "You set a place for me?"

"Of course," she said. "After all, you said you'd make every effort to return. Though I admit it was out of hope, rather than expectation."

"Then I'm happy not to have disappointed you."

He sounded weary, and any irritation she might have felt at his late arrival dissipated.

He was by her side, which was all that mattered.

AUGUSTUS TOOK HIS place at the high table next to his wife, then picked up the makeshift crown. He ran his fingers along the sprigs, inhaling the scent of pine.

"What do you think?"

He turned to see his wife staring straight at him, her chocolate-brown eyes crinkled into a smile.

"Is this part of the harvest tradition?" he asked.

She nodded and picked up her own crown. "The local children are tasked with making the decorations for the harvest supper," she said. "Last year they all vied for the honor of making the crown, and they were particularly excited this year at the prospect of being able to make *two* crowns." She lifted her crown to place it on her head. "Do you like our tradition?"

He caught her hand. "Yes, but for one aspect."

Confusion and disappointment flickered in her eyes as he removed the crown from her grasp.

He ran his fingers along the fronds of fir on her crown and lifted it to his lips. Then he raised the crown and gently placed it on her head. A stray tendril of her hair had worked loose, and he brushed it aside, tucking it behind her ear. Then he ran a light fingertip across her forehead, tracing the shape of her face, relishing the smoothness of her skin.

Finally, he leaned forward and brushed his lips against hers.

"There," he said softly. "A queen must be crowned by her king, as befits her station, and no one else. Only now can I say that the tradition is perfect."

A ripple of applause threaded through the hall.

"Did you do that for them?" she asked.

He took her hand and held it against his heart. "No, my love," he said. "I did it for you. All that I do is for you."

Her shoulders relaxed, then she gave him a shy smile. It was the smile that reminded him of the innocent young girl he'd fallen in love with—the girl he'd fallen in love with so quickly that the strength of his emotion had caught him unawares.

"It's only right that I return the favor," she said.

She withdrew her hand, picked up his crown, and placed it on his head. She lifted her hand to his face, as if to caress it, then the uncertainty in her expression resurfaced and she withdrew.

He might have a long road to travel to regain her trust, but tonight, he'd taken the first step.

And the second step awaited her in her chamber. He couldn't wait to see her face when she discovered it.

As soon as the meal was finished, and Augustus leaned back in his seat, patting his stomach—now filled with Mrs. White's game pie—several guests stood and began to clear the tables.

He leaned toward his wife. "What the devil are they doing?"

"It's part of our tradition," she replied. "Everyone is a guest here tonight, tenants and servants alike, and as such, we *all* help to clear the tables." She rose to her feet, holding her plate. Next to her, the parson followed suit.

Augustus suppressed a gasp. "You as well, Reverend Ilcott?"

"You know what the devil has in store for those with idle hands, Lord Hardwick," came the reply. The four of them, including the parson's diminutive wife, crossed the floor to a bench that had been set up by the door leading to the kitchen, where a small group of servants had gathered, collecting plates and scraping the leavings into a bucket, then setting the crockery into neat piles to take to the kitchen later.

As they returned to their seats, small groups, under the watchful eye of Miss Hinde, removed the dining tables, clearing the floor of the hall. A small band of musicians settled into seats at the far corner, and a set of discordant notes rang out as they tuned their instruments. Rather than return to her seat, Beatrice wandered among the guests, chatting to each in turn, taking their hands and smiling. Some she lingered on for longer than others, engaged in animated conversation, throwing out the occasional laugh, her eyes sparkling in the candlelight.

She had never looked more lovely than at that moment, though he couldn't help the twinge of jealousy as she lingered next to the blond-haired, blue-eyed, godlike form of Kit Atkin. But she then moved on to the young woman next to him, who was presumably his wife—and pregnant, by the look of it. The two of them steered the young woman to the perimeter of the room, where chairs had been set out, and sat her beside the parson's wife. Then they approached the floor, where couples had begun to line up, including the steward and his wife, the Atkins, and the Wiltons—which reminded Augustus that he needed to pay them a visit tomorrow to see about the roof repairs. Beatrice had admonished him about it before he left for London. Perhaps in seeing to the Wiltons' roof, he might take another step on the road to her forgiveness.

The parson approached Augustus, a young woman on his arm. "Well, Hardwick," he said. "There's plenty of unattached young ladies in the room eager for dancing. I trust you'll do your duty tonight."

Augustus glanced around the hall and caught sight of his valet's sister—whatever the devil her name was—sitting alone, and he approached her, hand outstretched.

"Miss Hever?"

She glanced up, and a blush crept over her face. "Y-your lordship?"

"Would you do the honor of partnering me for this dance?"

She placed her trembling hand in his, and he led her onto the floor, lining up beside Beatrice and her partner. Beatrice smiled and nodded her encouragement, then the dance began.

The musicians played a series of traditional country airs— quite unlike the staid notes of a Society ballroom in London— some of which Augustus remembered from his childhood. As the evening wore on, the guests whooped and cheered, clapping in time to the music, singing along in a variety of voices, ranging from the pure notes of Miss Hever, who had the voice of an angel, to the throatier, coarser warbling of Mrs. Atkin.

Beatrice, he noticed, moved from partner to partner, dancing with each in turn, young and old. At the end of each dance, she returned her partner to his wife or sweetheart. Her easy, affectionate air was that of a woman determined to ensure her guests were at ease, and Augustus only felt shame for his earlier suspicions. It seemed that men and women could enjoy a simple, straightforward friendship, with nothing untoward between them.

In turn, Augustus had followed Reverend Ilcott's example, and danced with as many unattached young women as he could, following the code of a gentleman at any Society dance when there was a lack of male partners. He noticed Kit Atkin doing the same, while the young man's wife continued to sit with Mrs. Ilcott. For the current dance, Augustus was partnered with Peg, the scullery maid who'd taken the message when Beatrice disappeared into the night to tend to Annie Atkin's confinement. The young servant had blushed so violently when he led her onto the dance floor that her freckles almost disappeared. But as they danced together, her eyes shone with pride, and when he handed her back to the young footman who was clearly smitten with her, a gaggle of young women surrounded her, no doubt eager to find out what dancing with the earl was like.

But a night's dancing was taking its toll, and he'd worked up a thirst. As the next dance began, he skirted past the onlookers and made his way to the punch bowl. He filled a glass and drained it, then dipped the ladle in for refill.

"I'd forgotten how well you dance."

He turned to see his wife standing before him, a gentle smile on her lips.

"There was a time when I could dance all night," he said, "but I'm not as young as I was. Whereas you…" He gestured toward the dance floor. "I imagine there's dozens of young men destined to be sorely disappointed tonight."

She approached the punch bowl, took a glass, and filled it. "How so?"

"You cannot partner everyone. Those who've had the privilege of partnering you tonight will be the envy of the whole room."

She smiled and sipped her drink. "I rather fancy the same can be said of you," she said. "I thought Margaret was going to swoon when you led her onto the dance floor."

"And Kit Atkin?"

She stiffened, her eyes narrowing. "He'd rather dance with his wife tonight, but she's expecting their first child."

"No, you mistook me, Beatrice," he said. "I only wished to remark on how capable a young man he's grown to be. Though he's clearly smitten with his pretty young wife, he's helped ensure that no young woman tonight has gone un-partnered."

The music stopped and a cheer rose as the guests cleared the floor and the parson moved into the center.

"My friends," he said. "We come here tonight to celebrate and to give thanks for a bountiful harvest. But I believe thanks must also go to our hosts, Lord and Lady Hardwick, without whom tonight would not have been possible. As I am here to tend to you, my flock, I know that the master and mistress of Hardwick Hall are happy to care for you all and ensure that all hereabouts are happy, safe, and fulfilled. Would you join me in giving thanks for the earl and his countess? To Lord and Lady Hardwick!"

"Lord and Lady Hardwick!" the guests chanted, then burst into applause.

Augustus's heart swelled in his chest, and, to his shame, his eyes stung with moisture. The sense of belonging had never been so acute in all his life. Hardwick Hall was his home in every sense of the word.

As was his wife. *Beatrice* was his home.

Beatrice leaned closer and whispered in his ear. "Naturally, Reverend Ilcott will be thanking the Almighty, rather than us, at church on Sunday," she said, "but for now, I suggest we accept our accolade with grace."

Augustus set his glass aside, checked the crown on his head, then bowed before her, offering his hand. "O, Queen of the Harvest."

Her eyes flashed with mischief, and she let out a giggle. Then she took his hand and let him lead her toward the center of the floor, where the parson stood, waiting.

"Dance with your wife, my lord!" a voice cried.

"Yes, dance with her ladyship!"

A fiddler played a few bars, then stopped. Several pairs of eyes focused on Augustus, and he looked at his wife and raised his eyebrows. "Well?"

She smiled and nodded, and another cheer rose.

He took her by the waist, and the music began.

Though a small number of couples joined then, Augustus only had eyes for the woman in his arms, whose soft body against his sent a firebolt of need through his veins. He spun her around, and she let out a laugh of pure joy and clung to him. This was not the hardened diamond who'd put a bullet in his arm, nor the broken angel who'd tugged at his heart when he first met her. She was a bright, vibrant soul, filled with love and laughter. Not the malleable young wife he'd sought, but an independent woman, capable of weathering adversity and giving of herself to the people she cared for and loved.

If only he could be worthy of her love!

The dance concluded, and they grew still, standing on the dance floor with eyes for none but each other. Pure liquid desire shone in her eyes—the warm, rich brown the color of Mother Earth. His pagan goddess was in his arms, and he was ready to worship and adore her, if he could seize the moment…

On impulse, he drew her closer for a kiss. She stiffened, and the wariness in her eyes returned.

He released her, and she glanced around the room, smiling at their guests.

The moment had passed.

CHAPTER THIRTY

A S SOON AS the guests had departed, Augustus followed his
wife upstairs, then they parted at her chamber door and she
slipped inside. A murmur of voices rose from inside her chamber
as she chatted to her maid.

There was a knock on his chamber door, and his valet appeared.

"Did you enjoy the evening, Simon?"

"Oh yes, sir," the valet said. "And so did Emma. She said it
was the most exciting night of her life."

"Emma?"

"My sister."

Emma—*that* was Miss Hever's name.

"She told me she had an offer for every dance after you sin-
gled her out for the first, sir. It's a wonder what a little jealousy
does to a young man."

Simon rattled on, and Augustus stood still like a compliant
child while the valet helped him undress.

Jealousy. Augustus knew enough of its effects to consider it a
state neither to be admired nor encouraged.

There was nothing wrong with a little healthy rivalry. An
uncertainty in the return of another's affections was the best
prevention for boorish behavior in a man—and shrewish
behavior in a woman. But jealousy, which festered like a canker,
brought about nothing but misery.

Simon held up a nightshirt, and Augustus shook his head. A knowing smile crept across the valet's lips, and his eyes sparkled. Then he deftly folded the garment and placed it in the chest of drawers.

After dismissing the valet, Augustus paced the length of his bedchamber, but he couldn't shift his attention from the low murmur of voices coming from next door.

Then the voices stopped. But the light coming from the crack at the bottom of the adjoining door remained. His wife hadn't extinguished her candle.

Did she wait for him to visit her?

Or might she visit him after she saw his gift? His heart rate increased as he waited.

Eventually, he could bear it no more, and he padded toward the adjoining door and opened it.

She was sitting in bed, the candle flickering on the table beside her.

"May I come in?"

She nodded, her eyes glistening in the candlelight. Her nightshift clung to her body, emphasizing every curve, and he lowered his gaze to her breasts, his mouth watering at the sight of two dark little shadows at the centers. She continued to watch him as he approached the bed, then she looked up and down, her gaze caressing his naked form, settling on his manhood, which was already straining with the need to claim her.

Her nostrils flared, and he drew in a sharp breath at the pull of lust, making his cock twitch with eagerness.

She was his queen, his pagan goddess, ripe for worship.

He sat on the bed, and it shifted with his weight, bringing her closer to him. Her eyes darkened, and she parted her lips. Her chest rose and fell, and he caught the sharp scent of female need.

She wanted him as much as he wanted her.

He reached out and placed his palm on her breast. Her nostrils flared, and she leaned into him. The peak at the center stiffened under his touch.

Then he took her face in his hands and brought their lips close.

She closed her eyes and turned her head—a slight gesture, but the rejection cut through his heart.

"Beatrice?"

Her eyes still closed, she unlaced the front of her gown, exposing her breasts, and his groin tightened with need, his cock swelling further.

Heavens! She only need touch him, and he'd spend.

But he didn't want her body. He wanted her heart. And her soul.

"Will you not look at me, my love?"

A tear beaded on her lashes and splashed onto her cheek.

He took her hand, and she curled her fingers around his. "Beatrice," he whispered, "do you know how much I want you?"

"Then take me," she whispered. "There's no need to ask."

"There's every need," he said. "I want to make love to you, Beatrice."

"You can do whatever you—"

"No!" he cried, and her eyes flew open. "No, Beatrice, I want to make love to you, not rut you."

She flinched at the coarse expression and drew back.

"Beatrice, it'll break my heart if we..." He hesitated. "If you..." He shook his head, his voice cracking. "I cannot weather anything like the other night, not when I love you as much as I do. My body may have relished it, but my heart... My love, I only want you if you wish to come to me completely, of your own free will—with your heart and your soul, not just your body."

She resumed her gaze on him, her eyes filled with moisture. "I-I don't know if I can risk my heart again..."

He placed her hand over his heart.

"My heart belongs to you, Beatrice, fully and completely. I would risk everything for you. Are not some risks worth taking?"

She closed her eyes and drew in a deep breath, then she opened them again, fear in her expression—the fear he'd first seen in her, his broken angel.

"Beatrice," he whispered, "am I never to be worthy of such a risk in your eyes?"

His heart broke at the fear in the depths of her eyes, and he lifted her hand and kissed it.

Then he released her and returned to the doorway.

"Forgive my intrusion," he said. "I'll leave you in peace now. But know this—I love you, Beatrice, and I always will, no matter what you decide."

He slipped back into his chamber and clicked the door shut, his heart thudding against his chest. For a moment, he leaned against the door, taking comfort from its solidity. Then he crossed the floor and slipped into bed—a bed destined to be cold and empty forever.

BEATRICE WATCHED HER husband leave. A part of her yearned to cry out.

Stop! Augustus, come back to me!

Perhaps he would. Her resolve had almost crumbled when he withdrew from her. He had only to return, to beg forgiveness again, and she'd give herself to him.

But he didn't.

She extinguished the candle, wriggled down under the covers, and leaned back against the pillow. She rolled over and felt something hard underneath the pillow. Reaching underneath, she felt a small box, like a jewelry box, with a metal clasp on one edge.

Had be bought her a gift in lieu of giving herself to him? If a plea for forgiveness didn't work, did he think she would spread her legs for a trinket?

Biting her lip to stem the tears, she pulled the box out from underneath the pillow and placed it on the table beside the bed.

She didn't want to be bought. She wanted a husband who trusted her, and loved her for herself.

CHAPTER THIRTY-ONE

AUGUSTUS LAY AWAKE as the first notes of the dawn chorus echoed outside.

Why did the birds have to be so damned cheerful? It was bloody cold. Even inside, his breath came out in sharp puffs, freezing in the morning air.

He climbed out of bed, shivering as gooseflesh rose on his skin, pulled out an undershirt, and rang the bell.

Eventually, Simon appeared, his hair only slightly tousled, rubbing the sleep from his eyes.

Augustus stared pointedly at the clock on the mantelshelf. "Did you forget I was due at the Wiltons' farm this morning?" he asked.

The valet raised his eyebrows. "At this hour? And in this weather? Surely it's wise to wait until—"

Augustus shot his valet a look, and, to his credit, the man ceased his tattle and silently set out his master's clothes for the day. He helped Augustus into his shirt and breeches, fixed his necktie, then slid on the waistcoat, which he buttoned up and smoothed down. Simon stood back, as if admiring his handiwork.

"Will you be taking breakfast before you leave?" the valet asked.

Augustus shook his head.

"Shall I send one of the lads to accompany you? Young Jonathan, perhaps?"

"No."

Simon eyed him with suspicion. "You're not thinking of anything foolish such as climbing onto their roof, are you?"

"Are you questioning my judgment?"

"It's *laborer's* work, sir," the valet said. "And no laborer in his right mind would clamber about on a roof on a day like this, not with a layer of snow on the ground."

"I made a promise," Augustus said.

"Mr. Wilton will understand."

"Not to Mr. Wilton."

The valet let out a sigh. "Nobody expects you to place yourself in danger to fulfil a promise," he said. A cautious expression entered his eyes. "Least of all Lady Hardwick."

Augustus winced inwardly. "Does the household have nothing better to do than gossip about the state of my marriage?"

The valet remained silent, but a slight blush crept across his face.

"I see," Augustus said quietly. "I suppose they laugh at me behind my back—whisper of how my first wife betrayed my trust, for which I punished my second, and she cannot forgive me. Do they say I've brought it upon myself and that I don't deserve her?"

"They say nothing of the sort, sir, I assure you."

"I wouldn't blame them if they did," Augustus said.

"Why, because you believe it yourself?"

The valet's words cut through his heart. As if he realized the enormity of what he'd said, Simon cleared his throat, waiting for the recrimination. When it didn't come, he resumed his duties and held up two jackets—one green, the other dark blue. Augustus gestured to the blue jacket. The valet nodded, draped the green over the back of a chair, and helped Augustus into the blue before adjusting his necktie and cuffs. Then he picked up a clothes brush and ran it along the jacket in smooth, sweeping motions, as if grooming a horse—starting at the shoulders, then moving along each sleeve, until he was done.

An uncomfortable silence stretched between the two men. Over the years, Simon had become something of a confidant, having familiarized himself with his master's particular likes and dislikes. More importantly, the valet knew when to speak and when to be silent—an important, if not the *most* important, quality in a gentleman's gentleman. But now, the unspoken words thickened the air, like the onset of a thunderstorm.

When Simon was finished, he placed a light hand on Augustus's shoulder. "Sir, may I speak out of turn?"

"I suspect you'll do that anyway," Augustus said.

"Lady Hardwick is not the sort of woman to bear grudges, and she loves you. I know it."

Augustus brushed the valet's hand aside. "You don't know what you're talking about," he said. "Have you turned into a gossiping milkmaid? You don't know my wife at all."

"Perhaps not. Emma told me that Kitty said—"

Oh, this is getting better and better.

"So I *am* the subject of gossip," Augustus said.

"N-no, nothing of the sort," the valet replied. "Emma told me in confidence. She and Molly have formed a friendship, and seeing as her ladyship's been so kind toward Emma and Ma, I suppose they speak of her."

And what do they say?

The question hung on Augustus's lips, but he resisted the urge to ask. For what would that make him? A desperate suitor? A man scorned, willing to take advantage of the servants in order to snare his wife's heart?

"Will you be wanting breakfast when you return?" Simon asked.

Augustus nodded. Then he exited the chamber and made his way to the stables, where a groom had already saddled one of the horses—a brown gelding who suited his temperament more than the fiery Heracles. Nodding his thanks to the groom, he climbed onto the mounting block and mounted the gelding.

Heracles stared balefully at him from his stall, then tossed his head and let out a snort. The horse vibrated with pent-up energy, but he was a little too wild for Augustus's liking. Each time he mounted Heracles, Augustus never knew whether the beast would turn his head and give him a nasty nip. But Beatrice always knew how to handle the animal, bewitching him with her tender care, as she had bewitched every soul at Hardwick Hall.

Including him.

What the bloody hell would he do if he never regained her trust?

I'll keep on trying until the day I die.

He spurred his mount into a canter and set off.

By the time he reached the Wiltons' cottage, the sun had risen from the horizon, casting its rays across the landscape. A thin layer of snow dusted the landscape, which twinkled in the sunlight as if Mother Nature had embedded diamonds into the ground—hard, bright gemstones forged from years of unrelenting pressure, to emerge stoic and unyielding.

He'd long since stopped comparing Beatrice to a diamond. Rather, she was like the small flowers that poked through the snow in spring, having weathered the frosts to emerge triumphant and relish her love of life and the land around her.

And if he had to crawl on his knees and prostrate himself before her every day for the rest of his life, he would.

As his gaze wandered over the cottage, he spotted a hole in the roof at the far end, near the chimney stack. Several tiles had worked loose, and a number hung precariously over the edge overlooking the yard. One sharp wind, and they'd come crashing into the yard. Or worse, they'd fall on someone.

He shivered at the thought of an unsuspecting child being killed by falling masonry, and the memory of Kathleen's child, the child he would have called his, threatened to engulf him. The Wiltons had three children. No parent should have to bury their child.

He strode to the door and knocked three times.

After receiving no response, he hammered on the door again.

"Hello there!" he roared.

"Who's there?" a female voice cried out from above, followed by a fit of coughing.

Augustus stepped back and looked up. A woman leaned out of one of the upper windows.

"Oh, mercy! It's *you*, your lordship," she said. "Begging your pardon…" She broke off into a hacking cough.

"Mrs. Wilton?" he asked.

"Aye," she said. "Forgive me, are ye wanting my husband? He's out in the field with our Tom." The woman coughed again.

"Are you all right, Mrs. Wilton?"

She shook her head. "I took a chill last night after the dance. Shall I come down?"

"No, don't trouble yourself. Shall I send for the doctor?"

"There's no need."

"There's every need, Mrs. Wilton," Augustus said. "I'll see to it as soon as I've taken a look at your roof."

"The roof?"

"Didn't your husband say I'd promised to look at it?"

She let out a snort. "He told me *he'd* look at it, the lazy arse…" Another fit of coughing. "Beggin' yer pardon, your lordship—he's been promising to look at it for weeks. All he's done is bring the ladder round."

"Does he know there's several tiles ready to fall down?"

"Oh, heavens!" she cried. "I *told* him! I'll give him a piece of my mind when he gets back."

"Let me do what I can," Augustus said, "then I'll go and find Dr. Pegg. You shouldn't be up with that cough. Go inside, Mrs. Wilton."

"Thank ye, your lordship." The woman closed the window, and the coughing continued, followed by the sound of a baby shrieking.

She needed the doctor. But first he had to deal with those tiles.

A long ladder was propped up against the wall, next to a pile of logs and several farming tools, including a small plough. A light dusting of snow had settled on the blades.

One of the advantages of the tenants' cottages was that the ceilings were half the height of those in Hardwick Hall, which meant that the roof didn't look *that* high up. It would take him less than a minute to remove the tiles. Lord knew what else he could do, but he had to do something useful, to prove to Beatrice that he kept his promises.

He removed his jacket and draped it over a barrel beside the logs. Simon would never forgive him if he snagged the finely woven wool on the ladder, considering how much he'd gone on about pressing the bloody thing last week. A material that thick was, apparently, nigh impossible to remove creases from, and that particular shade of blue showed the tiniest speck of dust.

The ladder was, thankfully, made of solid wood, and it stood firm when he tested the first rung. Gripping the sides, he swung his leg onto the second rung and began to climb, carefully testing each rung where the snow had frozen into the wood, rendering it slippery.

By the time he reached the top, his hands ached from gripping the sides of the ladder.

I'm getting too damned old for this.

The roof seemed sound, save for a hole near the chimney where the tiles had worked loose and slipped toward the edge. The cause was plain to see: several bricks had fallen from the chimney stack, too close to the base to be visible from the ground, and shattered a section of the tiles. Both bricks and tiles needed to be removed to render the roof safe.

After checking there was nobody on the ground below, he grasped the first few tiles and let them fall to the ground.

The bricks were just out of reach. He'd need to climb onto the roof to reach them.

Perhaps he should wait for the farmer to return.

No, don't be an ass. You're perfectly capable. Think how proud Beatrice would be!

He grasped the roof to haul himself up, and placed his foot on the next rung.

The rung gave way with a crack, and he lost his footing. He kicked out, trying to find purchase, but found nothing but air.

Dear God! He'd never survive a fall from this height.

Panic swelling inside, he reached out and managed to get purchase on the ladder, but he couldn't stop the momentum—he continued to slide down the ladder at increasing speed while he clawed at it with his fingers, ignoring the pain as splinters sliced into his palms.

He tightened his grip on the ladder, and the pain in his hands turned into an inferno, but the pace slowed, and he kicked out again, almost sobbing with relief as his feet found purchase.

For a moment, he remained still, gasping for breath, eyes closed, and clung to the ladder, thanking whatever deity was watching over him.

Then the ladder toppled sideways, and with a cry, he tumbled to the ground, landing in an explosion of pain.

Augustus lay on his back for a moment, panting, his breath forming puffs of mist that dissipated in the air. The ladder lay on its side, in Mrs. Wilton's flowerbed. Beside it, the pile of logs had disintegrated, as if it had exploded. He rolled onto his side, but save a few aches in his legs, the splinters in his hands, and a strange burning sensation in his left arm, he seemed unhurt.

The pile of logs must have broken his fall.

Saved by a woodpile! He smiled to himself. A woodpile, of all things! To think, children were always warned off playing near them or climbing them because they posed a hazard. And what would the logs get in return—the little saviors that had presented him from serious injury? They'd be rewarded by being tossed onto the fire.

Such was life.

He snorted with laughter. What might Mr. Wilton think if he came upon his landlord spread-eagled in the yard? Perhaps he might think an angel had visited him.

A wicked thought crossed his mind as he recalled the snow angels he used to make on the estate as a boy. If he moved his legs and arms, he'd make an angel in the farmyard. A man-sized angel.

He tried to move, but his upper body didn't seem to want to obey him, and a strange itching sensation threaded through his left arm, to accompany the burning that threatened to turn into an inferno.

The plough stood innocently next to the pile of logs. One of the blades glinted in the sunlight—a sharp, shiny edge, the color of a rose...

A deep red rose.

He caught sight of his waistcoat smeared with mud—bright red mud. And his shirt—one of the sleeves was covered in a dark red stain, which seemed to be spreading across the fabric. He tried to lift himself up, and bright red droplets spattered onto the ground, stark against the snow, in sharp contrast to the darkness swelling in his mind.

The blade of the plough curved into a sinister smile. Though the world had begun to fade around him, slipping in and out of focus, the blade remained, mocking him, as if—*she*—had returned from the grave to fulfil her curse at last.

No!

His first wife, the woman who had tried to destroy him, was long dead.

Only one woman existed in his world. Beatrice, his broken angel.

She was the woman he loved with the entirety of his soul, the woman he would die for.

As his life essence drained from him, he whispered the name of the only woman he had ever loved before the darkness claimed him.

"Beatrice..."

CHAPTER THIRTY-TWO

B EATRICE WOKE TO the sound of Kitty scraping about in her room. She yawned and stretched, then sat up.

"Oh, begging your pardon, Lady Hardwick! I didn't mean to wake you."

"No matter, Kitty." Beatrice swung her legs out and climbed out of bed.

"It's just that his lordship asked if you'd be joining him for breakfast," the maid said.

"Oh?" Beatrice glanced toward the adjoining door to her husband's room. "Is he already up?"

"Aye, he's at the Wiltons' farm."

Beatrice glanced out of the window. "In this weather? It must be freezing outside!"

"Oh, aye," Kitty said. "Peg said there was a layer of ice in the scullery sink. Now, how would you like me to do your hair today?"

"Something simple, please."

When Kitty had finished tying Beatrice's hair into a smooth chignon, she dipped into a curtsey, and Beatrice dismissed her.

To think—Augustus was visiting the Wiltons at this hour!

She had been too harsh with him last night. For her to truly move forward, she had to forgive what he'd done two years ago. Lord knew it was clear he regretted it, and he was doing everything he could to atone.

She glanced toward the window, and her gaze fell on the abandoned box on the table beside the bed. In a childish fit of pique last night, she had tossed it aside, thinking the gift was merely a way for Augustus to ingratiate himself.

But what if it was a token of his affection, a genuine peace offering?

She picked up the box and flipped open the lid.

Nestling among the deep blue velvet interior was a pocket watch—a very *familiar* pocket watch, fashioned in a rich, warm gold, with a white dial.

With trembling hands, she plucked it out of the box, testing its weight, curling her finger around the smooth, bulbous shape. She closed her eyes and stilled her breathing, and the familiar rapid ticking took over her senses. She could almost have believed herself a child of five, bouncing on her father's knee, exploring the watch in his waistcoat, holding it to her ear, and listening in wide-eyed amazement at the ticking noise, like a rapid heartbeat, as if the watch were alive.

Cradling the precious timepiece in her hand, she ran her thumbnail along the outer edge and flipped open the watch at the back. She ran her fingertips along the intricacies of the movement until she reached the familiar words.

T, Mudge, London.

Then she turned the watch over in her hand and traced the lettering on the back, whispering the words that had been carved into her memory.

To my beloved Anthony. Love is as eternal as time itself.

The breath caught in her throat as she stared at the words she never thought she'd read again—the inscription that spoke of the love her mother and father had shared. She closed her eyes and held the watch against her heart, biting her lip against the pain she'd endured, the day she'd handed the precious timepiece over to the pawnbroker, whose fat, greedy fingers had curled around it in glee.

When the Hardwick estate became solvent once more, she'd written to the pawnbroker, but learned that he'd departed for the Americas.

How she had grieved, then, for the one piece of her past that embodied the essence of love! But she had forged ahead, building her life here, at Hardwick Hall, determined not to lose her heart over a material object again.

But here, and how, that heart had been returned, and she held it in her hands.

Tucked into the side of the box was a note. She lifted the watch to her lips, returned it to the case, then unfolded the note and read its contents.

To my beloved Beatrice, with love, as always. Never think that your sacrifice went unnoticed or unappreciated. I only pray that in the years I have left, I will endeavor to earn your love.

Augustus

"Augustus…"

She blinked, and a tear splashed onto the back of her hand.

So, that was why he'd gone to London. He must have been sent news of the watch's whereabouts. But how had he managed to find it? And how had he known what it meant to her?

Was that why he'd not told her the reason for his trip to London, or how long he expected to be away? Not because he wanted to keep secrets from her, but because he had no wish to raise her hopes, only to dash them.

"Oh, Augustus, I have wronged you!"

He had no need to earn her love. She had always loved him, even if she'd been too proud to admit it.

Wiping her eyes, she exited her chamber and made her way to the breakfast room, to be reconciled with the man she loved more than life itself.

The breakfast room was empty, though the buffet was laid out, the aroma of kedgeree filling the air.

She approached the table, and a footman rushed forward to pull back her chair.

"Ah, Jonathan," she said. "Please tell his lordship that I await his pleasure. I'm eager to see him this morning."

"Yes, ma'am." The footman bowed and disappeared.

She sat back and waited. After a moment, she poured a cup of tea and sipped it.

Where was he?

But it mattered not. She would wait all day for him if need be. He deserved that consideration.

When she heard hurried footsteps, she smiled to herself. It seemed that he was just as eager to see her.

The door was flung open to reveal the footman, his chest heaving, distress lining his features.

"Good heavens!" she cried, leaping to her feet. "What the devil's the matter?"

"I-it's the master."

Icy fingers gripped the back of her neck. "My husband?"

"Th-there's been an accident"—he shook his head—"at the Wiltons' farm. Th-they…" He looked like he was going to burst into tears.

"Jonathan, tell me."

"They fear he'll not survive."

Not survive…

Her gut twisted with terror.

"What happened?" she cried, clutching the footman's arm.

"T-Tommy Wilton found him," Jonathan said. "He came as quickly as he could."

"Show me, quickly!"

They dashed out of the dining room and into the hall, where a farm boy stood, shuffling nervously from one foot to the other, wringing a cap between his hands.

"You there!" Beatrice cried. "What's happened to Lord

Hardwick?"

"H-he fell off a ladder, ma'am," the boy said, panting. "Da's sent for the doctor, then said to come to the great house to tell you."

"Have you brought him here?"

"No, ma'am. Da says he's too far gone to be moved."

Too far gone…sweet Lord!

"I must go to him…"

"No, if you please, your ladyship," the boy said. "Da says he's hurt bad. 'Tis no place for a lady."

"Then there's not a moment to lose." Picking up her skirts, she dashed toward the outer doors and sprinted toward the stables. "Where's the groom?" she cried.

A youth emerged from one of the stalls, in which she spotted the stallion's dark head.

"Saddle Heracles immediately," she said.

"He'll not take well to a sidesaddle."

"Saddle him astride."

"But—"

"I said *saddle him!*"

The groom's eyes widened, but he dashed toward the tack room. Moments later, he led the stallion out into the courtyard.

"Mind how you go, ma'am, he's had a fitful night—" the groom began, but she brushed him aside, hitched up her skirts, then grasped the reins and swung herself onto her mount. The groom's face turned the color of beetroot as he glimpsed her bare legs. Ignoring him, she steered Heracles into a tight circle, then rode out of the courtyard and set off.

As she urged her mount into a gallop, she glanced toward the heavens, uttering a silent prayer.

Please, God, don't let him die!

CHAPTER THIRTY-THREE

T HE SNOW-COVERED GROUND was untouched, save for hoofprints and a single set of footprints. The air remained cold, and clouds had begun to gather in the sky, hanging heavy with a dark purple hue.

More snow was coming.

As Beatrice neared the Wiltons' cottage, she saw a pale brown horse tethered to the farmyard gate. The animal lifted its head as she approached, and she dismounted and tethered Heracles next to him. Then she made her way to the cottage—and froze.

A pile of logs was scattered beside the building, and next to it, a plough lay on its side. The ground in front had been scuffed, with several footprints merging into each other. As Beatrice drew closer, she spotted smears of dark red on the ground, and her stomach churned at a sickly metallic smell in the air.

The stench of blood.

The cottage door opened, and Mr. Wilton appeared.

"Where's my husband?" Beatrice cried.

"We took him inside, your ladyship. But you shouldn't be here. I told my Tommy to stop you from coming."

"My place is by his side." She strode up to him and made to push him aside, then he rolled his eyes and stepped back.

"Don't say I didn't warn ye. He's upstairs. Doctor's with him."

She sprinted up the stairs. At the top, she spotted two bright-eyed children staring at her in silence, one with his thumb jammed into his mouth.

Then a low moan of pain came from behind a door.

Stifling a cry, Beatrice pushed it open.

The room was a low-ceilinged chamber, with a tiny bed at the far end.

A dark-haired man stood beside the bed, shirt sleeves rolled up. He was washing his hands in a ceramic bowl. Next to the bowl, a solitary candle flickered. The thin figure of a woman stood by the doctor. Her face had a sickly hue. She bent forward and began coughing, her chest rattling with each spasm of her body.

Beatrice caught sight of the motionless figure on the bed, and a cold hand clawed at her heart.

"Augustus…"

He lay on his back, his eyes closed. His hair was plastered to his face, which glistened with sweat. He was naked from the waist up, and his breeches had been ripped, one leg tightly bandaged from ankle to knee. On the floor was a white cloth. Or it *had* been white, once. Now, it was a dark red color, and the air in the room was thick with the same metallic odor as outside.

Then she saw it, and the breath caught in her throat.

A long, jagged gash ran along his arm, from shoulder to elbow.

The doctor looked up, and his eyes widened. "Lady Hardwick! What are you doing here?"

The urge to faint swelled in her mind, like a thundercloud. She only had to close her eyes and succumb. But as she watched the inert figure of her husband on her bed, the hardships and adversity she'd triumphed over in the past paled into nothing.

Here, and now, was the real test of her fortitude. She had risen to the challenge of her duty to Hardwick Hall and all those who served it. But today, a greater duty lay before her—the duty to the man she loved.

And she would not fail him.

She pulled off her gloves with a snap and entered the chamber.

"What must I do, Dr. Pegg?"

He gestured to the woman beside the bed, who had resumed coughing. "Mrs. Wilton—"

"Is not fit to assist you," Beatrice interrupted. "Any simpleton can see that." She turned to the woman. "Good lady, please take care of yourself. Go and rest. We'll call you if we have need of assistance."

The woman bobbed a curtsey and fled, coughing. The doctor raised an eyebrow.

"Don't question me, Dr. Pegg," Beatrice said. "Just give me a task, and I'll do it."

He nodded, recognizing the sharpness in her voice for what it was—the need for an occupation to prevent her from shattering.

"I've bound his leg," he said. "The break is only minor, and should heal in a matter of weeks. His arm..." He gestured to the wound. "It must be stitched and cleaned, to avoid putrefaction. But the real concern is the loss of blood. It's left him very weak, and I'm concerned his body will withdraw."

"W-withdraw?" she whispered.

"Aye, sometimes a trauma such as the one he's suffered overwhelms the constitution."

"Is there nothing we can do?"

He paused, then nodded. "Talk to him. Give him something..." His voice trailed off, but there was no need to complete the sentence.

Something to live for.

"Can you withstand the sight of blood without fainting?" he asked.

"Of course."

"Good. Wash your hands, please, then you can mind his arm while I stitch the wound."

The crisp command gave her a purpose, and helped to temper the panic rising within her. Beatrice followed the doctor's instructions, lathering soap on her hand, rinsing—and re-rinsing—them until he was satisfied. Then she dried them on a towel.

"Now, take his arm," he said. "It's important that you hold it steady, no matter how hard he struggles. I've given him a little laudanum for the pain, but I would prefer him conscious, in case…"

He glanced at her, a flicker of sympathy in his expression.

In case he never wakes.

Dear Lord, he was testing her mettle! But he respected her enough not to cover his words in a veneer of lies merely to reassure her. Sometimes, only the brutal truth would do.

She sat beside the bed and took her husband's hand, interlinking their fingers. Out of the corner of her eye, she saw the doctor holding a long, thick needle in the flame of the candle.

The man on the bed stirred, and though his eyes were closed, his lips moved.

"Beatrice…"

"Yes, my love," she said. "It's me, Beatrice."

"Must tell Beatrice… I'm sorry."

"No…" She shook her head, fighting the tears. "There's nothing to be sorry for, my love. I'm here, and I'm with you. Every part of me. Always and forever."

Did she imagine it, or did his fingers tighten their hold on her?

She brushed the hair from his eyes, then placed a kiss on his forehead. "Augustus, my love."

"Lady Hardwick."

She glanced up and saw the doctor standing beside her, needle in hand.

"Hold him steady."

She grasped her husband's forearm, uttered a silent prayer, then nodded.

He flinched as the tip of the needle touched his arm, then he arched his back and cried out as the doctor pushed it through the flesh and secured the thread with a knot.

Beatrice tightened her grip, then dipped her head and placed a kiss on his shoulder. "Be still for me, my love, and it will all be over very soon." She gripped his wrist again and nodded to the doctor. "Be quick," she said. "Not for my sake, but for his."

The doctor nodded, then placed another stitch through the flesh and pulled it tight. The patient groaned and shuddered, but Beatrice kept a firm hold of his hand. By the time the doctor had finished, the patient's arm was adorned with twelve neat stitches.

Beatrice leaned over and placed her lips on her husband's forehead. His skin was cold and clammy. His eyes remained closed, and his chest rose and fell with each breath.

"He's unconscious," she said.

The doctor reached inside his bag, pulled out a handful of bandages, and began to wrap one around the patient's arm. "No, he's just asleep," he replied.

"Is there a difference?"

"Oh yes," came the reply. The doctor placed the unused bandages into the black bag that lay open on the washstand. Then he rinsed his hands and wiped them on his breeches.

"What do we do now?" Beatrice asked.

"We wait. We must keep him warm, but he mustn't over-heat." He placed the back of his hand against Augustus's cheek. "He feels a little fevered already." He glanced at Beatrice. "You look distressed, Lady Hardwick. Perhaps you should go home and rest. We can send word if his condition changes."

She shook her head. "Nothing will persuade me to abandon him," she said.

"It could be days before he recovers."

"Then I'll wait here for days. I'll not be deterred, Dr. Pegg. He's my husband."

The doctor nodded, then pulled a small phial from his bag. "Laudanum," he said. "Give him a few drops, but only if he's in pain."

"Anything else?"

"Water," he said. "Just water."

"Thank you, Dr. Pegg."

"You did well, Lady Hardwick," he said. "In my experience, a woman cannot withstand the sight of such an injury."

"Not even for the man she loves?"

He dropped the rest of his instruments into the bag and closed it with a snap. "I'll send Mrs. Wilton up with some clean water," he said. "Is there anything else you need?"

Beatrice shook her head. There was only one thing she needed. And he lay motionless on the bed before her.

"I'll return tomorrow morning," the doctor said, "but send for me if his condition worsens."

After the doctor exited the chamber, the farmer's wife appeared with a tray carrying a pitcher of water, a glass, and a cup filled with a steaming liquid.

"I took the liberty of bringing you some tea, your ladyship," she said. "I stirred a little honey in. You've had a fright, and will be in need of the sweetness." She set the tray down, then stood before Beatrice, distress in her eyes.

"Mrs. Wilton, is anything the matter?"

The woman's lip wobbled, then she nodded. "It's just… Oh, forgive us! It's our fault Lord Hardwick hurt himself!"

"How so?"

"He was fixing our roof! I-I was in bed at the time, on account of having taken a chill, or I should have been there to help. Oh, forgive me!"

Beatrice took the woman's hand. "Nobody's to blame, Mrs. Wilton," she said. "It was an accident."

"But to think that such an act of kindness could lead to such tragedy!"

Tragedy…

Beatrice caught a breath as an invisible hand squeezed her heart.

What if he never recovered?

"Go and rest, Mrs. Wilton," Beatrice said. "I'll take care of my husband. Thank you for your hospitality."

The woman bobbed a curtsey then exited the room, closing the door behind her.

Beatrice took her husband's hand and lifted it to her lips.

She'd not been truthful with the farmer's wife. Someone *was* to blame for Augustus's accident.

And that someone was her.

She alone had spurned his peace offerings, instead accusing him of ignoring his duty. Whereas he had searched all of London to find Papa's watch, then risked his life to undertake a chore she'd been so insistent on him doing.

He had acted out of love for her. And now, he lay before her, his life in danger, because of it.

Would she ever forgive herself?

CHAPTER THIRTY-FOUR

T HE DAY WORE on, and Beatrice remained by her husband's side, occasionally dipping a cloth into the washbowl and pressing it to his forehead.

Each time he stirred, she tipped his head up, cradling it in her arms, and held a cup of water to his lips. Most of the liquid trickled down his chin, but he managed to swallow some, his throat rippling. When he let out a low moan of pain, she shook a drop of laudanum onto a spoon and held it to his lips, following it with another sip of water.

As darkness fell once more, he grew quiet. His forehead burned to the touch. She took his hand and threaded her fingers through his, willing him to react. But his fingers remained limp and weak.

Only last night, he'd swept her across the dance floor in his magnificence, the harvest king holding court among his subjects. She closed her eyes, willing him to hold her as firmly and tenderly as he had when they danced—to feel his hands around her waist, and his lips on her skin…

As night fell and the light faded, she remained by his side. The candlelight cast sharp shadows across his features. She studied his face—the wide forehead and strong brow—and ran her fingertips along the straight nose that had a slight indent halfway down. How had he come by it? An accident as a boy, perhaps? Finally, she traced the outline of his mouth, the strong, yet sensitive mouth capable of rendering her breathless with fiery kisses—yet those lips could be soft, tender, and sweet.

How many times had those lips uttered tender words of love and devotion? Would they ever speak again?

She blinked, and a hot, fat tear splashed onto his lips. She leaned over him and pressed her lips against his, tasting the salt and her desolation.

What would she do without him?

"Oh, Augustus, my love, forgive me," she whispered. "I've been a fool, a proud fool, unwilling to reveal my heart out of fear. You have weathered my temper, and my mistrust, and borne my ill humor with more grace than I deserve. Will you not wake and come back to me?"

He slept on, while she surrendered to her sorrow and let the tears roll down her cheeks. This beautiful man who had weathered heartbreak and betrayal had opened his heart to her, placing it on a platter as a gift. He was unlike any other man. His suffering had given him wisdom. But it was not just his experiences that had shaped the man he was. Hs heart was larger than the greatest ocean. He gave her freedoms that few women had in the world—to live her life as she chose.

He wasn't a man to shower her with trinkets, then leave her to indulge in the pursuits of a gentleman. He valued the unnoticed gestures—the small, light touches that did more to show his love for her than any grand gesture might have done.

To think that such a man loved her—it was too much to bear, and her heart ached at the mere thought of it.

She lifted her head and opened her heart.

"Please, let him live!" she cried. "He's the best man that ever walked upon this earth—kind, caring...never asking for anything for himself... He gives so much of himself—gives to others, with no thought for himself, and..."

Her voice cracked, and she lowered her head and placed it on his chest, squeezing his hand as if she feared he would slip away from her.

"Oh, Augustus!" she said. "It breaks my heart to think that you might believe you're not loved. But you *are* loved…so much! You are loved by everyone here. All on the estate love you." She drew in a shuddering breath. "And none more than I. Augustus, *I* love you. I always have, and I always will. Please come back to me! I couldn't bear to lose you—to never again have you hold me in your arms."

She clung to him, listening to the sound of his breathing, and the rapid heartbeat in his chest.

Please, please stay strong…

She willed his heart to keep beating. "If one must be claimed today, let it be me," she whispered. "I would gladly take his place if it would save his life. If that is to be my punishment for treating him so cruelly, then I'll accept it, for his sake. I love him more than life itself. I loved him from the first day I looked into his eyes—the kindest eyes I had ever seen, and ever will see."

"Whom?" a voice whispered, and she jerked upright.

Her husband lay motionless on the bed, his eyes closed.

Beatrice lifted his hand to her lips. Perhaps she'd dreamed it— a dream born of hope.

She closed her eyes and kissed each of his knuckles in turn, then her heart tightened in her chest as his fingers flexed then curled around hers.

No, she must be imagining it. Fate was playing a cruel trick on her, denying her dearest wish.

"Beatrice."

She opened her eyes and found herself looking into pure liquid silver—two luminous eyes, filled with love.

She let out a soft cry, her heart swelling with hope.

His throat bobbed as he swallowed, then he caressed her fingers with his thumb. "Whom, Beatrice?" he asked.

"Husband?"

"Whom do you love more than life itself?"

"Can you not guess?" She placed his hand against her breast. "Can you feel my heart?"

He blinked, and his lips lifted into a smile. "Aye, I can."

"It beats for you, my love," she said. "My heart, and my soul, have always been yours."

He tried to sit, and she placed a hand on his chest. "No, my love, you must stay still. You've had an accident."

His eyes narrowed, then he gave a slight nod. "Yes, I remember," he said. "I fell, then I thought I'd died. Then I heard a voice. I thought it was an angel, and I heard her offer her life for mine." He swallowed again, then let out a sigh. "And it *was* an angel," he said. "My angel—my beautiful, broken angel."

"I would gladly have offered my life if it would bring you back," she said. "I love you, Augustus."

"It was your voice that brought me back," he said. "It was you I thought of every day. Even when I abandoned you, I couldn't erase you from my mind. My love for you was too strong."

"Oh, Augustus!" Beatrice leaned over and placed her lips on his. "I never want us to be parted again, not even for a day."

"Forgive me for abandoning you when we married, my love," he said. "Not a day goes by that I don't regret it."

"Hush, my love." She placed a finger on his lips. "I was a child when we married. In those two years, I grew up, learned to take care of myself, and learned to love this estate, our home, and everything in it. It made me strong—*you* made me strong. We mustn't waste time on regrets. We must look toward, to our future, not back."

"Then let us start anew," he said. "Let us pledge to one another, here and now—reaffirm the vows we spoke."

"Augustus, you must rest."

"And so I shall, but first…" He took her hand and kissed it. "I, Augustus Henry John Hardwick, hereby pledge, in the sight of the Almighty, that I shall love, honor, and worship my wife, Lady Beatrice Millicent Hardwick, and remain by her side for all eternity."

She smiled, her vision blurred by tears. "And I, Beatrice Millicent Hardwick, pledge to love and honor my beloved Augustus until the end of my days."

"And obey?" A glint of mischief shone in his eyes.

"If my lord wishes."

"Then honor your vows and lie with me now."

"Augustus! You're not well. I—"

"Just in my arms," he said. "I want you in my arms. I'm afraid your thirst for pleasure will have to be quenched when I'm up to the task. But never fear, my love; I will do my utmost to see to my lady's pleasure. In fact, there's a rather pleasant spot in the woods in need of a little attention."

A fizz of anticipation rippled through her, and she lay beside him, relishing the warmth of his body against hers. She drifted into a peaceful sleep, lulled by his breathing and the strong, steady beat of his heart—a heart that beat for her.

EPILOGUE

Hampshire, April 1818

A UGUSTUS LAY BACK, replete with satisfaction.
Not just satisfaction, but pure, unbridled pleasure.

There was something so *primal* about making love out of doors, in the open air. Whether it was the freshness of the wind cooling their sweat-glistened bodies as he thrust inside her, or the frisson of excitement from the prospect of being caught, he couldn't tell. But his wife's little cries of pleasure as she writhed beneath him, parting her legs wider and arching her back to meet each strong, hard thrust, told him that she relished it as much as he.

Light fingertips caressed his chest, following the contours of his muscles, then they followed a line along his arm, tracing the scar that ran from shoulder to elbow. Then those featherlight fingertips returned to his chest, making wide circles around the nipple, moving tighter and tighter, until she reached the little bud and flicked it.

He drew in a sharp breath, and she gave a low murmur of satisfaction. Then her hot, sweet lips came down on his chest. Her tongue flicked out, tickling his skin. She shifted against him, and he caught a surge of sweet perfume. The bluebells were in full bloom, a violet carpet adorning the woods—a soft carpet into which they had dived, tearing each other's clothes off in their urgency for each other.

"Oh, Beatrice, you unman me!" He sighed.

She placed a kiss on his nipple, and a jolt of fire ripped through his blood as she nipped it with her teeth. His manhood, which lay flaccid against his stomach, twitched in anticipation of further pleasure.

"Quite the contrary, I assure you," she said, her wicked little fingers tracing a path toward his stomach. "You are all man, my love."

Then she curled her fingers around his length and caressed his sensitized skin with the tip of her thumb. A low whimper escaped his lips.

Witch!

In her eagerness to please him, his wife had discovered all manner of ways in which to evoke ecstasy with her hands and mouth. To think—the innocent little angel he'd spotted possessed such an exotic talent for lovemaking.

And she was his—all his.

"Now I have you at my mercy, husband, there's something I must tell you."

Her voice had taken on a deeper note, and he opened his eyes. She stared back at him, her eyes like liquid chocolate, the sunlight highlighting the gold flecks in the irises.

"What is it?" he asked.

"I fear that, at your age, the shock may be too much to bear."

"Impudent chit!" He laughed. "I should bend you over my knee for your insolence."

A wicked smile glinted in her eyes. "Oh, husband, you should never make a promise that you're not prepared to keep."

She sat and stretched, her long-limbed body glistening in the afternoon light. His mouth watered at the silhouette of her frame against the light—the curve of her throat and the swell of her breasts, with the delicious little peaks he'd tasted just moments before.

Then she met his gaze, her expression filled with love. Slowly, deliberately, she placed her hand on her shoulder, then moved it along her body, palm open, until she reached her stomach, her fingers splayed out, as if to protect…

Sweet Lord! As if to protect the life growing within.

"Yes, Augustus," she said. "I'm carrying your child." She reached forward and took his hand, then placed it over her stomach.

He blinked, and a tear beaded on his eyelashes.

"Hush, my love," she whispered. "There's no need to be sad."

"I'm not sad," he said. "I'm happy, so happy! I never thought I could be as blessed as I am with you—my beautiful wife, and now with a child on the way. How can I bear such happiness?"

"Because you deserve it," she said. "You're the best man in the world, and I love you."

"I love you," he said, "and I intend to show you just how much."

"How much you—Oh!" She let out a squeal as he grasped her hand and pulled her to him. Then he rolled her onto her back and straddled her, his manhood hot and hard against her thigh. "Augustus!" she cried, in mock horror.

"'Tis your fault, wife," he growled. "I find I'm ready for you again."

"And I you."

With a swift, sharp movement, he claimed her again, and they made love under the canopy of the forest, where the bright blooms heralded the onset of spring—the season of new beginnings.

Acknowledgements

Thank you, to Family Royal, as usual, for all your support, and to the Scottish Chapter of the Romantic Novelists' Association for all those writing days that helped me get the words down. To my Beta Buddies, your support and encouragement always spurs me on and thank you, as ever, to Sarah, for the moral support, and chats over wine and nibbles.

About the Author

Emily Royal grew up in Sussex, England, and has devoured romantic novels for as long as she can remember. A mathematician at heart, Emily has worked in financial services for over twenty years. She indulged in her love of writing after she moved to Scotland, where she lives with her husband, teenage daughters and menagerie of rescue pets including Twinkle, an attention-seeking boa constrictor.

She has a passion for both reading and writing romance with a weakness for Regency rakes, Highland heroes, and Medieval knights. Persuasion is one of her all-time favorite novels which she reads several times each year and she is fortunate enough to live within sight of a Medieval palace.

When not writing, Emily enjoys playing the piano, hiking, and painting landscapes, particularly the Highlands. One of her ambitions is to paint, as well as climb, every mountain in Scotland.

Follow Emily Royal:
Website: www.emroyal.com
Facebook: facebook.com/eroyalauthor
Twitter: twitter.com/eroyalauthor
Newsletter signup: mailchi.mp/e5806720bfe0/emilyroyalauthor
Goodreads:
goodreads.com/author/show/14834886.Emily_Royal

www.ingramcontent.com/pod-product-compliance
Lightning Source LLC
Chambersburg PA
CBHW072026220726
48293CB00016B/451